MATTER DEEP AND DANGEROUS

A NOVEL

Lawrence G. Burch

MATTER DEEP AND DANGEROUS

Published by Wheatmark®
610 East Delano Street, Suite 104,
Tucson, Arizona 85705 U.S.A.
www.wheatmark.com

ISBN: 978-1-60494-469-3
LCCN: 2010935429

● ● ●

Acknowledgements

To my wife, Bev, for her encouragement, help and patience.

To Mary H. Smith, for her computer skills and unflagging assistance.

To Gene Kunz, for his photographic expertise

And to the Editors at Wheatmark , for very constructive suggestions.

● ● ●

Dedication

This book is dedicated to those who do
what needs to be done to preserve our
safety and freedom, you know who you are.

"And now I will unclasp a secret book,
And to
your quick-conceiving discontents
I'll read you matter deep and dangerous."

Shakespeare, *Henry IV*

CHAPTER ONE

BEVERLY WITTMOND HAD JUST finished a phone conversation with her youngest son, who had called from college to wish her a happy birthday. He was two days late, but that wasn't too bad for an eighteen-year-old. She was rinsing her toothbrush when a point of light entered the extreme right of her peripheral vision and disturbed her bedtime ritual. As she turned to face the bathroom window, the point became two headlights and grew as the car came down the driveway toward the house. The car approached rapidly, and this stirred up anxiety within her. Entering the bedroom, she alerted her husband that someone was coming.

"Connie, there's a car coming down the drive. Are you expecting anyone?"

There were only two people in the world who could call Conrad Wittmond "Connie": his wife and his mother.

"No, I'm not, but whoever it is, he's in a goddamned big hurry," he replied, hearing the car coming to a screeching stop. "Who in the world could it be this time of night?" After a pause, he added, "I'll check it out."

Pulling himself out of the recliner from which he had been watching Jay Leno, Wittmond slipped on his boots and purposefully strode to the closet. Reaching in, he retrieved the Remington 870 shotgun, partially opened the breech to be sure it was loaded, closed it, and proceeded down the hall to the stairs.

"Do you really think that's necessary?" Bev called after him, just as the doorbell rang.

A brief backward glance over his left shoulder followed by a raised eyebrow answered her question.

The Wittmonds did live out in the country in a rather isolated area. It was 11:20 p.m., and they weren't expecting anyone. Maybe it was, if not necessary, judicious.

Connie had always been more, well … cautious than Bev. Some would say paranoid, but cautious was accurate.

Almost as curious as she was anxious, Bev elected to follow at what she considered a safe distance.

"I'm behind you," she notified her husband in a stage whisper. She was sure he had heard, but he gave no response.

Wittmond stepped to the side of the door before switching on the porch light. Across the room, Bev mimicked his move in compliance with the wave he gave behind him.

"Who is it?" Wittmond inquired through the still-closed door.

"Rhaspberry," came the reply. "We have to talk."

Using the muzzle of the shotgun, Wittmond pushed back the sheer curtain on the french door and peered at the caller through the small slit. After a full second of scrutiny, he unbolted the door.

"Come in," he said. Bev caught the cold edge to his voice. In stepped a well-dressed, slender, balding man of about sixty. With Rhaspberry inside, Wittmond stepped halfway out the door and scanned the area.

"I'm alone," Rhaspberry reassured him, eyeing the gun. "There is no need for that."

"I'm not so sure," Wittmond countered as he propped the gun in the corner of the entryway. Bev thought she caught a trace of a smile on her husband's face. If so, it was just a trace. There was no smile on Rhaspberry's face. Bev felt it was safe and stepped forward out of the darkness. Both men simultaneously turned toward her.

"Bev, this is Mr. Rhaspberry." Wittmond then nodded toward her. "My wife, Beverly."

"Very pleased to meet you," Rhaspberry said. She smiled and nodded. The introduction didn't calm her fear, however. "Connie…" she started.

"Mr. Rhaspberry is a very old … acquaintance of mine," Wittmond interrupted.

She noted Connie's purposeful avoidance of the word *friend*. "Who is this guy?" she thought. "Why have I never heard of this… *acquaintance* before?" She thought, "Why did Connie call him *Mister* Rhaspberry?"

There was urgency in Rhaspberry's eyes. With the introductions concluded, he turned to Wittmond and stated, "We have to talk. Alone." Wittmond started with an "Ah ..." but, sensing the awkwardness of the situation, Bev suggested they sit in the music room.

"I'll make you a pot of coffee," she said as she exited.

● ● ●

As soon as she was out of earshot, Rhaspberry said, "We've got a problem."

"You mean *you've* got a problem," Wittmond countered.

"No, if anything, you've got the problem," Rhaspberry said. "Actually, it's Wolkert that has the immediate problem, but you're next."

"What the hell are you talking about?" replied Wittmond, a little angry but more confused than anything.

"I will explain the details on the way, but you have to believe me that it is imperative that we leave now. Wolkert's and his family's lives depend on it."

● ● ●

"What the hell is going on?" mused Bev to herself as she fired up the Mr. Coffee. "Well, Connie will certainly explain everything after what's his name, Rhaspberry leaves." Pensively, she watched the thin stream of black, steaming liquid fill the carafe.

Bev put two mugs, creamer, sugar, and the carafe on a tray and made for the music room, quietly and with ears perked. Unfortunately, the conversation ceased before she could hear anything intelligible. "Damn," she thought.

As she placed the tray before the men, Wittmond rose and gently took her by the elbow. "Come out to the kitchen with me. I've got to tell you something."

Rhaspberry said, "Try to hurry, will you? Time is critical."

They made for the kitchen in silence, but as she crossed the threshold, Bev turned to Wittmond with fire in her eyes.

"Connie, what the hell is going on? Are you in trouble? What?"

"No, Bev, I'm not in trouble, but a very close friend is. You don't know anything about him; he's from the past. At one time, he was my most trusted comrade, and now he is in very deep sh— trouble. I owe him. You have to trust me on this; it's something I have to do. I can't explain because I don't even have the particulars."

"Is this one of those hunting trip things?" Bev asked.

"Yeah, kind of," he replied with more than a slight look of surprise.

"I'm not an idiot, you know," Bev urged.

"I know you're not an idiot, and if you had any misgivings or suspicions about some of my activities in the past, I truly appreciate that you never pressed me for answers I couldn't give you," he said, unblinking.

"Well, how do you parry that?" she thought, returning his gaze. "Can you tell me anything?"

"I can only tell you I have to go now. Lives are at risk, dear lives. I may be gone for a week or more, but I swear I'll explain everything when I get back. But there's no time now, I have to go."

Wittmond turned and raced up the stairs to his office. Bev could hear him rummaging through his office closet and then, three or four minutes later, he bounded down the stairs. He placed a black duffle bag on the floor to her right.

"Trust me, this is the last time," he pleaded as he placed his hands on her shoulders. The bottom line was that she did trust him, so she smiled, and they kissed briefly.

"For Christ's sake be careful, Connie." It wasn't very original, but what else was there for her to say?

As she followed him to the door, Bev noticed the butt of a stainless-steel .45 protruding from his duffle. This did little to calm her anxiety. As they reached the threshold, Rhaspberry was getting into the car.

Connie turned to Bev and they briefly kissed again.

"I'll be okay. I'll be back as soon as I can. Oh, and please call Ed in the morning and tell him he'll have to cover for me? Tell him it's a family emergency." He turned away and got into the passenger side of Rhaspberry's car. Bev stood on the porch and half-heartedly waved at the taillights as they faded into the darkness. She looked at her watch, 12:07 a.m. In less than an hour, a stranger had come in the middle of the night, persuaded her husband of thirty years to leave without explanation, and turned what had been an ordinary evening into a nightmare of confusion and anxiety.

Bev went inside, locked the door, and turned off the porch light. She spied the coffee tray and noticed that it was untouched. This was definitely not a Suisse Mocha moment.

Deciding to clean up the tray in the morning, Bev ascended the stairs. At the top, a shaft of light shone through the door of Connie's office.

"In such a damned hurry, he forgot to turn off the light," she muttered. She glanced at the things scattered on the floor in the office as she felt for the light switch. She went in and picked up the field jacket and Wellington boots. Her mind was formulating a sentence about men and messes when her eye caught the safe. The door was ajar. In all the years that they had lived here, she had never seen the safe open. She knew that the combination was taped to the bottom of the desk chair, but she had never seriously considered opening it.

There the door stood open. She paused to consider whether she should investigate or just close it and twist the dial. After a full thirty second's reflection, she decided to do neither. Bev hung up the jacket, turned off the light, and closed the door. This was no hour to be making decisions of this magnitude. Boots in hand, she went to the bedroom at the other end of the house. Her mind was flitting from one unanswered question to another. The night was as restless as it was lonely, but finally, she fell asleep.

CHAPTER TWO

VICTORIA CHARLES WAS PICKING at her lunch, not really enjoying it. This was a slow time, and she didn't handle slow time well. She enjoyed being busy but she hadn't had a job in over three months. Contract killing was a somewhat sporadic enterprise. She often mused about how easy her occupation was. Her victims, exclusively men, never expected or suspected a woman. They usually looked very surprised when they died.

She paid her bill and left a generous tip; she had found the waitress pleasant and attentive. Hot air blasted her as she left the air-conditioned restaurant; summer in Indianapolis could be hell. The inside of her Ford Escort was hotter still. The black vinyl seat burned her backside and the steering wheel was too hot to touch. She rolled down the windows and waited for the A/C to show some sign of life. When the air blowing out of the vents turned cool, she closed the windows and headed to her apartment. "Goddamn this heat!" she thought. She hated perspiring. It made her feel unclean.

Her apartment was spartan, but it was very well kept. She ran her mail service from here, not for the income, which was minimal, but for the cover it afforded. One did have to have a visible means of support. Entering, she scanned the room and found nothing alarming. She unbuttoned the top two buttons of her blouse and kicked off her shoes. With one foot, she moved the shoes against the wall and fanned herself with the front of her blouse to get the apartment's cool air next to her skin.

She fixed a glass of iced tea, punched the Play button on the answering machine, and sat on the sofa, propping her feet up on the coffee table.

There were two messages. The local newspaper wanted to know if she wished to have the newspaper delivered to her door, she didn't, and an "employment opportunity" awaited her if she called 1-305-555-1963 at eight o'clock that evening. She wrote the number down and looked at the area code, then retrieved the phone book from a drawer. After thumbing through the first seven or eight pages she came to the area-code map, which showed 305 to be in the Miami area.

"Miami," she thought. "I hope this isn't one of those Cuban drug deals. Those people are so unpredictable, so volatile, so dangerous."

She had passed on that type of employment opportunity before because of the one that had nearly killed her. She would pass up this, too, if it involved drugs.

"Just not worth it," she muttered. Eight o'clock was hours away; she had things to do.

Her first task was to catch up on the mail service work. She set her PC in motion to generate the mailing labels for the five thousand brochures from a local travel agency. While the machine was busy with this, she stripped down to her panties. She moved to the bedroom and began her exercise routine in front of the full-length mirror. She enjoyed seeing her muscles strain.

"That belly's as hard as steel," she thought. As she flexed her pecs, she enjoyed seeing the definition of the muscles in her arms.

"Not bad for thirty-eight. Not bad at all," she remarked aloud. She knew she didn't have to be muscular to pull a trigger, but being in shape could be very useful at times. And she was definitely in shape. She liked being strong.

Thirty minutes later she was in the shower rinsing off the inevitable but despised perspiration. Afterward, refreshed and powdered, she sat at the desk in her robe with a towel around her head, doing more mailings, the "idiot work," as she called it.

After applying a few hundred of the labels to brochures, she boxed them for mailing. Checking her schedule, she saw that this batch was to go out in three days. Plenty of time.

This irksome but necessary task completed, Victoria carefully placed a frozen meal in the microwave and set the timer.

With a glass of white wine in one hand and the remote in the other, she sat down to watch the news.

She must have dozed off because the microwave buzzer startled her. As she got up, she saw that she still had about two hours to kill before she could make the call. She was anxious to make the call. When supper was over and she had tidied up the kitchenette, she still had an hour to wait.

"They said eight, so it'll be eight exactly. Have to appear businesslike," she thought, looking for a diversion.

She picked up this morning's paper. She had finished the crossword puzzle, except for 63 down, "Swiftian brute," when the clock chimed eight.

"Swiftian brute, Swiftian brute," she muttered as she looked for the Miami phone number.

She dismissed the puzzle and carefully dialed the number. On the third ring, a male voice with a Hispanic accent answered, "Yes."

"Damn!" she thought. "Cubans!"

"I'm calling in regard to the employment opportunity," she said.

"This would be ...?" the man asked.

"Primrose, Catherine Primrose."

"Ah yes, Ms. Primrose. If your services are not presently engaged, my employer would like to retain you for an urgent transaction."

"The schedule is clear providing the transaction does not require relocation to the Southeast," she said.

"Not at all, Ms. Primrose. The position is in the very middle of the Midwest," he reassured her.

"Fine, just send the information to Box 478. The Zip is 46240." The background noise led her to believe that he was at a pay phone in a bar, probably a strip club, judging from the whistling. Disgusting animals.

"Excellent," he replied. "The information will be in the mail tonight, sent overnight express. Good night, Ms. Primrose." He terminated the conversation.

"All in under two minutes," she noted. Satisfied, she hung up the phone and went back to watching TV. She was anxious to see what the mail would bring.

On Tuesday afternoon, Victoria approached the post office box near closing time. She observed the patrons for a while and then, deciding all was okay, she retrieved the large envelope. Prize in hand, she hurried to her car and drove back across town to her apartment.

Almost ritualistically, she sat on the edge of her chair with the envelope on the coffee table. Deftly, she slit the top with the letter opener. Carefully removing the contents, she separated the items and laid them out in front of her: the packet of one-hundred-dollar bills in one stack, the photographs in another, and the typed letter in another.

First she counted the money. The whole ten thousand dollars was there. Then she moved on to the letter.

> *Ms. Primrose:*
>
> *Though I have never availed myself of your services, you came highly recommended. The man in question is one Conrad C. Wittmond. His address is on the back of the enclosed picture. He appears to be a physician but was involved in a very un-physician-like enterprise that resulted in the death of the son of our mutual employer, so beware. When you have finished the job, submit proof of completion to P.O. Box 5815, Miami, FL 33014-1815, and the second half of your commission will be forthcoming.*

After reading the letter, she was upset by the stipulation of "proof of completion." "What the hell does he want? Pictures, body parts, what?" she speculated.

She didn't do body parts, so pictures would have to do. With this, she picked up a page from a Saint Louis University Medical School yearbook that she had taken from the envelope. One of the pictures was circled in red.

"He looks pretty ordinary to me," she said to herself as she turned the page over. On the back was a list of data.

Conrad C. Wittmond MD, PhD

8881 Bachman Ln.

Godfrey, Illinois

Age 52, Wt 190 Ht 6'3" white male

Hair Br Eyes Hz

"They must have gotten this off of his driver's license," she mused. "This picture must be ten years old, too." She was unfamiliar with Godfrey, Illinois, but her road atlas showed it just north of Saint Louis, Missouri.

In a matter-of-fact way, she packed her bags. She'd leave in the morning. Her destination was only five hours away by car, so she would drive instead of flying. Neat: no paper trail, and no giving the pistol over to baggage handlers. She was fond of the suppressed Ruger .22 automatic. She had used it on numerous occasions without a hitch. The airline losing it would present a real problem; replacing it in a strange city would be difficult if not dangerous.

She filled the gun's magazine with eight Winchester-Western subsonic hollow-point rounds and inserted it into the handle of the pistol. She always left the chamber empty for safety, and she double-checked it before packing the weapon in her suitcase. The silencer—illegal—would ride in the spare-tire well of the trunk.

That night she drifted off to sleep asking herself, "How did a doctor get messed up in something like this?" It really didn't matter.

On Wednesday, the clock radio came on as scheduled at 7:30 a.m., and Victoria performed her morning ritual just as she did every other morning, but today was going to be different. She had a contract. She smiled inwardly each time she thought of how she had gotten into the business. Her late husband had been in the murder-for-hire line before they had met. Theirs was a perfect match: he had money and didn't like to screw, her ideal man. She provided him with something, although she wasn't quite sure what it was. Perhaps she gave him a cover, heterosexual legitimacy, whatever. At any rate, they were a match. They liked each other. She had been unsure of his sideline until a year after they married, when suspicion led to acceptance, which led to participation. Not participation in a direct sense, but in the aiding and abetting sense. He made good money and all went well until he was killed in an car accident. The calls for employment continued to come in; the employers were apparently unaware of her husband's death. She toyed with the thought of picking up the family business. She knew the ropes and had the equipment but had never actually killed anyone. After six months, with finances dwindling, she finally decided to try it. She accepted a contract on an accountant by directing the employer to send a dossier to a post office box, just as she had done for her husband many times before. Several days later, just before closing time, she went to the post office and retrieved the package. The large envelope contained all the pertinent information on the victim and ten thousand dollars, half the fee. She would receive the other half after the job was completed. Looking at the photograph, she thought her first victim was a disgusting pig.

David Hansen, CPA, was at his home in a suburb of Denver by himself; his wife had taken the kids to her mother's as she did one weekend a month. He was watching the Bronco's game on Sunday afternoon when the doorbell rang. Victoria, posing as a distressed young lady, told him about the trouble she was having with her car and asked to use his phone. He leered at her and directed her to the kitchen. He turned to watch the replay of what the announcer claimed was a close call by the referee. The single shot from the silenced .22, which entered his head just above his right ear, caused him no pain. He just slumped to the floor, a pulsating jet of blood spraying the back of the off-white sofa. Victoria picked up the ejected shell casing and exited the house without touching anything. Sitting behind the wheel of her rental car, she assessed her feelings. Her heart rate was still rapid but slowing. Her hands were a little shaky, but not very. Her face felt flushed but not at all uncomfortable.

"Not unlike after an orgasm," she thought as she put the car into gear and pulled away. She dropped the car off at the airport in Denver and caught the bus back to Indianapolis.

One week later, the other ten thousand dollars arrived. It was easy when you had no conscience. People with a conscience rationalized their misconduct; Victoria saw no need for that.

The drive from Indianapolis to the Saint Louis area would be easy. Highway 70 connected the cities. Her target's home was just north of the city. Victoria felt good about this job. A fat-cat, middle-aged doctor. She didn't care for men with authority; they reminded her of her father.

CHAPTER THREE

BEV AWOKE WEDNESDAY FEELING anything but rested. She busied herself with chores and continued to ruminate about Connie. Around noon, the issue of the safe came to the top of her mind. The events of the last twelve hours engulfed her. She couldn't concentrate on her book, there was really nothing that would hold her interest on television, and for once she didn't want to talk to any of her friends on the phone. Like a tiny piece of apple skin stuck between teeth, the thought of the safe and its contents poked at her until something had to be done.

"Why not?" she reasoned. "Probably nothing in there anyway. I'll just take a quick peek."

She proceeded to Connie's office. As Connie had left it the night before, the safe door was open. She placed one finger on the top corner of the door and gently pushed it open wide. Now she could inspect the contents without touching them.

As ever, Bev made the moral distinction between looking and touching. Predictably, though, looking did not yield enough satisfaction for her, so she employed the eraser end of a pencil to poke around a bit. This, too, proved unacceptable, so finally she gave in and sorted through the contents with her hands. She quickly decided not to rummage randomly; she would inventory the items methodically from the top to the bottom.

The top shelf contained two items: an antique Luger pistol and a square Tupperware container that held, according to the label, two hundred ten Krugerrands.

"Let's see, at about three hundred fifty dollars per, that would be about seventy-five thousand dollars. Jesus!" she muttered.

The next shelf held their respective wills and the deed to the house. A pigeonhole to the left held a few laminated cards, a ham radio license, a pilot's license for rotocraft, and school diplomas… nothing exciting there. She was on the brink of disappointment.

A small drawer contained dog tags, a Zippo lighter, and an assortment of Boy Scout pins. As she closed the drawer, her eyes fell to a maroon leather folder shoved back in the corner. Its brass hasp opened at a touch, revealing several hundred typed pages stacked perhaps an inch thick. The first page, addressed to her, read:

> *Dear Bev,*
>
> *If you are reading this letter, it means that I am missing and possibly dead. This folder contains documentation of several events that have occurred throughout my life about which you know little or nothing. I have put this journal together to provide an account of these adventures. This was done so that you and the children can get a full understanding of what I have done and, more important, why I have done it. I feel a certain pride in these undertakings because I had, in each case, the required skills. For several reasons, all of which will become obvious, I have chosen to keep the details of these events form you—that is, until now. Try not to judge me too harshly.*
>
> *Forever, Connie*

As she flipped through the pages, the words "Tam-Ky," "drug dealers," and "blood streak" jumped out at her. She didn't stop a moment to reconsider reading the document; she knew she had to know what this was about. Bev went to the kitchen to prepare a pot of tea. Then, with the teapot, a cup, and the folder in hand, she headed to the sunroom.

CHAPTER FOUR

IN THE WEDNESDAY TWILIGHT, Rhaspberry and Wittmond sped south on Highway 367 across the Mississippi and then the Missouri River. A few miles later they picked up Highway 270 west, which linked them to 44 west. This would take them to their destination.

Wittmond was still disturbed about leaving Bev so abruptly. He ruminated about the anxiety the unexplained event must be causing her. Without fail, as it had a hundred times in the past, the memory of their first meeting came to mind. That morning in April 1969 had changed his life forever.

He had been in Huntsville about a year. That particular morning, a Monday, he had left the engineering bay at Boeing/NASA and caught the shuttle bus to the Redstone Arsenal Library. He needed to research and review a new computer program that had been generated by Sperry-Rand for the detection of radiation heat transfer from a geometric body to a point. He saw a possible application of this program to his project, which was to determine the heat flux generated by the Saturn V SI-C stage rocket's plume to various points on its base. If he could apply the program, it would save him months of work. Papers in hand, he left the bus and expectantly entered the library. The facility was laid out with rooms like a series of railroad cars. Wittmond entered into the building's general information area and proceeded down a series of security checkpoints where guards checked patrons' ID badges for the correct clearance for that section. The first point bore the sign CONFIDENTIAL, marked with a blue stripe; the second read SECRET, with a red stripe. The last checkpoint was vaulted and marked TOP SECRET, with a black stripe.

Wittmond stopped at the SECRET section to peruse the new paper. He was very encouraged by what he read and went to find the Xerox machine to copy it. He was engrossed in his work as he fell into the line of people waiting to use the machine. He hardly noticed the young lady in front of him.

When his turn came, he pulled back the copier's cover and found a page still lying on the glass. He picked it up and called out to the departing woman.

"Oh, miss, I think this is—"

She turned, and her green eyes penetrated his and locked onto his soul. She smiled at his awkwardness and took the paper. Her soft, "Thank you," finished him off.

Bev was from Salina, Kansas. She worked at Redstone/NASA translating Russian technical papers and evaluating their relevance to the space program. Her background as a math major and Russian minor made her ideal for the job and she enjoyed it.

Bev allowed Wittmond to pursue and eventually capture her after their typical courtship.

Approximately a year after their Xerox meeting, they married. A year after that, the space program fell apart and they decided that Wittmond should go to medical school. Bev took a job as a math teacher at a private girls' school not far from the medical school, and things went well.

Rhaspberry's gruff voice interrupted Wittmond's woolgathering. "I'm retired, you know," he said. Wittmond didn't know.

"Yes, I hung it up about a year ago. I was basking in leisure until last week, when Sherlock, my old protégé, called me and wanted a meeting. He flew to my place in Carolina and brought me some disturbing information. You, of course, remember the last time you and Wolkert went out to play."

"Of course" Wittmond replied.

"You'll recall that the brother of that kingpin, Cerro, was hatching a plot that you and Wolkert terminated. With both brothers dead, Old Man Cerro was pissed. He never appeared to be a major player in the drug business, but that turned out not to be the case. He was actually the brains behind the two brothers."

Wittmond nodded. "I guess that makes sense."

"According to Sherlock, who has been monitoring the situation, the old man has spent a lot of time and money over the last two years to find out who killed his second son. He traced the hit back through the aid station to the doctors whose names you two assumed. Those doctors were each contacted, but a man named Lupe, who apparently has seen your faces, cleared them. Now Sherlock says that somehow Old Man Cerro has gotten a handle on Wolkert and is planning retaliation. Cerro doesn't know about you yet, but if he gets hold of Wolkert, he will."

Wittmond frowned. "So what's your plan?"

"This is not an Agency problem. We have to handle it ourselves, and we have to do it now.

"Wolkert had to get his family to a safe place, and he chose to take them to their summer place in the Ozarks. That's where we're headed. No doubt the bad guys will find out about the retreat and he will need help."

Rhaspberry had a dossier on the hired help but no picture of the old man. Wittmond looked through the dossier and said, "The team members are very professional and very dangerous." He flipped through the pages describing the team leader and two assistants. The leader was a forty-three-year-old white male. He had been involved in the killing of at least twenty-three people. Most of his victims were involved in drugs; some were family members of someone involved in drugs. There was a paragraph about one instance in which he murdered two children with plastic bags; it inscribed itself indelibly on Wittmond's brain. This guy was a real shitbum.

The first crony was a twenty-three-year-old black male who had a long record of petty crimes but had been implicated in only four killings. However, his style of murder—cutting out various organs of his victims—made up for his lack of numbers.

The other crony was a twenty-six-year-old white male with no police record at all. According to the dossier, he had been involved in at least five killings. An amateur with aspirations.

Unlike hit men Wittmond had seen on TV, these guys looked average. Rhaspberry cautioned Wittmond to memorize their faces well and, when the moment came, to act without hesitation. "Rhaspberry need not worry," Wittmond thought.

"They will probably try to take Wolkert alive to question him, and that's to our advantage. What tools did you bring along?"

"Just the .45 and a knife," Wittmond answered.

"Not the goddamned Boy Scout knife?"

"Oh, yes. It has mystic powers, you know."

"Bullshit," Rhaspberry scoffed.

"Well, I'm alive and without any extra openings in my body after having known you for thirty years. How many other people can say that?"

"You might have a point," Rhaspberry conceded with the slightest grin.

It took nearly six hours to find Wolkert's place. *Remote* was an understatement. As they drove up to the cabin, Rhaspberry honked the horn and flashed the lights.

"We don't want him to think we're sneaking up on him," Rhaspberry said.

Rhaspberry parked the car, and they waited. After perhaps five minutes, a camouflaged figure emerged from the woods to their left. He held an H-K MP-5 at his waist, pointed at them.

"Put your hands on the dash," prompted Rhaspberry. "This is always the most dangerous part."

Wittmond agreed.

A smile cracked through the man's face paint as Wolkert recognized them. He lowered the weapon after he checked the backseat. Rhaspberry lowered the driver-side window, and Wolkert leaned over to it.

"Pull the car behind the cabin," he said, pointing to a grass path to the left side of the structure.

Rhaspberry parked beside Wolkert's Taurus, and he and Wittmond climbed out. Wittmond, very stiff after hours of confinement, was stretching when Wolkert came around the corner.

"Goddamn am I glad you guys showed up! I've got my family in the basement, and I've been awake for three days, expecting the worst. Come on inside."

They gathered their gear and followed Wolkert into the walk-out basement.

CHAPTER FIVE

CURLING UP ON THE sofa, Beverly examined page one of the manuscript.

I was still living at my parents' home while attending college. It was around the first or second week of January 1963. I recall that I purposefully used an uncomfortable chair; it kept me from falling asleep while I was studying. Leaning back, enjoying a brief pause, I noticed the tea in my cup had become tepid. I was thinking of getting up to get a refill when a seemingly innocuous phone call became the first true disruption of my rather complacent life. The caller was a Mr. Jerome Rhaspberry.

"Jesus, that long ago!" Bev said.

He said that he was a representative of Lowe Chemical Co. and that he wished to meet with me in the next few days to discuss a possible job opportunity. He explained that he knew I was in my senior year at Saint Louis University, completing a BS in chemistry. He thought that his company could extend a very interesting offer. We agreed to meet in the Campus Club at the university in two days, at 7:00 a.m., before classes.

After we hung up, I filled my teacup and sat at the window watching the snow fall through the halo of the streetlight. I felt quite pleased with myself. Lowe was a large company and seemed interested in me. After a few more minutes of contemplation, I returned to the books. Lowe would be interested only if I graduated.

At breakfast the next morning, I told the folks about the phone call. My father thought it sounded like a great opportunity and a much better idea than going to graduate school. After all, one did have to work sometime. Fortified with this subtle piece of philosophy, I set out on the twenty-three mile drive to the university. I calculated that I had done this about six hundred and thirty times over the last three and a half years. It wasted a lot of time, but it saved a lot of money. Like most twenty-one-year-olds, I thought I had a lot more time than money.

During the course of the day, I told several of my classmates in the chemistry program about the phone call. Each thought it sounded like a great deal, and each denied having received a similar call. It was then that the first, but by no means the last, wisp of concern entered my brain. Academically, I was good, but I wasn't the best student in the program. I had no business connections, and I wasn't lucky. Why was I the only one being extended an offer? While driving home that evening my thoughts were not occupied with the usual cheerleader in the '57 Chevy fantasy. The time after supper passed slowly. It was difficult to concentrate on the books, so I walked uptown to get an unnecessary pack of cigarettes.

I was up early the day of the interview. The sun was blinding as it reflected off the snow. The air was so cold that it made my face feel tight. It took forever for the heater in the Chevy to warm up. As I reached the outskirts of Saint Louis, I set aside all of my feelings of paranoia and actually looked forward to my interview.

The blue-gray haze in the Campus Club was thicker than I had expected for that early in the day. The eternal bridge game was changing players, and I could hear the usual philosophical bullshit in the background—some sophomore trying to impress a freshman girl. Coffee in hand, I awaited Mr. Jerome Rhaspberry. Looking at my watch for the fifth or sixth time in as many minutes, I determined that he was now one minute late. As I opened a fresh pack of Pall Malls, I noticed the lipstick on the opposite side of my coffee mug and wondered who the left-handed honey was that had left her mark, and how long it had been there. Since Rhaspberry had called two days before, I had been trying, albeit in vain, to figure out how Lowe Chemical had come to know about me. I had made no application to their, or any, firm for a job. It was my intention to go to graduate school and get an advanced degree in chemistry. I had several graduate school applications pending.

Then in came a man of about thirty wearing a tan topcoat. He was short and slight, and he had a searching expression on his face. With his black-framed glasses he could easily have been mistaken for an English professor. My upward nod caught his eye. I extinguished my cigarette and introduced myself.

He started his part of the conversation with a brief introduction and quickly moved to questions about my plans for the future. I told him I had decided to attend graduate school unless something exceptional came along. The ball was now in his court. He then inquired about my draft status. I felt he must have known that I had a student deferment, and I was now sure he was going to pitch me a draft-deferred job with Lowe. He said he was certain the student deferments would end in a year or two and that it would be a shame to have a couple of years of postgraduate research interrupted by being drafted. A shame? Hell, it would be a disaster. I would have to start all over, if I could even get back into a program.

Having secured my attention, Mr. Rhaspberry produced a folder with my name on it. At first I couldn't see what it contained. As he leafed through it, he casually asked if I still had the DMC-1903-A1 rifle. At this point I was thoroughly confused and becoming slightly alarmed. The conversation was not going to end in a job offer. I asked him politely but directly what was going on, and he handed me the folder. In it was a varied collection of my personal papers: copies of grades, my high school diploma, my Eagle Scout certificate, reference letters from neighbors, teachers, employers, scoutmasters, and the parish priest, some as recent as December 1962. Also enclosed were five-year-old score sheets from a rifle club I had belonged to as an Explorer Scout. They weren't copies, but the actual goddamned score sheets.

Rhaspberry then asked if I had done any one-thousand-meter shooting recently. I said he probably knew the answer and firmly asked again what was going on. He offered me a cigarette with a filter. "What kind of pussy smokes filtered cigarettes?" I thought. Declining his offer, I lit up a Pall Mall, and he went for more coffee.

Returning, he said he was not with Lowe Chemical Company but was with the government interviewing special people for a special job. I didn't know if it was him or the coffee, but I was beginning to get queasy. He said his agency needed some long-range marksmen for a short period of time. He further explained that if I were interested, he could extend three guarantees: I would be gone no longer than six months, I would receive ten thousand dollars in cash, and I would never be drafted and could attend graduate school without interruption. With reservation, I indicated that I was interested (ten thousand dollars for six months' work!) and wanted to know more, like who he really was.

He produced an official-looking card with his name and picture on it. It indicated he was with the Central Intelligence Agency. He said that all he could tell me was his outfit, a covert operation group, or COG, was code named THOR. The members were to receive brief basic training and to be sent to Southeast Asia to engage in a short-term aid program. He also made it clear that all this was unofficial, and I, of course, should speak of it to no one. I was to think it over, and he would contact me in about two weeks. The man's manner was officious, but I detected an underlying thread of malice.

He gathered his papers and departed. Lighting a cigarette, I tried to ponder the possibilities, but the din of the crowd made this impossible, so I, too, departed. Hell, I had two weeks.

During the last week of January 1963, I read all I could find about American involvement in Southeast Asia. There was very little in the newspapers or on TV about Vietnam and absolutely nothing about any U.S. activity there. This operation of Rhaspberry's obviously had a low profile and was of little significance—probably a Peace Corps variant to teach the villagers how to defend themselves.

Rhaspberry called me on February 4. (Every time I heard the guy's name I thought of the raspberry sound made while sticking out your tongue.) Having given the idea as much thought as I could, I told him it was a deal. Actually, I was afraid to get on his wrong side. All he had to say in return was, "Get your degree, and you will be contacted."

The subsequent three months were filled with study, exams, and efforts to learn more about Vietnam. The atlas showed it to be a slender coastal nation bordered on the east and south by the Pacific Ocean and on the west by a mountain range that separated it from Laos and Cambodia. The atlas went on to explain that the climate is tropical. In recent history it had been colonized by the French, who battled the Vietminh but called it quits in the mid 1950s after their last and largest defeat at Dien Bien Phu. The truce divided Vietnam into North (Communist) Vietnam and South (colonial) Vietnam. From that time the north had been sending supplies and men south to organize guerilla bands, attempting to effect the overthrow of the government and reunify Vietnam. Apparently South Vietnam had all the good farmland. The French, British, and, it turned out, the United States had all made token attempts to assist the government of South Vietnam, but their less-than-vigorous support had only stiffened the resolve of the north.

I read an account of the Dien Bien Phu fiasco. It seemed that the North Vietnamese had competent, confident, and tenacious leadership. The troops seemed to be disciplined and effective. Not a good combination in an enemy. I wondered at the wisdom of teaching a bunch of people to shoot if they had such a superior enemy.

On May 5, I received another call from Mr. Rhaspberry. He informed me that within the next week I would receive, by mail, papers indicating that I had been accepted for graduate study in the Department of Chemistry at the University of Missouri at Columbia. He said this was to be my cover story and that I was to proceed as if the offer were legitimate. I was to be at 613 Gentry Place in Columbia by June 1, 1963. I would be contacted at the pay phone on the second floor at 8:00 a.m. that day.

At the graduation at Kiel Auditorium in Saint Louis on Saturday, May 25, my classmates and I received the usual pep talk about how we had an obligation to change the world and make it a better place. I wondered if I were going to make it, period. I hoped that I, the first of my family to graduate from a university, was not going to end up perforated in some shithole whose name no one could pronounce.

With a degree of resignation, I decided that if I were going to do this thing, several things had to be squared away. First, the spiritual: confession and Communion. Who knew when my next chance would come? After that, the supernatural had to be dealt with. I definitely had to take my lucky T-shirt and Boy Scout knife with me. Having dealt with the intangibles, I packed the rest of my junk, including the Luger I had received as a birthday present. One never knew; the need for protection might well arise.

Loins thus girded, on May 30, I set off for beautiful Columbia, Missouri. The '52 Chevy was running smoothly. It was filled with a lot of stuff I knew I'd never need but had to take to make things look right. I had told the folks I might be home for Christmas break but certainly not before. I also said I would be very busy; however, I would try to write or phone whenever I got the chance. I felt bad about deceiving them and wondered what I'd say if they ever found out. I also pondered how they might find out.

From Saint Louis, it was a straight shot west on Highway 70 to Columbia. I'd never been there before, and it took quite a while and two stops for directions to find 613 Gentry Place. What a dump! The place was a two-and-a-half-story white frame house located behind a crumbling sidewalk and a postage-stamp yard that was trying in vain to grow crabgrass. The sole redeeming feature was that I wasn't going to be there long. I rang the doorbell, and a lady in her forties who seemed to be a little too well-spoken for her role as landlady answered. I must have been getting paranoid again.

After a brief explanation of the amenities, she showed me to my room on the third floor. The decor was in keeping with the house's exterior. The door to my room had a large hasp on it for a padlock. The lady gave me a lock and one of two keys, stating that she would keep an eye on my things. Her smile won my complete trust. As she left, she mentioned that there was a pay phone on the second floor.

After I unloaded the car, I had a look around. Aside from the landlady, I was the only one there. The third floor had three rooms with sloping ceilings and a common bath. The second floor had five rooms, a common bath, a pay phone, and an ancient refrigerator in the hall. This was off-campus housing at its very best. As I stood by the pay phone, a sudden movement caught my eye. I wasn't alone after all. A solitary roach, a full one and half inches long, had been disturbed by my presence and had made a dash for the safety of the darkness under the icebox.

After I called my folks to let them know I had arrived safely, it was time for supper. I drove around town for a while looking for a place to eat and settled on the Wigwam Cafe. The only thing that looked good was the french toast and sausage. After eating, I headed downtown. En route I passed a movie theater showing *PT*

109 and decided to see it. Later, I reflected that if someone who had played such a minute role in World War II could become president, perhaps there was hope for me. I stopped at the all-night market for tomorrow's breakfast and headed home.

The house was dark except for a light in one of the landlady's windows. My footfalls echoed in the empty second floor. I wondered who she really was, what she really did, and how many more like her there were. I also wondered how many more like me there really were. I put the milk in the fridge, stared at the pay phone for a second or two, and then proceeded up to my room. Awaiting me was a note directing me to address five envelopes to my folks and write five vague letters about my scholastic endeavors; no dates, please. I took about forty-five minutes to write them. As I stacked them on the dresser, I thought about how easily I was adjusting to deception. Only mildly troubled about being mildly troubled by this, I bathed and turned in. Sleep came easily on the narrow cot. I had had a lot of experience sleeping on this type of rack in the Boy Scouts.

The alarm obediently sounded 7:30 a.m. I poured milk over the Sugar Smacks in the Kell-Bowl pack, ate the cereal, and then drank the rest of the quart of milk. I had just brushed my teeth and was draining the tank when the phone rang downstairs. I checked my watch; his call was ten minutes early. Rushing down the steps, I caught the phone on the fifth or sixth ring. It was, of course, Rhaspberry. He told me to pack everything I wanted to take along in a knapsack that I would find in the dresser of the room next to mine. I wouldn't need extra clothes, he said. I was to lock my room and be in front of the house by 8:15. The landlady would watch my stuff and field any calls or mail from my relatives. That's how it would work.

I found the knapsack and proceeded to pack it with what I thought I would need: my lucky T-shirt, two cartons of Pall Malls, a bag of Tootsie Pops, the remaining five small boxes of cereal from the six-pack, a razor, deodorant, a toothbrush and toothpaste, a bottle of Vitalis hair tonic, my Boy Scout sheath knife, and the Luger. I told the landlady the keys to the car were on the dresser if she needed to move it. She smiled and told me to be careful. "Nice smile and a nice sentiment, but the time for being careful may have already passed," I thought.

Rhaspberry drove up in a stock '59 Buick with black-wall tires. It was so plain that it drew attention. I got in and we drove to the Columbia airport. Passing through, I picked up a newspaper before boarding a nondescript twin-engine Beechcraft. In addition to the pilot, two other passengers were already aboard. The door closed, and we taxied off to my first airplane ride. We left Rhaspberry alone on the air strip, staring after us but not moving. A strange man, Rhaspberry.

Flying was not what I had imagined. I had thought that it would be like riding in a car, only higher off the ground. Actually, it was very noisy and a little closer to the elements than I cared for. The interior of the plane was certainly spartan. The seats were hard and the whole thing vibrated in a subtle but unnerving way. My Chevy rode better, and it was a lot less drafty. After we leveled off, I loosened my death grip on the seat and tried to appear casual. I made some pithy remark about a good takeoff to the man seated next to me. Somehow I got the feeling that he was trying to appear casual as well. The ensuing exchange revealed that he and the other guy were from Omaha; they had left very early this morning. The pilot had told them that we were headed for Texas but were going to stop in Columbia and Little Rock to pick up passengers and fuel. With the baggage, there was barely room for one more. My two traveling companions were civil but reserved, so instead of straining at conversation, I busied myself with the paper's headlines concerning the Pope's illness and the *Thresher* photos. The crossword puzzle and a nap occupied the next hour and a half. We then landed in what I assumed was Little Rock, Arkansas. The pilot said this would be a thirty-minute stop, so get some lunch, hit the john, and be back on time.

Having done exactly what he had said, in the order that he said it, we came back to the plane to find our last sheep already aboard. The takeoff was mercifully uneventful, so we were on the next leg of our journey. This last fellow was measurably more friendly than the other two men, and he and I exchanged stories of how we ended up here. The other two were presumably contemplating the karmic implications of their absence from Omaha.

Bev put down the journal and rubbed her eyes. What had Connie gotten himself into? And after all these years, why had he never told her about it? She got up to stretch her legs and pour another cup of tea. She definitely had to read more.

CHAPTER SIX

BEV PICKED UP CONNIE'S journal again and continued reading.

My new companion's name was Wolkert; his story and mine were disturbingly similar. He was an engineering student at the Rolla School of Mines and was also interested in graduate school. He also had demonstrated long-range shooting skills. I wondered how many times this pattern appeared throughout the United States. I guessed that I was going to find out.

It was a wretched afternoon when Wolkert and I first set down on the very busy landing strip in a desolate part of Texas called Fort Hood. As I left the plane, a blast of hot air reminded me just how far south I had come. We were told to take our gear and stand by an olive green bus until further instructions. There were already about twenty people by the bus. Over the next two and a half hot, boring hours, more people drifted in for a total of twenty-nine. A short time later, a middle-aged man with the demeanor of a wolverine showed up and invited us to board the bus. Wolkert commented that he didn't see why it was necessary to talk to educated people with such vile language. The thirty-five-minute bus ride terminated in front of a group of "mature" Quonset huts nestled in the shadow of a hill called Henson Mountain. In short order, we were given a physical examination, measured for evening wear, and fed. After a decent hot meal, our escort from the bus informed us that this area was going to be our home for the next two weeks. Though he did not believe we could be molded into his image in that length of time, we would all die trying. (I wondered what my folks were having for dinner.)

Awakened gently but firmly by our ill-mannered keeper at quarter to six the next morning, we were told to dress in the uniforms in the lockers at the end of our bunks. The uniforms were of camouflage material and not brand new. The only markings on them were a three-inch circular red patch on each shoulder. We were instructed to refrain from talking to anyone not wearing this red ball patch. We were led to a mess hall where we ate in our own roped-off area. There were other groups of people there with different patches. Curiouser and curiouser.

After a distinctly military breakfast, we retired to a classroom. There sat a knowledgeable-looking gentleman who seemed to be in charge, and next to him, our keeper. Our class numbered twenty-nine, not counting the keeper. The man in charge proceeded to give us the scoop, or at least his version of it. We, the chosen, were a group of experienced marksmen who were to be used in hit-and-run ambushes to stem the flow of supplies from North to South Vietnam. The supplies were coming to the Viet Cong by way of pack trains winding through the passes of the mountains separating Laos and Cambodia from Vietnam. To reassure us, he told us there were several groups like ours with similar intents, though their methods may be a little different. He also said that our training would be brief, as we were needed immediately. Only the necessities—marksmanship, physical conditioning, and survival techniques—would be stressed. He said that our attacks would usually be from a distance great enough to preclude effective return fire. The words "attack" and "usually" bothered me a lot, but the idea of few casualties on our side did calm me somewhat.

After dismissal, we were taken to the armory to select our rifles. Seeing the variety of weapons, I saw three constants: large scopes, heavy barrels, and .30-06 caliber. I chose a rifle I had lusted after for years: a Winchester model 70 bull gun. It was fitted with a Unertl twenty-four-power telescopic sight. The gun was slightly used; the scope was new. It looked good. It felt good. When I put it to my shoulder, I felt we were one. Outfitted with my prize, I boarded a bus to the firing range.

The initial targets were set at five hundred meters, and the results were less than gratifying. It had been a while. The recoil of the unpadded buttstock was beating the hell out of my shoulder and destroying my concentration. At five hundred meters, I couldn't see a twelve-inch bull's-eye with the naked eye. The twenty-four-power scope made it quite visible, but all movements from my breath and heartbeat made the crosshairs dance all over the target. Only with deep concentration could I squeeze the trigger between heartbeats while holding my breath. I needed to become oblivious to all other external stimuli, such as pain and the noise of other guns firing. I had done it in the past, but I could not do it that morning.

A little depressed and a little sore, I got on the bus and went for noon mess. After lunch, I looked under my shirt and saw that my whole goddamned shoulder was red-streaked from the buttplate. Back at the range, we were instructed in the basics of the AR-10, M-14, and Colt .45 pistol. We fired a number of rounds from each gun to gain familiarity, if not some degree of proficiency, in using them. When the instructors were satisfied that we were more of a threat to the enemy than to ourselves, we went back to base camp.

The keeper, decked out in a sweatsuit, met us there. He marched us over to a clear area and introduced us to physical exertion. The old bastard was as tough as he was obnoxious. Our physical fitness was probably a few rungs below that of an urban Brownie troop. After about five minutes, I was sure I had inflicted permanent injury upon myself. It was a battered wreck that dragged itself to bed that evening.

On the second day, the keeper revealed new depths of his sadistic nature. We got up at five forty-five, ran in and out among the buildings for a half hour, and topped it off with some puke-inducing calisthenics. We then ate and went to the range. I did somewhat better on the targets after fitting a recoil boot to my rifle butt. After fifty rounds, I could hit the five-hundred-meter bull's-eye about every other time, and the misses were near misses. My ability to really concentrate had still not returned, although I now felt I had cause to believe that it would. As we prepared to return for a light brunch, we noticed the limo was missing. We were then obliged to carry the rifles and all the unfired ammunition back to camp on foot. The brunch faded into a late lunch after two and a half hours of hiking and listening to nearly constant bitching about what a bunch of physical decadents we were. (Not his exact words; the keeper had but one adjective in his vocabulary.) One thing was sure: there would never be unfired ammo again.

After lunch, we began classes in jungle lore. The things likely to bite us were all listed under the title "Survival Hazards." The mosquitoes and black flies topped the list. They carried malaria, yellow fever, dengue fever, and filariasis. Any one of these aliments would completely incapacitate the victim. Spiders, my backup phobia after heights, presented little danger. All snakes, especially those in the water, were to be considered venomous and avoided. Asian leeches were divided into two categories: the water leech and the blood-sucking land leech. The land leech lurked on wet vegetation, awaiting the opportunity to attach itself to a warm passerby. Both were minor pests unless accidentally swallowed in drinking water. Jesus!

Around midafternoon, we went back to the range, shot up every cartridge we had, and then attended a class on self-defense. The class taught us what to do if we had no firearms. The knife was the basic weapon. We were shown how and where to insert the blade. We were told how to doggedly grip the enemy until he was lifeless. We were told how to avoid a surprise counterattack by giving the knife a twist before releasing the body. I was sure this was the acme of antisocial behavior. I was wrong. That title went to the methods of separating a body from its soul using a machete, which we also learned.

After we had supper, we engaged in polite conversation, recalling the events of the day for about an hour, and then retired.

Day three found me paralyzed in my cot. Only a superhuman act of will got me into the hot shower, and only the keeper's dulcet tones got me out. After the first agonizing mile of running, I actually started to loosen up. Things went better at the range. After lunch we learned about edible life-forms in the jungle and its streams. The instructor divided these potential meals into two groups: plant and animal. In the jungle, there were always plenty of plants; some could be eaten raw safely. Others, such as tubers and roots of the taro, cassava, and palau plants had to be boiled to remove the poisons. Pandanus trees bore a red fruit similar to a pineapple, but its pulp had to be cooked as well. The lesson: boil the hell out of everything. The final rule of thumb for plants was, "If you see a monkey eat it, you can eat it."

Animal food sources presented two different problems. They

were usually riddled with parasites, and they usually balked at being eaten. Well-boiled or roasted frogs and snakes were the best bet. This old Boy Scout could handle that. One guy said he would die first, and the instructor agreed that he probably would.

Day four bore a distinct resemblance to Boy Scout camp. The better part of the day was spent renewing our campcraft skills. We brushed up on celestial navigation, map reading, and use of the compass. In the afternoon, fire building, signaling, water purification, and first aid were the topics of instruction.

After supper, we had a few hours' instruction in the Vietnamese language. No grammar, just a collection of potentially useful phrases:

> *Coi chung!* Look out!
> *Di! Di!* Hurry, get out!
> *Cho!* Wait!
> *Rat cam on.* Thank you.
> And my personal favorite:
> *Dung lo!* Don't worry!

After a while, this last phrase sort of became the official motto of my group. It sounded like "Gung ho!" but carried a message more in keeping with our state of mind.

Day five, the anniversary of D-day, found me on the brink of physical disintegration. I didn't think I could last much longer. The medic for Redball, our group, said he thought we were doing fine and that things were about to get better. I thought he was full of shit; I knew I was dying. That evening there was free beer for everyone. D-day was a big deal around there: "6-June-63," very military. At least my body was not getting worse. Maybe, just maybe, I would live.

So, the next day, in a strange ritual celebration of possible survival, we jumped off ten-foot-high platforms into sandboxes. The guys who were leaving the area as we arrived were talking about parachutes, and my worst fear started to well up inside me. I really hated heights, even more than spiders. A short time later, in addition to having had my spinal column rearranged playing in the sandbox, my left ear was starting to ache.

On day seven, my ear was only mildly aching until we went to the range, where the gunfire made it excruciatingly painful. The medic examined it and said it was infected from the muddy water I had gotten in when I had fallen off a log in the obstacle course two day ago. He proceeded to lance it and put me on some antibiotics. It felt a lot better after being drained.

Day eight. "Death, where is thy sting?" This day claimed casualties but, fortunately, no fatalities. A guy named Gilson broke his right ankle on the platform jump, and Eilbacher crunched one of his back bones. Brown had an eye injury from a blown cartridge primer. By the end of the day, we were down to twenty-six.

On day nine, the routine changed somewhat. After the usual running, eating, and shooting, we went to a new area of the base where we were introduced to the "captive chute." This ingenious device was a parachute attached to guy wires. One jumped off a hundred-foot tower wearing the parachute and fell at a controlled rate. The puppet master worked us swiftly from floating feather to streamlined rock. Even at its worst, the impact of the landing was less jarring than after jumping off the platform. The whole trick was controlling my hysteria.

The other change occurred in the afternoon. We went to the range, where targets were set up at one-thousand meters. They were full-sized horse-shaped steel plates. Perhaps our employer had not wanted to prick our consciences prematurely.

I awoke on the tenth day with a strange sensation: the absence of pain. Actually, it was more than that—I almost felt good. The morning was routine, the afternoon found us learning to rappel down the face of a cliff. Most of my colleagues thought it was the first fun thing we had done since arriving. I disagreed.

Day eleven. Diarrhea! The medic claimed it was due to the antibiotics. Just goddamned wonderful! Rappelling out of a helicopter in itself can cause a certain loss of sphincter control, but with my bowels already loose, I experienced a most extreme result from the impact. Of course this was followed by the expected derogatory tirade from the keeper. As training wore on, I more frequently pictured the crosshairs on him.

Day twelve. This whole training exercise was starting to

resemble a cross between the Bataan Death March and the Stations of the Cross. At least my bowels were now controlled. The helicopter rappel went fairly well for me, but not so well for Brown. He had just recovered from an eye injury, and now he descended the line too rapidly and badly blistered his hands and thighs. "Brown may yet come to his end within the borders of the United States," I thought.

Back on the range, the steel targets were now made to move from left to right at three miles per hour for about thirty yards before reversing. This made them difficult to hit, at first. At this speed, the horse covered about four and a half feet in one second. The bullet traveled at twenty-eight hundred feet per second at the muzzle but slowed to eleven hundred by the time it had gone the distance to the target. So the target covered a little over six and one half feet from the time the bullet left the barrel. At that range the lead was calculated in body lengths, so I would aim at about one body length ahead of the mule . . . and hope I had compensated for, or doped out, the wind speed and direction correctly.

Hitting a target at 1,000 meters does not happen by chance but with the skilled application of the scientific principles collectively referred to as "ballistics."

The bullet's point of impact was principally affected by two factors: angle of elevation and crosswind. Shooting up or downhill from 1,000 meters exposed the bullet to gravity. The marksman had to calculate the equivalent distance of 1,000 meters times the cosine of the angle from the horizontal. At small angles, the effect was small. However, at 45 degrees, the cosine is 0.70, so the target should be shot at as though it were only 700 meters away. If the marksman failed to make this compensation, he would grossly overshoot, to the tune of about 13 feet.

The wind's effects were the largest unknown variables. The wind could change direction and velocity in an instant. With the bullet in the air for 1.5 seconds, the wind could considerably alter its path. The wind could even be blowing in two or three different directions over a course of 1,000 meters. Only wind blowing across the bullet's path affects it; the head- and tailwinds have little or no effect.

I knew that there would be little point in trying to shoot accurately at long distances in wind speeds at or greater than 5 miles per hour. However, if I applied these principles within their valid ranges, they would considerably increase the probability of a hit.

Day thirteen remained in my memory as the day that my mother's idiot son jumped out of a perfectly functioning airplane. The jump instructor said we only had to do it once to be "jump qualified" and that it was unlikely that we would ever need to do it again. "Bullshit," I thought.

As it had taken us to other disasters, the bus dutifully took us to the airfield. On the north side of the runway stood a very long, narrow building. Inside, men were busily rigging parachutes. I hoped that they were as proficient as they appeared to be. We each received a chute and reviewed its proper use. After everyone had their chute on correctly, we marched out on the tarmac. Awaiting us was a vintage C-47, or DC-3, as it was better known. As we boarded the plane, I noticed smoke issuing from the port engine. We sat on the wooden plank benches on each side of the craft, facing each other. The door remained open as we took off because there was no door! It was probably just as well; within minutes the air had become laden with various odors usually associated with fearful men. As in the movies, there was a red light next to the door leading to the cockpit. Under it was an unlit green light. It didn't take a genius to comprehend their significance. The guy across from me was very sweaty and looked very nervous. He looked very much the way I felt.

It took the plane about thirty minutes to level off. As we neared the jump site, the red light started to blink. With this, we were ordered to stand up and face aft. The next order had us check the chute of the man in front of us. Finally, we hooked our ripcords to a cable that ran the length of the bay. As we jumped out, the ripcord would automatically open the chute as we left the plane. No one could see the lights from our vantage point. Suddenly, the keeper yelled, "Go! Go! Go!" and someone behind me started pushing. I closed my eyes as I shuffled toward the door. The last words I heard as my turn came were, "Watch your step." This prompted me to take a peek. I saw the keeper's smiling face just before he pushed me out the door.

"Jesus, Mary and Joseph!" gasped Bev.

CHAPTER SEVEN

RECALLING CONNIE'S FEAR OF heights, Bev was astonished as she continued reading about the parachuting experience.

With my arms folded and my eyes and jaw clenched, I prayed for the jerk of the deploying chute. I could have read half of *War and Peace* in the time it took to open. Following the lifesaving tug on the harness, I chanced a look about. My body oscillated under the chute, and my view of the countryside was like that from a rocking Ferris wheel car, but one hell of a lot higher. The ground didn't rush up to me until the last few hundred feet. I tried to remember all the stuff I was supposed to do to prepare for impact. I guess I got it right because in a split second I was on the ground, unhurt. Dirt and I had just become inseparable friends. That little exercise in madness cost the team two men. One suffered a badly fractured ankle, and the other a fractured wrist. We were now twenty-five.

After mess that evening, instead of enjoying our usual free time, we went back to the range and were introduced to the AN/PVS night scope. This device used a set of lenses and photomultipliers to enhance light sixty thousand times and magnify the target four times. And, unlike the old infrared scopes, it was completely undetectable. It had a useful range of about five hundred meters, but this could be stretched a little with practice, we were told. The scope operated on a small hearing-aid-type battery pack. Each pack had a life of ten hours if used continuously. As I looked through the scope, I saw an all-green field with shadows moving on it. It took a while, about three minutes, for my eyes to get used to it. Things then became quite clear, even with the stars as the only light source. As marvelous as the scope was, it had a number of big drawbacks. It only magnified four times, it was bulky, a muzzle flash blinded it for about five seconds, and it cost about twenty thousand dollars.

The mount for this device attached to the side of the rifle with thumbscrews for fast mounting and removal without upsetting the rifle's point of impact.

From five hundred meters, we fired at the steel horses, which were illuminated by a light so weak it was not visible to the unaided eye. The muzzle flash blinded the scope when I fired the shot, so there was no seeing if I had hit the target. After some practice, I made hits regularly, and we discovered that by focusing on targets of known range and marking the spot on the focus ring, we could easily estimate the distance to targets at night. The scope's crosshairs were marked with graduations that made leading and holding over easy.

I learned a few potentially valuable lessons on the fourteenth day. With great effort, I could throw a hand grenade thirty yards. The grenade itself had a potential kill radius of thirty-five yards. Something about that didn't make a whole lot of sense. We also learned that, though a claymore mine had certain directional properties — THIS SIDE TOWARD ENEMY — , anything twenty feet behind it was also likely to be killed when it detonated. This was all very nice, but for wholesale destruction, the satchel charge just couldn't be beat. The user threw it like a giant grenade, fired it remotely, or rigged it to a tripwire. Its blast was fucking monumental. This device appealed to a little dark corner of my soul.

Day fifteen started out with a rumor that we were leaving this accursed place. My colleagues and I spent the time going through brief reviews of everything we had been taught in the last two weeks, including the captive chute business. At the end of that day, we were spent.

The opening of day sixteen seemed to confirm the rumor of the previous day. We were issued new—truly new—uniforms. Our last names were sewn over the right pocket, and in the place of the red ball on the shoulder there was a roundish patch with a wavy edge and a blue field with thirteen stars. Lucky number thirteen. We received dog tags bearing our names, rank, and social security number. Interestingly, they all had us at the rank of captain. Someone said that status might help if we were captured. Captured, huh? It seemed as though we were really going to leave this place. Just as well; May's *Playboy* was getting pretty ragged.

On 18 June 1963, the real adventure began. We were awakened for the last time by the keeper. It was 4:00 a.m. He explained that due to the interest of the press in an unrelated activity at the base's airfield, we were to be taken by bus to an alternate point of departure. He said he was sure they would have no interest in a bunch of assholes like us, but he had his orders. He was such a warm, caring person. We arrived at a large bus loaded with all of our stuff—rifles, scopes, ammo, everything. Then the twenty-five of us boarded. With a hiss of the closing door and a rev of the diesel engine, we left the keeper in a cloud of blue-black smoke. Served the son of a bitch right.

The driver said we were headed to Fort Bliss, just north of El Paso. Around dawn, we reached Fort Worth and turned west. Four hours later we had lunch in a diner in Big Springs. Just how big was this goddamned state? At seven thirty that evening, we pulled into El Paso and had dinner. We then hopped back on the bus, and about an hour and a half later, we reached our destination, an airfield within the confines of Fort Bliss. We loaded our own stuff into another C-47 and took off. This one had a door. Never get on a plane without a door. About four or five hours later, we landed on a very desolate runway in southern California, part of the Fort Irwin complex. Here we changed over to a large jet aircraft and were on our way west in less than an hour. At 8:00 a.m. Texas time, we refueled in Hawaii. On the stretch to Guam, we crossed the international date line and changed the day. Then I knew neither the right time nor the right day. I decided not to mess with my watch until we got to where we were going, and then I'd ask someone for the correct time and day. So I measured the whole trip was in Texas time. Around 4:00 p.m., we refueled in Guam and even got a chance to get out and stretch a little. What a dump. But then, we might not have been in the resort area. Five hours later, which was 11:00 a.m. 20 June 63 local time, we arrived at our Asian vacation spot, Chu Lai. Chu Lai was located on the coastal highway about one hundred kilometers south of Da Nang. The airfield was on the south end of the city. We got off the plane and right onto a truck, and within an hour we had covered the twenty-five kilometers north to the village of Tam Ky.

Our accommodations consisted of a group of nine large Quonset huts and a few wood-frame buildings. Next to the structures was a paved area where a number of UH-1 helicopters rested. We were assigned bunks then told to unpack and meet for lunch at the mess hut. This whole place had a peculiar acrid, moldy smell; the dirt wasn't the right color either. After lunch, we met in a briefing room. There, a Col. McCaffrey informed us that we would be given the rest of the day to adjust to the time change but that we were to go to work in the morning at dawn. We were divided into five four-man groups and one five-man group. Each group, now referred to as a hunter-killer team, would have a leader assigned who was "experienced." We viewed aerial photographs showing the mountain passes and trails used by the North Vietnamese to bring supplies to the south. The areas where we would be deployed were in the mountains. We would be overlooking trails exposed at long range, usually across a river or valley. The areas had been selected so the ranges were four to six hundred meters, which would prevent the enemy from effectively returning fire with the small arms they carried. We were warned to watch for mortars, however, as these could most certainly reach us. The basic job was to "neutralize" (such an inoffensive word) any pack animal, bicycle, cart, or human of any age, creed, or gender carrying anything south or east. The plan involved hit-and-run ambushes, but if we got into trouble there was airstrike capability, although it was very limited. We were told our commanding officers would make every effort to avoid casualties on our side, as these were most difficult to explain back home. We met our group leader, Gerhardt Roiger, Jerry, for short. Jesus, this guy, though diminutive, looked like he ate Cong balls for breakfast. He seemed pleasant enough at our first contact.

After the orientation, I walked around the compound and found the mini-PX. I bought a paper, June's *Playboy*, a bag of Tootsie Pops, and a beer. The beer was warm. For some reason the goddamned beer was always warm. I got into the habit of drinking it over ice. This had the added advantage that when you were finished, you could put the ice in the back of your hat. Why they couldn't use the ice to cool the beer, I never understood. Anyway, the newspaper said that the political situation in Vietnam was nearing violence. No shit. Perhaps that knot in my stomach was a manifestation of anxiety. Two more beers didn't help, so I went to chow. Oddly, after mess there were two types of people occupying the room: those who were withdrawn, and those who talked incessantly. Different coping mechanisms, I guessed. I didn't know if it was the food or the fear, but I thought I was going to puke. I left the mess hall for some air and then went to the bunk.

We had finished breakfast an hour and a half before dawn. There was no sun, but the air was still thick and humid. We had stowed all the gear aboard the baby blue helicopters while they warmed up on the pad. Our foursome was assigned to the second Huey on the pad, and we found our leader already aboard. The thing supposedly had room for eight, but our junk took up most of the extra space. Our target area was about 110 kilometers away. The Hueys could do a little under 200 kilometers per hour, so the trip would take about 40 minutes. This would get us there 30 minutes before sunrise. The Huey's engine revved up, and the blade tips fanned upward as the rotor caught up with the engine. The chopper seemed to give a little grunt and then, in a dust cloud, jerked into the air a few feet, and then proceeded forward. Having achieved a speed of about 20 miles per hour, it bobbed up into the air. We leveled off at about 1,000 feet and followed railroad tracks northwest. After a bit, the tracks turned due west and then a spur took off to the north. We followed the western route to a village named An Hoa, where the tracks ended. The plan then called for a 75-kilometer flight due west out of An Hoa. The terrain first became hilly, then mountainous. The green-black valleys were filled with mist, and looking back I could see the mist being swirled by the prop wash. Everyone was quiet. It seemed that if no one broke the spell, the descent phase would not begin. The spell was broken. Screaming to be heard over the engine noise, Roiger told us we would be landing in a few minutes and that it was imperative that we get clear of the chopper as quickly as possible. To avoid detection, we would land on the opposite of the mountain from which we would be shooting, then we would climb up to our position. We swept wide to the south and came up on the landing area through a small valley, just 30 feet off the ground. The ship's nose abruptly flared up and then craft gently dropped on its skids, and we scurried off. Roiger made sure we had all our gear and signaled the pilot. The chopper was away in less than a minute.

After the chopper had faded to a small speck in the predawn sky, Roiger called us together. He wanted to take this opportunity to bestow upon us some useful information, no doubt gleaned from his years of combat experience, now that we would be on our own. He said that we had already broken the first rule of survival: never go into the jungle.

Now, if we were going to get out of the jungle, we had to abide by Roiger's Eight Don'ts:
1. Don't question commands, execute them.
2. Don't think you have the situation under control; you don't.
3. Don't talk while headed toward the enemy.
4. Don't bunch up on the trail.
5. Don't yell if you get lost; stay put.
6. Don't drop trash.
7. Don't hesitate to fire if you see the enemy.
8. Don't *ever* let yourself get captured, no matter what.

He made it clear that if we failed to adhere to rules one through six, he would make us very sorry; if we failed to obey numbers seven and eight, someone else would make us very sorry. After asking, in a condescending tone, if anyone had difficulty understanding, he placed us in file and took the point. We were on our way. With our scoped rifles in their cases and strapped to our backpacks and an AR-10 or Remington 870 shotgun in hand, we almost looked like we knew what we were doing.

Looking north, the mountain loomed at least thirty degrees above the horizon. It was all green, except near the top where the trees thinned out, which was rocky and gray. The sun had already risen up there; I could see it reflected off the ledges and boulders. It was still very dim where we were, and there were many hours between us and the top. I was sweating already, and we hadn't even begun. My throat suddenly became dry, so I took a chunk of ice out of my hat to suck on. Single file, fifteen feet apart, we followed Roiger northward and upward. As the foliage thickened, the air became more humid and heavy with the smell of decaying vegetation. Underfoot, the ferns were so dense I couldn't tell exactly what I was stepping on or into. Where were those goddamned bloodsucking land leeches? Within minutes, our clothes were soaked from sweat and dew from the foliage. As it became lighter, the bugs began to find us. The small, black, biting flies had us flailing ourselves like a procession of monks during Lent. Every now and then we would startle an animal that, in its flight, would scare the shit out of us. This thing was definitely turning into a re-enactment of the Bataan Death March. The goddamned hill got steeper and steeper. As we tired, we began to fall frequently. We were getting nowhere. Roiger called a break with some under-his-breath muttering about a bunch of pussies. Nothing shows disdain like "pussies" in a German accent. The bugs seized this opportunity to dine on all our exposed flesh. After twenty minutes of water, rest, flies, and some vicious ants, we pressed on. The rest of the trip was as delightful, and we arrived at the tree line looking like rejects from a leper colony.

With the rocks came hope. There were only a few hundred meters to go. As we neared the top, Roiger warned us to stay below the ridgeline. Looking around, we saw that others had been here before us a long time ago. There were old slit trenches, sandbags, and timbers, but there were also obviously new boxes of equipment. When asked why they couldn't have dropped us in as well, Roiger said the equipment drop had to be done at night, and that clarified the issue immediately.

After regaining our strength, we set up camp, sandbagged up fire pits, and set up the flashers— not perverts, but battery-operated strobe lights set away from the real fire pits. We controlled them remotely, turning them on when we needed to draw fire away from ourselves. We set up the flashers directly across from the area we were going to fire on. This was about one hundred meters west of the camp.

Our squad set up the range finder and determined the exact distances and angles from the horizontal for three likely areas across the way, designated A, B, and C, each about thirty meters apart. We wrote this data on ammo boxes for quick reference. Each man zeroed his scope at the middle range and calculated hold over and hold under for his particular weapon for the other areas. We used a sixty-power, two-eye scope for spotting. It could easily pick out anything on the trail across the way. From where it was situated, we had a view of a quarter mile northeast and northwest of the fire zones. After all was set up, we established four-hour shifts at the scope—much longer than that and the spotter started to see things that weren't there.

We ate cold meals; there could be no fires. The bugs had abandoned us at the tree line, and as night closed in, we were within a klik of comfortable.

I had slept for about four hours when I was awakened to take my shift. It was 11:00 p.m., and the moon was rising. It was about three-quarters full and bathed the opposite side with enough light to make it seem like noon through the night scope. The trail on the mountain face was about ten degrees below us. It ran roughly east to west and parallel to our ridge a few hundred meters; then it turned north on both ends and disappeared around the mountain. Below the trail, just across from us and about seventy feet down was a small outcropping, and below that, there was a sheer drop, probably two or three hundred feet, to the rocks at the river's edge. The river flowed east. It too came from behind the mountain on the west and then ran around to the other side.

The rifle pits were hidden behind a façade of stone in front of sandbags laid out in the shape of graves. Each pit was about eighteen inches deep and had a slit in the north end so the rifleman could shoot from nearly complete concealment. For protection from the glaring sun, a camo poncho was stretched over the bags to shade the rifleman who preferred baking to broiling. The big rifles, coated with protective grease, were cradled in sandbags for stable firing. With extra ammo boxes at hand, all the riflemen needed was the alarm, and they could be in the pits and ready to shoot in a few seconds. The spotter's pit was deeper, allowing him to sit up while scanning the trail. It had a battery-powered buzzer button that, when activated, set off an alarm, causing all the other miscreants to run to their positions at full tilt. My shift lasted until 3:00 a.m. and passed without incident. After I closed my eyes, I could still see white scintillae's from staring through the night scope.

Bev heard the phone ring and glanced up. She ignored it, the answering machine would get it. She was not going to stop reading the journal.

CHAPTER EIGHT

THREE HOURS INTO MY sleep, the alarm sounded and we all hurried to our positions. As he was switching from the night scope to the sixty-power day scope, the spotter picked up fifteen men and six pack animals slowly winding their way south, directly toward us. It would be perhaps ten minutes before they could turn east and be in the midfire zone. We checked and loaded our rifles, made ready extra ammo, wiped lenses clean. Lastly, Roiger assigned target priorities. The pack animals were first, then the armed men—the one with a pistol (an officer) was the highest priority, then the other men. The animals carried the most gear, the armed men could run faster to get away. The rest could either drop their loads and run or be shot with them. With a few minutes left, we slipped into the rifle slings and tightened them. It took a minute of shifting and adjusting until man and machine molded into one. The light wasn't bad and there was no wind this dawn. In fact, it was disturbingly calm. I easily acquired my primary target, the second pack animal, in the scope. After some minor focusing to get the image just right, I slipped off the safety and awaited the fire order. While waiting, it occurred to me that this was going to be an irrevocable act and that we might not be able to finish what we were about to start. I mean, what was the point of looking for trouble? Too late for that. The deck had been cut, and the cards were being dealt. I had to concentrate. I opened the bolt slightly to make sure the weapon was loaded. The gold glint of the brass case reassured me that all was ready. We waited.

Suddenly the silence was broken buy a harsh Teutonic, "Now! Now!"

Just before I pulled the trigger, the man riding the animal gave it a few taps on the rump with a stick. The gun recoiled, and in the time it took the bullet to get there, I reacquired the target and saw the animal buck violently and bolt right over the edge of the goddamned trail, taking himself, his driver, and the cargo to their respective ends on the outcropping below. My next target was looking about, no doubt trying to figure out what the hell was happening. I felt the rifle recoil, and he dropped like a rock. Within seconds, all the animals were down and so were five men. The rest had dropped everything and were hightailing it back from whence they had come. Upon further inspection of the area, the spotter at the big scope found a survivor furtively peeking out from behind some small bushes. He was the center of attention for about five seconds and four shots. Then all was quiet.

It was obvious our targets had never determined the source of the incoming fire. They made no attempt to return fire. They might not have even heard the shots. So far, so good. I made a quick inventory and found that I had fired five shots and accounted for two men and one ox. We stayed in position, and about forty minutes later, one man came walking cautiously down the trail. He stopped at the ambush site, looked around, examined the bodies, and proceeded east. We let him pass. He continued around the bend, but ten minutes later he reappeared and went all the way back to the west and out of sight. After another hour, everyone but the spotter went back to camp. We congratulated each other on the job, and I was more than a little surprised at my emotional detachment considering I had killed two people. Perhaps it was because I thought that they were really not people like us after all. They were so far away I couldn't see their faces. That seemed to be it. If it had no face, it was just a target. Targets don't have children, grandchildren, birthdays, or futures.

Later in the afternoon, the alarm sounded again. This caravan was more heavily armed and moving much more cautiously than the last. There were two pack animals, nine coolies with very large packs, and ten armed men. Nahle doped the wind at three miles per hour, west to east, and Roiger assigned targets. Mine was the leading soldier who had his pistol in his hand. I guessed that it made him feel secure. As they approached the pile of debris from the last go-around, birds eating some spilled grain flushed and flew away. As the men paused at the wreckage, Roiger gave the signal; my man spun and dropped. Next to him, a wounded man was crawling. The pack animals were down. The coolies ran west; two dropped, then a third. Someone's frustrated fourth shot finally finished off the wounded man. The areas was now littered with all sorts of bags, boxes, and bodies. Our targets did not seem to know where we were. No return fire. Only three targets escaped.

Roiger, in his ever-observant (some would say paranoid) state, had the spotting scope trained on the river and had one man watch it while another watched the trail. Not fifteen minutes later, the spotters saw two dugouts with five armed men each crossing toward us. They had known where we were. When they were midway across the river, we opened up on them, and the man I shot did a back flip out of the boat, just like he had been flicked by the finger of God. I must have hit high. My next target was already in the water making for shore. It took two rounds to sink him. None of them made it out of the water. After that, it was very quiet. I didn't feel like eating, so I sucked on a Tootsie Pop for supper. The first day ended. I had fired thirteen rounds, killed six men and an ox. The first casualty of war is not innocence, it's your underwear.

I passed the night in fitful sleep. There were no alarms, only a few outbursts caused by those awakened by troubled dreams. Though not really loud, they were more than enough to disturb those sleeping lightly. My shift came again with daylight. The scope revealed literally hundreds of birds feeding across the way. Close inspection showed some kind of animal feeding on the bodies of men and oxen alike. It appeared to be some kind of large rat or opossum. Little else appeared on the trail that shift, or that day, for that matter. Perhaps they were waiting for dark. If so, it wouldn't be a long wait. We prepared supper by mixing dried rations with water from a canteen left in the sun. At least it was warm. Dusk allowed us to drift into sleep.

The moon had been up for an hour or two when a call came. With the night scopes, our range of vision did not encompass much more than the center fire area. So when the alarm was raised, the VC were already there. It took a few minutes to get into position; then, as our starlight scopes warmed up, we could see ten to fifteen VC trying to clean up the mess across the way. It was too dim for Roiger to assign targets, so the plan was target of opportunity. The flashers were activated to draw any return fire to the spot a hundred meters west of us. Our own rifles with their long barrels and low residue powder made very little flash. That was enough, however, to blind my scope for a few seconds after shooting before I could acquire a new target. About thirty seconds into the foray, Roiger, who was on the spotting scope, yelled, "Mortar by the shrub!" and everyone frantically searched for it; its shells could reach us. The man with the mortar got off two rounds that fell in the area of our flashers. He then became our main attraction, and by the way he flipped and jerked around, I figured he must have been hit by three or four rounds simultaneously. No one came to take his place. I probably hit three in that exchange, and another one-third if counting my piece of the mortar man. The way it was going, the debris alone would soon block the trail. It must have smelled horrible over there; the jungle sun could rot a body pretty fast. We were starting to smell pretty horrible over here, and we weren't dead—yet. There was no more action that night, and there was also precious little sleep.

At daybreak, our opponents tried another ploy. Nine unburdened but well-armed men walked to within fifty meters of the first body on the trail. They stopped and looked our way with binoculars, and then they started to run like hell. Someone must have seen something that unsettled him. Bad move. Only two made it to the bushes on the west side of the main trash pile. Under the cover of the bushes, they tried to return fire. Another bad move. Their rifles were too weak and their cover too thin, and in a few seconds they were Communist martyrs. My body count now was eleven unassisted, and I had used up one box of twenty cartridges. This must have been a pretty cost-effective operation, as there had to be thousands of dollars worth of junk littering the path.

All of us except the spotter returned to camp for breakfast. We took this opportunity to become a little better acquainted. It was really the first time we could.

Roiger broke the ice by relating that he had been a soldier for over twenty-five years. He had been in the Waffen-SS on the Russian front and later, fortunately for him, was captured by the Allies. He then joined the French Foreign Legion, no questions asked. He fought for the French in 1954 at Dien Bien Phu and was one of the thousand or so captured. He subsequently returned to France, where he was recruited by the CIA in 1960. He harbored a deep hatred for Communism and Communists that I suspected had more than ideology at its root.

The next soul in this purgatory to open up was Robert Hoehnfeld, a twenty-one-year-old premed student from La Crosse, Wisconsin. He admitted to being pretty tense all the time, or as he put it, high-strung. He wanted to eventually go back to La Crosse and be a family practitioner.

Larry Wolkert was the twenty-one-year-old engineering graduate who had accompanied me south on the plane out of Little Rock. He was rather pragmatic. His goal was to work for NASA.

Mike "Spike" Nahle was a nineteen-year-old marine out on loan to this operation. He was here because he really wanted to be, if you could believe that.

Just before noon, a shot startled everyone in the camp. As it turned out, Nahle had been watching the scavengers across the way and noticed that the birds were staying away from one of the bushy areas. After about thirty minutes of patient surveillance, he was convinced that one of those men in the brush wasn't dead after all, and Nahle had fixed that.

After the noon meal—and I use the term "meal" in the loosest sense—it was time to search for shade. The sun bore down on us and the humidity soared. Sweat did not have any cooling effect; it didn't evaporate. It just ran down the small of my back, paused for a while at my beltline, then trickled down the crack of my ass, on to the insides of my thighs, and finally collected in my boots. The little rivulets often felt like crawling bugs, and I found myself swatting what later proved to be an uninhabited area. The heat, the sweating, and the fact that the water supply was limited to drinking, had us soon smelling like a bunch of hogs. It was just after lunch that I noticed the red blotches on my elbows, each about the size of a quarter, raised and a little scaly. I showed the rash to Hoehnfeld, the premed, and he thought it was a fungus. Just what I needed, leprosy. I then showed it to Roiger, who confirmed that it was fungus that came from digging my elbows into the soil to shoot. He had it too. He also said I'd never get rid of it. He had tried everything to no avail. Shit. If it spread over my whole body, I could write off the cheerleader in the '57 Chevy.

Later in the afternoon, Roiger said that the air recon had confirmed his suspicion that the opposing team was up to something. If they couldn't cross the river below us, the next place that they could cross was about six miles northwest, and that meant they had to cross two mountains to get at us. He figured that would take them two to two and a half days. Hell, it took us a day to get up the side of one mountain, but Roiger said they were more motivated than we were. Nahle said, "Bullshit."

All in all, June 23 ended quietly. The night, too, was quiet, and I found that disturbing. This was a real mental catch-22. If it was not quiet, I was extremely scared; if it was quiet, I was extremely apprehensive.

June 24 opened with a furrow of concern on Roiger's brow. That, in turn, caused a flare of distress in four sets of bowels. After a radio conference with air recon, Roiger was now sure that trouble was on the way and that the best outcome would result from our taking the fight to them in the form of an ambush. He, from either experience or outside information, felt they were planning a coordinated effort. As the flanking attack began on us, they would rush all the supplies they could over the trail. This meant a preset attack time or a signal. If we could disrupt the attack, it would be a turkey-shoot across the way. He said the recon photos gave him reason to believe that the forces sent against us would be a small patrol of six to eight men. Figuring they had been underway for twelve hours or so and traveled about twice as fast as we did, he decided our ambush should be set about twelve hours out from camp. Here we would intercept them at dusk a day and a half from now and then we would hurry back in time for the festivities. It sure sounded like he knew what he was talking about, and wasn't that really half the battle? In any event, Roiger decided that he and I were going to head west early in the morning. The rest would watch the trail and, I hoped, pray that I would survive this honor.

Roiger and I spent the remainder of the day preparing equipment for the trek west. This was a job for high explosives and automatic weapons. We made ready the AR-10s and stocked our packs with ammo, claymore mines, satchel charges, and four rations of MREs. After topping off our canteens, we went to sleep for the next ten hours.

At 4:00 a.m., Roiger woke me. Christ, I had really slept well, and I felt pretty good. I went through my duffle bag and retrieved a clean pair of socks and my lucky T-shirt. If there were a time for luck, it was then. I made a cold breakfast in the dark and visited the latrine hole; I didn't want to carry any more than I had to. After the group's emotionally awkward but well-meaning send-off, we made our way down the slope, below the tree line, and into the jungle. When we hit the tree line, we picked up our traveling companions, the bugs.

We had been in the undergrowth about an hour when the rain started. It cut our already diminished visibility down to just a few feet. The idea of heading toward the oncoming enemy in that shit had me swallowing almost continually to keep from puking. I became oblivious to the bugs in my single-minded effort to see that extra few feet. The foliage-covered ground was slippery and uneven, causing a few falls and many near falls. When the rain stopped, the whole jungle became misty. As Roiger walked ahead of me, he seemed a man on fire with smoke rising from his body. The visibility was now zero, and we had to stop to keep from injuring ourselves.

We paused on a stream bank swollen from the rainfall. It was definitely time for a Pall Mall. This would have made a great commercial. "After a grueling day in the jungle, killing Cong for Christ, there's nothing like a Pall Mall." After waiting about fifteen minutes, a slight breeze picked its way through the trees and thinned out the fog to the point that we could see well enough to go on. I unwrapped one of my chocolate Tootsie Pops, and we were away. A short distance upstream we had to ford. Roiger made a point of telling me to cover all body parts that would come in contact with the water. The waterborne parasites could bore into unprotected skin. Entering the water, I noticed a small green snake swimming away from me a few yards downstream, and I quickly checked to see if it had any companions. After stepping on a few suspicious objects in the water, we made it to the opposite bank. Getting up the bank must have taken a whole five minutes it was so goddamned slick with mud. At the top, we looked like we had just climbed out of a latrine. Roiger said not to worry; it would keep the bugs off. He was right. Five minutes later I wished I had more mud. The fucking bugs were out with a vengeance. The buzzing was unbelievable, and the way they hovered in front of my face kept me constantly fanning my eyes. I even inhaled a few of the bastards.

A short while later, two good things happened: the bugs thinned out, and Roiger found an animal path headed in the direction we were. This meant we didn't have to do a lot of chopping with the machete, a very strenuous activity. As we went along, we hacked marks on the trees along the path. We would be returning this way in the dark, in a hurry.

About noon we broke through the jungle onto a ridge. From here we could see the junction of the bases of two mountains about three miles west-northwest of us. Roiger said that would be the spot for the ambush. The enemy would have to come through there. "What if they've already been through there?" I thought. Somehow, being in the opening in the jungle made the feeling of imminent vomit go way. As we reentered the trees, the feeling immediately returned.

The fear was an amazing thing. Unlike other emotions, which come on, build, peak, and then subside, the fear continued to build, and when I thought it couldn't get worse, it did. My gut muscles fatigued from being continually tensed; my ass was so tight I thought I'd never shit again. I felt an intestinal quivering that only those who have felt it could understand. Only two things kept me glued together: I didn't want to look like a chicken shit, and I didn't know the way out. Prayer turned into undisguised bartering. I promised anything to be delivered. I'd stop indulging in any vice, real or imagined. As a Catholic, I had a lot of bargaining chips. Only some last vestige of pride kept me from completely decompensating. Having drawn up what I considered a generous contract with the Almighty for my safety, I plodded through the jungle quietly, continually reminding Him of his obligation.

The last three miles were almost dreamlike. All I had to do was follow Roiger. God was with me. Exhausted, we reached what Roiger called "a good spot." We took off our packs and scouted the area. No one had been through there lately; the vegetation and spiderwebs were undisturbed. The trail continued up the ravine between the two mountains. There were two large rocks on the left side of the trail and one on the right. Roiger said that the lads would be coming through there in their typical half run. We placed the claymores in a zigzag from one side of the trail to the other and set them to self-trigger. The idea was that the lead man would trigger one in the middle of the trail, and the survivors would jump to the sides of the trail and touch off the remaining mines. Just to be sure, we put remote-detonated satchel charges under each of the big rocks on the side opposite us. This was for anyone who made it there for cover. I jokingly asked Roiger if he thought we had used enough explosives, and he assured me that we could never use too much. We then prepared cover for ourselves about fifty meters down the trail, where we could observe the festivities. Finally, we rested.

Bev sighed, "Oh my God." She had to stop and take a break. Putting down Connie's journal, she went to the kitchen and fixed a turkey sandwich and pulled a bottle of apple juice from the fridge. She wondered how Connie had managed to survive this ordeal. And why had he kept it all to himself? Not even a slip of the tongue, ever. She'd give him hell for not telling her if she ever saw him again.

CHAPTER NINE

BEV POLISHED OFF HER sandwich and returned to the sofa with the rest of her apple juice. She turned the next page of Connie's journal and continued.

Under our cover, we had a little to eat and took turns napping. We had to get some rest because the trip back would start right after the upcoming encounter. Nightfall came swiftly but without company. The moon was on its way up and was nearly full. The evening was cooling off and the bugs were thinning out a bit. As our eyes adjusted to the moonlight, we could see the trail all the way back to the scene of the impending disaster. My intense observation of the area gave birth to imaginary forms darting here and there. This brought the acid to my throat again, and I had to sip almost continually from the canteen to keep my mouth wet and my supper down. I kept wondering if they could see or sense the trap. If so, were they about to turn the tables? If only I had put a few more leaves on the mines and the wires. I decided Roiger had been right; we couldn't use too many explosives. All of a sudden, my bowels had a terrific urge to move. I guessed I had finally relaxed a little, or I was losing all control. Roiger said to hold it. Moving would be dangerous, and if I defecated around here, they might smell it and be tipped off. The moon was up now and the night birds and other unknown beasties were really carrying on. Roiger said it would be easy for us now; when the noise stopped, the party would begin. I thought my bowels were going to explode, the cramping was so intense. As a matter of fact, I had to puke too. Maybe I belonged in a different line of work.

Then the worst happened. The jungle became quiet. Oh, fuck. About ten seconds later the first claymore went off, then a second and third in rapid succession. All was quiet. It was then that I noticed that I had pissed my pants. There was no sign of movement in the area illuminated by the small grass fires caused by the mines. Five seconds later, Roiger gave me the signal to detonate the satchel charges. The dark corner in my soul brightened as I twisted the detonator handle and the whole area in front of us roared. We had planned to lie quietly, watch, and listen for about thirty minutes. About halfway through the waiting period, the birds started up again. Taking this as a sign of safety, we then cautiously, and I mean cautiously, approached the blast area with the AR-10s ready. Even by the moonlight it was difficult to determine the exact number of casualties. There were two bodies on the trail. They had been shredded by the first mine. Off to the left was another—actually a half. A few yards back on the left, a fourth victim. Behind the rocks, or what was left of them, were still smoking holes about four feet across and eighteen inches deep. We found only one sandal and two battered rifles there. Christ only knows how many VCs had used the rocks for cover.

Roiger said I could relieve myself. Even though things had tightened up again, this took about three seconds. Then we packed up and tore out for camp. It was easier going back, as we had left everything but our rifles and water. I no longer feared running into VC. That helped the climbing puke situation a lot. We took the wrong path a few times and had to backtrack but made pretty good time. When we got to the ridge opening in the jungle, I looked back. The moonlight reflected off the mist hovering over the trees looked just like snow on a harvested cornfield. As we moved on, I had trouble keeping up with Roiger. The old son of a bitch was in pretty good shape. He had to slow for me and complained that we had to move as fast as the party we had blown up or we would be late for their supply run. Heaven goddamn forbid. When we arrived at the stream, we found it had drained to barely a trickle, so we crossed in just a few seconds. During the crossing, I looked intently for my buddy the green snake. The moon was going down, and it was getting darker and more difficult to see where we were going. I fell into one of the goddamned holes that I had fallen into going the other way. Mercifully, we stopped for a drink and a smoke, which allowed the pain in my side to decrease to bearable. I unwrapped my Tootsie Pop, and we resumed the Roiger marathon.

At daybreak, we were still hours away from camp. The signs were easier to read, I could see where I was stepping, but I was dead on my ass. We took a break. I caught a fifteen-minute nap after a skimpy breakfast. With about four hours to go, we discarded everything but our rifles and one canteen and hauled ass for camp at a trot. Roiger figured that noon was the earliest that the VC would reach our camp, but they probably had a built-in waiting period of a few hours to allow for contingencies, so the push could come any time after two or three o'clock. Their boys across along the trail would likely wait to hear sounds of combat before they ventured out. We would supply these sounds at two o'clock sharp. Even if the hour was wrong, they would figure there had been a mix-up and start out anyway.

We spotted the tree line below camp at about one o'clock. We went in yelling, "It's us, you assholes! Don't shoot!" to the guards waiting in case we had not been successful. We were welcomed with yells and hugs. Things got a little emotional again. Roiger explained the whole scheme to the rest of the group while I got into my rifle pit and went to sleep. I figured they would wake me when the time came. They did.

About ten minutes to two, we prepared. Roiger went down the hill with five grenades, an AR-10, and a flare gun. At two o'clock on the money, he launched a flare, heaved grenades, and fired the automatic weapon at the crest of the ridge just west of the flashers. Sure as hell, those fuckers across the way came running. Our game plan was for three rifles to open up on the head of the column after it got well past the trash pile, into the east most area. The fourth rifle would start at the back and work its way forward.

Those bastards were bent on getting through. There were oxen, horses, coolies, bicycles, and armed guards, all coming on at full speed. There were so many coming so fast that we didn't make any attempt to count them or assign targets. Unfortunately for them, the wind was doped at less than two miles per hour, west to east, and they were traveling west to east about four miles per hour. They were so close to each other that it was going to be difficult to miss them. All this translated into about a 70 percent probability of a hit for each round fired at a man and about a 90 percent chance for a hit on the animals.

We opened fire when the men were about thirty meters past the pile of debris. No doubt their leader's last thought was that they had once again outfoxed the Yankee pigs. He had no opportunity to change his mind, but his compatriots did. Pack animals went down, men went down; the head of the line was soon blocked by the accumulation of wreckage. Wolkert was working up from the back of the line. The men in the middle just kept pressing forward until they were stopped by either traffic or a bullet. When all forward motion stopped, there was mass confusion. Some tried to hide behind the dropped cargo, some tried to turn around and force their way back. Some either jumped or were pushed over the side of the cliff. They were firing back, and for the first time a few small-arms rounds landed near us. They knew where we were now. Our gun barrels were getting hot, and the mirage over them was making it harder to get hits. Suddenly, a ten-foot section of trail blew up and cleared off an additional ten feet of debris on either side of the blast. Four or five VC put up their hands as if to surrender. No dice.

After it was over, I guessed that about five of them made it through to the east and perhaps ten made it back to the west. All seventeen of the animals were down. All the bikes, seven to ten, were down, and I estimated that thirty-two coolies bought it, judging by the number of bundles. To this tally had to be added an unknown number of armed guards as well. I expended thirty-nine rounds, one short of two boxes. I put the last one in my pocket to keep as a good luck charm.

Wolkert kept an eye on the trail while the rest of us cleaned the spent shells out of our pits, wiped the cordite residue off our faces and hands, and got a drink. The guns were too hot to clean.

Everyone jumped at a delayed explosion across the way. Wolkert yelled out that there was nothing to worry about, and I went back to treating the burn on Nahle's neck. During the fracas one of his ejected cases went down his collar and blistered him good. He said he hadn't noticed it until he was wiping the soot off his face. Concentration was the name of the game.

Leaving a spotter, we adjourned to the luxuries of the camp. It would be dark soon, so we ate, and then I told the rest of the guys about Roiger's and my field trip over coffee and cigarettes. Roiger said that today's little set-to was really going to piss off the opposition. They would probably send a fucking regiment up here as soon as they could. It was time for us to get our collective asses out. There were no dissenting votes. After making radio contact, Roiger told us the chopper was to pick us up at dusk tomorrow at the same site where we had been left off six days before. I like a man who knows when to fold.

I could hardly move the following morning. The air was thick and damp. It smelled old. My clothes were saturated and my muscles were stiff as boards. Nevertheless, June 27 was going to be an all right day because we were getting the fuck out. We ate, policed the area one last time, packed up the junk, and, as a parting gesture, set up a few surprises for anyone who sought us out. Everything we couldn't carry we tossed over the mountainside. After all the housekeeping chores had been attended to, we took off down the mountain.

It was easier to quick-march away from the action than toward it. I imagined everyone was thinking of showers, shaves, clean cots, hot food, cold beer, and undisturbed sleep. A month ago I had all of this as givens I took for granted. Now it was all I could think of. The old saying is true, "You don't know how good you've got it." Around ten o'clock that morning it started to rain again. This had two beneficial effects: one, the bugs let up, and two, we made better time falling down the mountain than walking down it. Around noon it was really coming down hard. I couldn't even keep a cigarette lit. My poncho didn't keep me dry, but it sure kept me warm. I didn't know if the liquid filling my boots was rain, sweat, or urine. My thirteen-pound case rifle now weighed in the tons. No matter how I had it slung, in a few minutes it was digging into me painfully and I had to change position again. Nahle commented that at least we'd all smell better after this drenching. "You couldn't wash a dog turd enough to make it smell better," Wolkert responded.

At about two o'clock the rain let up and the bugs were on us for a late lunch. We took a break and attended to our bodily functions— well, all but one. Except for Hoehnfeld; I think he did them all. By four o'clock, we were at the landing site for a few hours of rest before the chopper arrived. We slept the sleep of the pursued and were easily awakened by the rotor noise of the incoming helicopter long before its arrival. We loaded the gear and were airborne in five minutes.

That was a deus ex machina if there ever was one. Plucked from a horrible situation by an envoy from the gods and swiftly delivered to safety on his wings. The orange sky with its red-gray gashes was behind us as we skimmed along a few hundred feet above the ground. I saw the pinpoint fires of a tiny village off to the southeast. The pilot found An Hoa and the railroad tracks, which we followed back to Tam Ky.

Back in the barracks, I grabbed my toilet kit and headed for the shower. I immediately ran into a problem. The sweat and grime had dried, fusing the hair on my body to my filthy clothes. The hair came off with the clothes. The remedy was to step into the shower dressed, and as the water loosened the bond, the clothes would come off a layer at a time. The shower was ecstasy. The only problem was that the shower watered down my beer quickly. It also precipitated a strange phenomenon. Before I went into it I was not sweating much and smelled mildly ripe. After the shower, I sweated like a pig and smelled horrible. I had to reshower and change underwear twice before the stench abated. It must have been something to do with rehydration.

The subsequent hot meal was ambrosia, and the sit-down latrine was the pièce de résistance for the day. Maybe that's why those VC were so obnoxious: they had to squat in the woods. "Perhaps if we used our foreign aid to provide them all with toilets, they would curb their antisocial behavior," I thought as I dozed off.

During breakfast the next day, a chopper looking pretty shot up, landed on our pad. The rifle team it carried was okay, but one of the crew was dead. They said they had drawn fire while passing over a village around dawn. Hell, I thought, those assholes in the villages were supposed to be on our side. I guessed that the only ones we could really be sure of were the dead ones.

The rest of the day was composed of naps and beers so that by nightfall no one was very sleepy or very sober. This led to the beginning of the Tam Ky Hearts game marathon. The weather had turned bad enough that the choppers could not take off, so that left us grounded. To pass the time, sixteen men were divided among four tables. Each played to a thousand points. Things went pretty well for about six hours, then the betting on the winner started to get out of hand. An "accidental" misplay of a reneged club triggered the goddamnedest fight I had ever seen. That pretty much ended the social activities for the evening, so I went to bed uninvolved and uninjured. At breakfast, there was a lesser rendition of last night's fight. It was as if those idiots didn't remember how bad it was out in the bush and how good it was at the base. I think the slow time was getting to them, and some of them would rather be out shooting. Not me, goddamn it, not me. Their memories had to be about as long as their dicks. They'd get their wish for action soon enough; the sky was clearing.

July! One month down and five to go. At lunch, Roiger brought air recon photos of our ex-camp. It seemed that our air arm had been watching it for the expected counterattack, and when the VC arrived, the air team plastered the shit out of them. The weather people claimed that we would be able to fly in the morning; how delightful. After supper we were called to the briefing room and were told about our next mission. It was to be a one-day job. All we would take along were the rifles, a few rounds of ammo, and water. We would be back by noon. Well, it beat being out a week. We were to learn about the particulars after we were underway at first light the next day. I went to the mini-PX and stocked up on cigarettes and Tootsie Pops. I wished that I could get a bag of only chocolate pops. I hated the grape and the orange ones. After a few beers, it was night-night. In the darkness, all I could hear were cot-spring noises coming from Hoehnfeld's bunk, followed by a few rather strident comments, and then humid silence.

The next morning the sunlight woke me. What happened to leave at first light? Roiger said there had been a change of plans and that we would be leaving at midafternoon. In the middle of the morning, a chopper landed and unloaded a really grungy-looking rifle team. Apparently they had been stranded by the weather and had run out of supplies and become a bit peckish about the whole mission. As they passed by, one rather unkempt individual was heard to mumble something about a motherfucker named Rhaspberry. Ah, another fan.

After lunch we were directed to zero our rifles for special ammo. Roiger specified exactly 640 meters, 10 degrees down, and don't clean the barrel afterward. It sounded as though the first shot really had to count. After the zeroing in, which took all of thirty minutes, I was leafing through the July *Playboy* on my bunk when the word of imminent departure came. The gear had been on the chopper for hours, so all we had to do was hop aboard and press the penthouse button, and up we went.

Our course took us almost due west to the sizeable village of Kham Duc. The pilot landed and turned the engine off, and we remained in the chopper listening to the very gradually slowing *whup-whup* of the rotor blades. Within a few minutes, we were joined by two men, one Vietnamese and one American. This was the first native I had seen close up. He was short, maybe five-six tops, with straight coal-black hair and a build Charles Atlas couldn't have helped. Christ, if they were all like that it was a wonder we could hit any of them. Coming from a small Midwestern town, I had never seen an Oriental person. My impression of them were primarily based on 1940s John Wayne movies. This guy was a dead ringer for the son of a bitch that shot down Scotty in *The Flying Tigers;* he was probably a distant relative. The Vietnamese stood outside and the American got in. The pilot came back and they pored over some maps and information sheets. How they knew this shit I'd never know, but they knew that two ranking NVA officers were going to visit a VC encampment just inside the Cambodian border. They were going to arrive by motor launch around eight tomorrow morning. We were going up to a rocky prominence 640 meters upstream from their dock this evening. We would sleep in position and provide a welcoming salute as they landed. For some reason, it was quite important that only the first two that got off the launch be nailed. I guessed the guy who gave us all this information was going to be aboard. Or maybe they just wanted the VC to know they could kill anyone of them whenever they wanted to. Or ... who knows?

The American, who was inexplicably wearing cowboy boots, and his faithful Vietnamese companion, Tonto-San, departed. After a few minutes of engine warm-up, we were off again. The chopper flew due south about eight miles to Dak To, then southwest for twenty minutes or so. The pilot then did an evasive maneuver by going south, circling west to north, which put us in position to come up on the river from the south. It was nearly dark, and we were flying so low that I could actually see individual leaves on the trees. We were dumped off at a flat spot about eight hundred meters south of the prominence from which we would be firing. As the chopper hightailed it south, we started north and in a few minutes were at the base of the prominence. Nahle was sent up the cliff to drop a line for the rest of us. It made climbing that sixty vertical feet a hell of a lot easier for the not so fit. On the top, Nahle dropped more lines to facilitate a hasty exit. We crawled over the rock looking for the paint marker that the helicopter crew had dropped to give us the exact distance to the dock. Locating this, we settled in for the night. We could see small lights in the camp, and every once in a while the wind would bring us a whiff of smoke and cooking food. We slept in position to avoid any detection. We covered ourselves with the gray-green ponchos with all loose ends tucked in. We painted black camo streaks on our faces, pointed our rifles in the correct direction, and double-checked that they were unloaded. It was then that Nahle noticed that the bolt was missing from his rifle. That meant there would be two rifles on one target and only one on the other. Roiger decided that Hoehnfeld and Wolkert would shoot the lead man as soon as his feet touched land and that I would shoot the second when I heard their shots. That way there would be two rifles ready for follow-up shots, if needed. After a Tootsie

Pop, I tried to sleep, but the rock was very uncomfortable and I was worried about rolling off the cliff, among other things.

Bev looked up from her reading. Connie's discomfort made her uncomfortable as well. How long had she been sitting? She looked at her watch. Six hours! She had to get a drink but didn't want to stop reading.

CHAPTER TEN

BEV STRETCHED HER ARMS and her back before turning the page and forged ahead.

Nothing takes longer to come than dawn. At about 5:00 a.m., the wind picked up. If it had rained, I would definitely have broken my neck on that rock. I had another Tootsie Pop. After the long night I was now down to the orange and grape ones. Three hours and seven pops later, Nahle spotted the launch coming down the river. We hunkered down to wait for them to pass. The sun was up and hot. The air had stilled. It got very uncomfortable under the tarps, but on the plus side, there were no bugs; they had died of heat stroke. The launch passed within a hundred meters of us and proceeded down the river to dock. There were four officer types and one crewman aboard. As the boat slowly made its way to the dock, the people at the camp came down to greet the passengers. There was a lot of arm waving and, no doubt, cheering, but we couldn't hear that. We loaded the rifles with special 168-grain hollow-point boattail bullets and waited with our scopes trained on the dock. It was narrow, maybe two feet across at the widest part. They would be disembarking single-file. Perfect.

We had our rifles resting on rolled-up ponchos and were going into concentration mode as are targets tied up the boat. After taking a few deep breaths, I held my breath and picked up on the rhythm of my heartbeat by watching the crosshairs bounce. I was ready. As the first man's foot hit the bank, Hoehnfeld and Wolkert touched off their rifles, and a heartbeat later, I fired mine. I had the crosshairs on the target's left shoulder blade, but as I fired he turned slightly toward me, probably reacting to what had just happened to the man in front of him. My bullet must have hit him in the left armpit, and he fell sideways into the water. The lead man was obviously dead, sprawled facedown on the ground with his feet on the dock.

All three of us took one follow-up shot at the man floating in the water, and then we hauled ass. We slung our rifles and rappelled down the cliff. The chopper pilot was on his way in for us as we hit the ground. Running as fast as possible, we covered the distance to the chopper in about five minutes and got aboard in about two seconds. As we lifted off, I noticed there was still a wisp of smoke drifting up out of my gun barrel. I pursed my lips and blew across the muzzle. I glanced at Roiger and found him looking at me; then he looked down and shook his head. I think he was smiling. After we cleared the area, we ascended a few thousand feet and made no stops on the way back to Tam Ky.

Lunch was a quiet affair. We four sat at one table and discussed the recent job. Nahle, of course, didn't see any difference between it and anything else we had done, and perhaps he was right. We other three, however, felt there was a basic philosophical distinction. It was one thing to ambush armed men but quite another to engage in assassination, and for profit, at that. Maybe it was that we got away clean. Perhaps if they had come closer to killing us we wouldn't have been indulging ourselves in this moral masturbation. Maybe it was guilt. If guilt were going to enter the picture, it had best hurry. Our consciences were becoming less receptive by the day. What could guilt do to someone who had personally and deliberately killed over twenty people and had been intimately involved in the demise of many more? It was best not to mention that this had been accomplished in our first two weeks on the ground and that we were committed to five more months. Hoehnfeld got a little weird during this speculation and started to talk about divine retribution. No one wanted to hear that shit, so we left him sitting alone. The guy was a jackoff.

During the afternoon, Roiger called us together to inform us we were going back to our first camp in a few days, so we had better rezero our rifles. He then collected all the hollow-point ammo— it was against the Geneva Convention. I had to keep one for a souvenir.

Supper was very tense. We discussed only the lightest and least controversial of subjects, the weather, this month's Playmate, that kind of shit. Wolkert and I went for a walk afterward. He was really the only one I could talk to; a mirror, of sorts. We agreed that Nahle and Hoehnfeld were both nuts; they differed only in specific pathology. We also agreed that the chances of us surviving would be better if we covered each other. It was then that our friendship was forged, and from that time on it was us against the universe.

That night, Hoehnfeld was quietly praying at the foot of his bunk, head in his hands. I had nothing against praying—I was doing it more frequently myself—but that mother was coming loose.

The next day was the Fourth of July, and I wondered if these Vietnamese clowns could ever have a Fourth of July. In all likelihood, all they would have was a continuous Chicago version of Valentine's Day. Their historical conflicts never end. They may cool down for a while, but they never end. There were a hell of a lot more of them than us, and the implications of these facts certainly gave me pause, unless I thought about nuclear or CBW solutions. But more to the point, what the hell was I doing here shooting at them with a weapon that had been patented in 1898? It must have made sense to someone, somewhere, but not to me.

We weren't shooting that day, so Wolkert and I decided to make a firecracker and celebrate. You know, relieve some tension. We scrounged around for components and came up with five pounds of C-4 explosive, two five-gallon plastic cans of gasoline, and three detonator caps. We figured that after dark would be the ideal time for our pyrotechnic display. We didn't let anyone else in on what we were up to. It was to be a real surprise. Surreptitiously, we dug a shallow hole at the edge of the landing pad, at least one hundred meters from the nearest manmade object. We placed the C-4 in the hole and put the cap in place. We placed the gas cans, all with their own detonator caps, on top of the pile and wired everything together. We then strung the detonator wires inconspicuously out to the steps of the mini-PX. There we sat after supper, sipping beer and recalling Fourths past. At first there were only the two of us, Wolkert and me. Then the group grew in size by ones and twos until we were about fifteen. It was getting dark, so the PX porch light was turned on so the bugs would know where the meat was, and the chatter continued. The ideal time for the display came when

Hoehnfeld brought up retribution again. In midsentence, Wolkert stood up and called upon the Prince of Darkness to sweep down and claim us for our transgressions, and with this, I touched the wires to the battery. Hoehnfeld's objections were drowned out by a mighty roar. The sky was filled with a spray of red-orange flames that replicated what I had always imagined hell to look like. It took the group about five seconds to figure out what had happened. I figured it was the convulsions that Wolkert and I were having that gave it away. Someone uttered some unkind words concerning our sexual preference, so we took off. Hoehnfeld may have suffered permanent psychic scarring from that episode. The prank had only a very transient uplifting effect, and soon boredom came to sit with us again. The *Playboy* had become mildewed; the staples were rusty. The beer was giving me indigestion, the cigarettes were making me gag, there was no relief from the tedium. I went to bed.

In the briefing room after breakfast, we found out that a recon team had been sent to check out our old camp and sanitize it, as we were going back this afternoon. Roiger looked directly at me and said he did not want to know who was responsible, but he didn't want a repeat of the bullshit that had occurred last night. Duly chastised, I began my preparations for the trek with my usual run on the PX for pops and cigarettes and then packed all the essentials for the trip. Nahle got a new rifle, and we tied the bolt to the trigger guard with a string so he wouldn't lose it again. He did not appreciate that at all. The boy took himself much too seriously. Marines. Around two o'clock we boarded the helicopter, and we were off to the office. I napped during the flight. I guess a human being can adjust to just about anything.

The chopper set down on almost the exact spot as before and we disembarked. While unloading, Hoehnfeld's pack fell open and a couple of cans of beer fell out. Holy shit! Roiger was on him like a mink on a chicken. He stomped the beer cans flat, spraying beer all over. He then knocked Hoehnfeld to the ground, called him a motherfucking idiot, and said if he ever brought booze or beer out on the job again he would personally kill him. Well, that really threw a wet blanket on the gaiety of the outing. Roiger then took the AR-10 from Hoehnfeld, and we were underway. We had barely seen the surface of that man's capacity for violence.

This trip up the mountain was every bit as delightful as the first. It was nice to renew acquaintances with the insect population, soak up some of the local moisture, and fall into some familiar holes. We covered the distance thirty-five minutes faster than we had last time. I asked Nahle if we could now qualify for the Marines. He just said, "Shit," and turned away. We sacked out just outside the tree line, as the sun was down when we arrived. We wanted to be able to see everything when we went into the camp area. At this location, there were two ways to sleep, and both were bad. Number one, cover up everything with a poncho and suffocate; number two, leave your face exposed to the bugs and lose it. I decided that suffocation was the lesser evil.

At sunrise, we ate, cleaned the ants out of our clothes, and proceeded up the last hundred or so meters to the camp. We got to the top with only one incident. Nahle had almost stepped on what he thought was a snake, but it turned out to be the tail of a turtle. The tail on that son of a bitch must have been eighteen inches long.

We examined our old place and found it all shot up. Bullet holes and bomb craters were all over the place, along with some ominous dark stains here and there on the path. Roiger decided that we would put our flashers where our fire pits had been before and set up in the old flasher pits. It took about three hours to get squared away; then we rested.

Roiger then gave Hoehnfeld his rifle and turned to Wolkert and said, "If that crazy fucker shoots me, you have a direct order to kill him." Wolkert nodded an almost enthusiastic affirmation. Even more surprising, I was offended that Roiger had not chosen me to cover him. Things were getting weird. We redid the geometry of the fire fields and posted a spotter. Then we were open for business.

All of that afternoon was quiet. As a matter of fact, the next four days and nights passed without incident. Did the VC know our location? Were they coming after us? Had they taken a new route, leaving us to languish on that rock? For the hundredth time, Roiger reminded us to be patient.

Our patience paid off around noon the following day. Wolkert was on the scope and spotted a pack train coming down the trail. They weren't being too cautious, either. The first four men were carrying what appeared to be large boards. It soon became evident what they were up to. The explosion from the cart we shot up the last time had made about eight feet of the trail impassable. These guys were now putting heavy planks across the area. We waited. Roiger assigned targets; mine was on a bicycle. He had four AK-47s across his back and several large bundles tied to the bike. Those guys could carry more on a bike than the U.S. Army could get in a two-and-half-ton truck. He dismounted to cross the boards, and I fired when he was midway across. As he fell, he knocked off two of the boards. His comrades seemed to think he had just slipped, but when an ox dropped, five of them dropped everything and hauled ass back west. Perhaps they were the survivors of a previous engagement.

About ten minutes later, the flasher area was hit by rather intense mortar fire. They really had that spot zeroed in. We could not determine the source of the fire. After it subsided, the road crew appeared with more boards. We watched as they nervously placed the planks. Then one of them scanned our side of the canyon with binoculars. Their work done, the four men picked up some bundles and proceeded east. We let them go. A quarter of an hour later, one man with an ox came. We let him pass. It was like playing God, deciding who lived and who died. The man tested the board with the ox and then turned around and went back.

Shortly, another pack train arrived. Sixteen men, five oxen, one horse, one large pig, and four bikes. As soon as they reached the boards, we opened up with two rifles trained on the front of the line and two on the back. A wounded ox turned and ran west, knocking two men off the cliff before it too ran over the edge. In a few seconds, all the animals were down except the pig. The men that weren't dead sought cover among the corpses and rubble. We guessed there were about four or five left. Some of them fired their weapons blindly; they still had no idea where we were. One made a run for it. He had no chance; all four of us were waiting for such a move. We knew the others would be ours too, sooner or later. One, using a wicker basket and the pig for a shield, tried to inch his way west. It might have worked if Nahle had not shot the pig just for the hell of it. With the pig down, there wasn't enough basket to cover his ass, so he lost it. Some ten minutes later, I caught another man peeking over a cloth bundle and dropped him with a shot through the bundle. The last survivor came out waving a white rag in each hand. He was hit by one round in the chest, fell back onto a wounded ox, which bucked at the contact, propelling the man face forward over the cliff. I had heard these Asians were good gymnasts; that was at least a 9.2. Several hours passed with no sign of life across the way. If anyone were there, he wasn't moving until it was good and dark.

It was good and dark before we made contact again. They probably figured that we would let ones and twos get through to get the big score. So they started to come down the trail singly, about two hundred meters apart. It worked at first, and we let three through before we caught on. After that, our man with a starlight scope shot at anything he saw when he saw it. After five shots, they didn't want to play anymore. The rest of the night passed calmly.

At breakfast, our talk centered on our phenomenal luck. Without a single casualty, we had killed well over a hundred men, a herd of oxen, several horses, and one pig. The more I thought about it, the spookier it seemed. It was like that movie with William Bendix as a Seabee. He survived the big battle only to be shot in his moment of victory when he opened the pipeline valve. He never saw it coming. Did we see it coming? Even Roiger, who claimed it wasn't luck, but planning that kept us alive, felt we might have stretched it a bit. He called for the taxi, and we packed up. We'd be back. He knew it; we knew it.

On the way to the pickup point, Nahle and Hoehnfeld got into it over something. We broke up the fistfight, and Roiger said that if they wanted to fight, we could go back up the hill. Nahle said he wouldn't fight next to that chicken-shit bastard anymore. Nahle said that Hoehnfeld wasn't even shooting during the last engagement. That statement drew some somber stares in Hoehnfeld's direction. It was pretty quiet the rest of the way back, except for Wolkert's and my subdued speculation about our futures.

We had to wait about two hours for the chopper. Where was that mother? Roiger had Nahle watch the trail for any signs of pursuit. Had he really thought they were after us? Wolkert and I decided to help Nahle watch. We asked him what the earlier fuss was all about. He said that while they were walking, Hoehnfeld was carrying on about us being murderers and that we weren't going to get away with it. Then Nahle really got pissed off when he started harping about the unnecessary killing of the fucking pig. And that was when Nahle hit him.

We went through half a pack of cigarettes waiting for that bird. Fortunately, it showed up before any VC did. We boarded and lifted off cleanly. It was a relief to be above the jungle—the heat, the bugs, and the danger. Everyone dozed on the way back. I only shifted once to get more comfortable.

The helicopter had us home by suppertime. We had time to shower, shave, and take a turn on the crapper before we ate. I had really lost weight. At 6′ 2″, I had weighed 154 pounds when I left home, and I was at least 15 pounds lighter now from the exertion, lack of regular meals, and diarrhea induced by fear.

Hoehnfeld was conspicuously absent at mess. Roiger said he was gone—for good. I wondered aloud if he'd ever get it back together, and Nahle said that he never had it together in the first place. I doubted that. I thought he had it together enough for the real world but not for this shit hole. I figured that if a man had any loose ends, this place would unravel them. Conversely, if you could take this for six months, were you fit to return to the real world? Could you ever look at things in the proper perspective again? Wolkert commented that we'd learn the answer to that question in a few months. Roiger interjected that perhaps we were being a bit premature. We were barely into the task, so maybe Hoehnfeld was only the first to crack. A sobering thought; why did he have to bring it up? I slept fitfully that night; Hoehnfeld hadn't had a monopoly on unsettling dreams. At breakfast, we nervously discussed Roiger's comments and dismissed them as a load of shit.

Around 10:00 a.m., two helicopters landed at the pad; one had smoke coming out of its engine vents. We ran over to check it out and saw multiple bullet holes in both choppers. There was also blood on the floor of both. More ominous was the fact that only two guys got out of one chopper, and only one guy got out of the other. Each usually carried a crew of six. Wolkert's rapid, anxious interrogation of one of the pilots revealed that they had been hit by machine gun fire as they flew by a supposedly friendly village. No one was killed, but nine men were wounded, four seriously. The choppers had just dropped them off at the hospital in Chu Lai. I'll say. The fucking blood was still wet. I quickly took a few seconds to remind God of the contractual agreement we had made in the jungle a short time ago. After all, I was meticulously holding up my end of it. I wondered how the higher-ups would explain the men's wounds back home, since the Russian machine gun was not commonly employed in convenience-store holdups. I was nevertheless positive that they'd invent a plausible cover story.

I think it was 20 July 1963 when we were told we were going to replace a fire team that had been in place for over three straight weeks. They were on a pinnacle that could not be reached from the ground. The pinnacle was located at the confluence of two rivers and was a very busy place. The ranges of fire were fairly short, about three hundred meters, with the targets twenty to forty degrees down. The jungle growth was very heavy right up to the banks, which is all that saved the position from mortar fire. Command had spotters in the jungle about a mile upstream on each river, and they warned those at the post of oncoming traffic by radio.

We were going to get two replacements that day and head out to the pinnacle in the morning.

Bev noticed the light fading and turned on the lamp. She shook her head. She still couldn't believe her Connie had gotten tangled up in this mess. At this point in the story, he was still a youngster, but he was getting older by the day.

CHAPTER ELEVEN

SHIFTING TO A MORE comfortable position, Bev turned to the next page.

The day before we were to head for our new assignment, the new folks, Brenner and Sutton, arrived in time for lunch. These guys weren't new. Hell, they had scar tissue and tattoos dating back to the Second Battle of the Marne. Roiger said it was nice to have some experience aboard. Well, screw him! The old farts went off to talk about their muzzle-loading days, and we young ones were agonizing over the fact that at only three hundred meters from our targets, someone could get killed. We replaced our twenty-four-power rifle scopes with eight-power scopes and zeroed in at three hundred meters. At this distance, it would be a lot easier to hit. And a lot easier to be hit. It seemed that our role in this scenario was slowly but inexorably evolving into one for which we were ill suited.

Long-range rifle shooting is a solitary endeavor, not a team sport. With a good rifle and good ammunition, the results depend solely on the marksman's skill. His only competitor is himself. The type of person that takes up this sport is generally a loner; a person who does not depend on the adulation or consolation of others. He marches to his own drum beat. He does not confuse effort with results. Victory or failure is his alone.

A group of people of this type must, by definition, be loosely knit. Each has staunch confidence in his own ability and little interest in anyone else's. To mold this group into a fighting unit would be next to impossible. To attempt to do so would also put severe psychological stress on the participants, as it would be forcing them to act counter to their basic personalities. We had been together one and a half months and still knew very little about each other. We were hardly a bunch of buddies, except for Wolkert and me.

The next morning after a breakfast of Cream of Wheat that was lumpier than our mattresses, we took off. The chopper was positively crammed with supplies and it strained to get off the ground. There was hardly room to sit. It was a good thing Hoehnfeld was gone; there certainly wasn't room to whack off. The chopper had new accessories: door guns and gunners. Out of each side poked an M-60 machine gun operated by a guy with a dark, face-covering helmet. Things were rapidly changing.

Our chopper dutifully followed another that contained more supplies and the new geriatric arm of our unit. We headed north along the tracks, as usual. We turned west, as usual, in the direction of An Hoa. We then flew at least a hundred kilometers farther west. If we weren't in Laos, by God, we were close enough to spit on it. Right before we landed, we took a turn north for just a few minutes. There it was, a mesa with a top shaped like a bean. The narrow portion was about seventy-five feet across, and it was maybe two hundred and fifty feet long. The edge dropped off precipitously for more than a hundred feet on three sides. The fourth side, on the southwest, angled down about sixty degrees. Truly, the mesa was accessible only by air. Fortunately, the VC had no air force. At the base of the cliff was very dense jungle that extended to the river's edge some two hundred meters away. On the river's opposite shore was also jungle, extending as far into the mist as I could see. Two rivers came from the northwest and north and joined northeast of the mesa, where they continued to the south.

The choppers had to be landed and unloaded one at a time. The first one took about four minutes to land, unload, and take off. With the pad clear, ours landed. It took about fifteen minutes to unload us and load up the guys we were replacing. These guys looked rough—very, very rough. They were dirty, thin, and wild-eyed. One guy was biting the area behind the knuckle of his right index finger. He did not take his hand from his mouth even as he boarded the helicopter. It looked like Hoehnfeld was going to have company. It bothered me that this guy's buddies treated him so gently and not like we had treated Hoehnfeld. Maybe he was a nicer guy; maybe his buddies were nicer guys.

After the chopper lifted off, we went about dividing our supplies up into three piles, one on each end of the bean and one in the middle. This was to prevent a lucky hit from putting us out of business. We then laid out two rifle pits and a light machine gun on the northeast end, a heavy machine gun in the middle, and two more rifle pits on the southeast end. The big machine gun was a heavy-barreled .50 caliber made in 1951; Korean War vintage. The light one was an MG 34, a German weapon from World War II. After inspecting the guns, I asked, "What the hell is this, the budget tour?" Roiger answered my skepticism by saying that the MG 34 was the finest machine gun ever made and that if we got time, he would show me how to properly care for and feed it. I detected a mixture of prejudice and nostalgia in his voice when he said that.

The object of this operation was the same as our previous endeavors: stop enemy supplies. The method was as dangerous as it was different. The .50-caliber centerpiece, which Brenner would operate, would sink any boats, canoes, sampans, rafts, and other floating vehicles. The rifles and light machine gun would keep the fire off the heavy gunner. He would be the center of enemy attention. Of course, if he got hit, someone had to take his place. This fact alone ensured that everyone, and I mean everyone, was going to do his best to make sure that Brenner stayed alive and unharmed. We had parachute flares to illuminate the area below at night, so we were a twenty-four-hour-a-day shop. What unnerved me was that they knew we were here. There would be no element of surprise, no free first shots. I was starting to get nauseated again. The puke really climbed when I examined the rifle pits. I found chip marks on the rocks and leaky sandbags—the results of small-arms fire. After lunch, it seemed that everybody's bowels had to move at the same time. We couldn't dig a hole in this rock, so we had to go into plastic bags, knot them, and toss them over the edge. Maybe that would keep the VC away.

A half hour after lunch, the radio reported a convoy coming down the right (north) branch. It would arrive just after two o'clock. It was getting close to showtime when we climbed into the pits. These were very close to the edge of the mesa so we could get a good angle down at our targets. We shot through a notch about eight inches wide. The machine-gun pits had a wider opening, but a thicker wall of bags. Each man loaded and locked his gun. Roiger thought that maybe our targets were making a run because they had seen the choppers leave. In any event, none of us were getting close enough to the edge to be seen from below.

Just like the train at Kelly Square Station, at quarter past two they came. We waited until they were all in view so that no one could beach and run. The .50 caliber opened up first, and then all hell broke loose. The riflemen shot at anything on the boats that looked like it was trying to return fire. At a 275-meter range, shooting at men fully exposed on a slow-moving boat was not too difficult. The .50 was literally tearing the boats up. Pieces were flying into the air. Mayhem hopped from boat to boat as Brenner gave each its share of attention. Roiger was playing the MG 34 like a piano in short bursts of four or five rounds. His gun was just as effective as the rifle, and particularly so against men in the water because Roiger could use the spray to direct the stream of the bullets. Many rounds and four minutes later, all the boats had been reduced to their molecular components, all the men had been sent to their ancestors, and the jungle absorbed the last echoes of gunfire. God, that .50 was loud.

We watched for a while to see if anyone crawled out to the shore. No one did. I went over to where Roiger was cleaning the 34, and he showed me how the thing worked. It was an ugly masterpiece of engineering. I asked to try it, and he acquiesced. I fired about fifty rounds before I got the hang of it; after that, I wanted it for my own.

"Fine, bring her to our next dance," he said as I finished cleaning it and reloaded the empty belts. The belts held fifty rounds each, and any number of belts could be linked together. Each round was held by a clip that looked like the clip that holds a pen in a pocket. The end of the clip fit into the groove at the cartridge base to keep the rounds lined up properly. I linked two hundred rounds together, put them in a box just to the left of the gun, and fed the starter tab into the breech. All was ready. The key to using the 34 was to fire short bursts, as Roiger had done earlier, as firing the gun at its maximum rate of nine hundred rounds per minute would burn out the barrel. The gunner needed to exercise some self-control.

Supper was as uneventful as it was tasteless. We didn't have to hold our posts constantly because of the radio warning system, and we wanted to keep clear of the edge to avoid drawing fire.

So everyone congregated in the middle of the mesa and sat atop the huge supply of .50-caliber and 8-millimeter ammo. We kept the radio on and occasionally heard faint messages from other operations. If an operation's task had any relationship to its name, like "Thor" generating bolts from heaven, names such as "Bearclaw," "Brimstone," and "Gaslight" certainly primed the imagination.

Night set in and everyone except the radio monitor went to sleep. We had lived through yet another day.

The next day, July 22, passed without so much as log coming down the river. Everyone was entertaining the same unsettling thought: those shifty fuckers were up to no good again.

That night was a little more exciting. At about 10:30, the radio started to crackle. There was a flotilla of ten or twelve boats and rafts coming down the right side again. I wondered who the poor bastard back in the jungle spotting all this shit was. I could hardly imagine a more miserable existence. We prepared the parachute flares. It would be one man's job just to keep the lights on. The rest of us would engage our usual antisocial behavior. When Nahle spotted the bad guys with the night scope, they were hugging the opposite shore and punting as fast as they could. They probably shit when the first flare went off; they had to have shit when the .50 opened up. The first boat was sunk in seconds. It stayed in the shallows, so the wreck remained above water and initiated a traffic jam. The enemy's confusion prevented any effective return fire.. A few targets probably got by, draped over flotsam, but damned few. When we saw no more movement, Nahle halted the flares, and the night grew dark again. It was a long while before the jungle sounds resumed, and their sources were not disturbed for the rest of the night.

After breakfast, we cleaned the brass casings out of the pits and replenished each pit's ammo from the central supply. It was then time for a cigarette and a Tootsie Pop. I had only two chocolate ones left. Things were getting critical.

We had just completed our sumptuous lunch when the radio's crackle induced my stomach to nearly lose it. Once I heard that combination of static hissing and garbled speech I could never forget it. There were two guys trying to talk at the same time. Sutton told one of them to shut up, and we listened to the other. The first spotter told of a group of fifteen assorted vessels loaded with cargo coming down the left branch toward us. After we noted the details of the message, the other guy said that there was a group of nine boats headed our way down the right side. These were not loaded with cargo but were heavily armed. They had about forty men and a number of heavy machine guns. We asked about mortars; he said he had seen none. Our calculations indicated that both groups were going to arrive at about the same time. That was their stratagem: the armed convoy would try to keep us occupied on the far bank while the cargo boats would sneak by along the near shore.

This was going to be big. We packed even more ammo into the pits. I linked one thousand rounds together for the 34 and put two extra barrels within close reach. We all beefed up our pits with extra sandbags. We reinforced our flak jackets by stuffing our flak shorts inside them. When we got into the pits, it was just minutes before the guests arrived. Lunch was trying to crawl out of my throat. I had a few brief thoughts about the safety of my hometown, but with effort I dismissed them. I then reminded God that I had kept my part of our agreement to the letter and reverently suggested that it was incumbent on Him to do the same. I knew this was going to be bad. I was sure I saw a bead of sweat on Roiger's brow.

My knees were quivering so badly I don't think I could have stood up. Just one more click on the fear knob and my brain, bladder, and bowels would have been out of control. "Jesus H. Christ, what the hell am I doing here?" I asked myself. That question would be answered in less than ten seconds.

Due to some miscalculation, the cargo convoy arrived before the armed one, but only by a couple of minutes. The .50 opened up on them and drew mild return fire, which I helped subdue with the 34. About five of the fifteen boats were down when the armed convoy arrived. Boy, were they pissed. They fired everything up at us. To hell with the supplies, this was now a fight for survival. The .50 and all the other guns turned on the armed convoy. The noise was horrible. Bullets were whizzing overhead, thumping into sandbags, and zinging off rocks. The .50 tore the boats apart. Brenner was inspired; he was a maniac. In my enthusiasm, I had forgotten the short-burst rule and was pouring a steady stream of fire into the crowd below. The gun seized up after a couple of hundred rounds. It took a few seconds to replace the barrel before I was back at it, this time doing it right. The barrel jacket was smoking as the thin oil coat cooked off, but the gun operated perfectly. One back-and-forth sweep of a boat completely cleared the deck.

I had a near miss. The sand kicked up by the bullet sprayed in my face. I used up all one thousand of my rounds and had to get more. Now all I had were boxes of fifty-round belts. They went rapidly. It seemed like I was always reloading. Another near miss; my face really stung and I couldn't see for a few seconds, but I kept shooting. When I could see again, the armed boats had been reduced to splinters and ten or fifteen men were in the water, some alive, some dead. My sole purpose was to make them all dead. Brenner had now turned back to the cargo boats, nine of which had slipped by and were headed away from us. The crazy bastard picked up the .50 and ran to the southern edge of the mesa to set up shop. Roiger was running after him with the tripod and a box of ammo. In a few seconds, Brenner was chewing their asses off. Those old guys really took their killing seriously. The gun had a range of five thousand yards, and the ten minutes it took for the three surviving boats to get out of sight must have been the longest in the entire lives of the survivors. The crews of the six boats Brenner sank were in the water and fell prey to the riflemen. I was disassembling a boat that had been beached. Its crew was still very testy, and we traded ordnance for several minutes before I hit something that sent them two hundred feet straight up. This explosion punctuated the firefight, and then it was still.

I rolled over on my back and looked up. Sand from a leaking bag rained down into my face. As I wiped it away, I noticed blood on my hand. The whole pit was slowly shrinking. The bullet holes in the bags were letting the sand out, and they were deflating. I looked over the edge, and every fucking bag had multiple holes. Not only that, but the left leg of the 34's bipod had a hole in it, and I figured that the metal that was blown out of the back of that hole was what had perforated the skin on my forehead, cheek, and left forearm. I was shaking like a leaf, and a few minutes later, I threw up.

Bev again put down the manuscript. She too felt queasy. She needed to eat supper but didn't want to take a break, not just yet.

CHAPTER TWELVE

BEV WIGGLED HER CRAMPED toes and continued her reading.

Roiger, Brennar, Sutton, Nahle, and Wolkert had not fared too poorly. Brenner had been grazed by two bullets, one lightly in the neck and one deeply in the left shoulder. Sutton had been punctured by a round that had to have gone through a sandbag first, as one-third of it, a copper button, stuck out of his thigh. He pulled it out with his fingers. The wound didn't bleed much, but the area was massively bruised. Roiger was unscathed, naturally. Wolkert was okay, except for the stains in his pants. When I saw he had wet his pants, I checked mine and found that he was not alone.

We were all gray with soot and had an unnerving dead look. Roiger asked if I could see okay, and after an affirmative answer, he said I was very lucky. He had seen this type of thing happen before, and usually the victim ended up blind.

Nahle was not injured. His pants were dry, but he was really acting weird. He was pacing and yelling, "Fuckin' intense, man! Fuckin' intense!"

I too felt very strange. I could hear, feel, and see everything with incredible clarity. I noticed bug and bird noises; footfalls were as loud as drums; I could hear the sand running out of the bags. All this minutiae was crystal clear. I was extremely aware; I felt I was immortal. I would not, could not be killed. I would survive. I was tingling and I felt flushed. My heart was pounding. I couldn't stand still. I went up to the edge of the mesa and yelled at the dead below that they weren't good enough to get me, and I dared them to try again. I yelled at anyone down there to try. I called them and their ancestors some really nasty names. I was acting like Nahle.

After a while I sat down, exhausted. I must have carried on for thirty minutes. Nahle was down, too. We were still hyper but too weak to walk. In about an hour, I was asleep. When I woke I was very calm, but I vividly remembered the Feeling. It was scary, it was wonderful, it was better than sex. Like Nahle said, "Fuckin' intense." I wondered if I could get it again. Nahle and I talked about it, and our experiences were almost identical. Wolkert looked at us like we were nuts. Roiger said we had taken the step beyond fear. He said that it was addictive, and the actions of those seeking it were often mistaken for bravery or insanity. Like scotch, it was an acquired taste, and, by God, I had the taste. I would never forget July 23, 1963.

After the Feeling faded, reality came into focus. My ears were still ringing so badly that I could hardly hear. My eyes were watering and burning profusely from the dust and gun smoke. It was then I realized that the hyperawareness was a trick played my mind had been playing, caused by some kind of circuit overload. Hell, I couldn't have heard the guy next to me talk much less understand the conversation between insects. Nevertheless, it had felt very, very good.

We ate, cleaned the weapons, and restocked the ammo in the pits. By then, night had closed in and I was trying to ignore my septic-tank breath and get to sleep. I just couldn't rinse the burn of vomit out of my nose and throat with water. My kingdom for a beer.

I had been asleep for several hours when I was awakened by a scream that had to have come from hell. I grabbed my Luger and looked out of the pup tent cautiously, half expecting to see the VC swarming over the place. Instead, there were Roiger and Sutton restraining Wolkert. In his sleep, Wolkert had become entangled in the tent and in a panic had cut his way to freedom through the side of it, screaming all the while. He was extremely embarrassed after he was fully awake and figured out what had happened. I don't think anyone slept well the rest of that night.

The radio was quiet all the next day. It was really strange. Everyone in the group was depressed due to a lack of activity—or, lack of victims. We were becoming really fucked up. Wolkert was sewing up the slash in his tent and I was having a Tootsie Pop and leafing through the July *Playboy* when I heard a single shot. That idiot Nahle had been conducting an experiment to determine how well flak jackets would protect him. In addition to scaring the hell out of everyone, his test's results were downright demoralizing. A rifle bullet had gone through two vests, one atop the other, and had taken a large chip out of the rock he had laid them on before ricocheting into the jungle below. Any feeling of security my flak jacket gave me left with that bullet. I was glad my contract with Jesus was still in force.

Spirits were really down, and there was talk of the desire for action by some of the more demented. I, on the other hand, was ambivalent. I felt that I had an adequate amount of material for the entertainment of my grandkids and saw no need whatsoever to goad the gods of war, but the Feeling was enticing. For the next three days, the prayers of those who had petitioned for calm were answered.

Eventually, their clout ran out, and on July 27, around nine in the morning, the radio crackled and sputtered to life to inform us that boats were on the way. There would be four coming down the right side in a few minutes. As we got into position, it struck me that my prime emotion was not fear but anticipation. It was nothing like July 23. We blew the four boats were blown away in seconds and killed the crews. There was no return fire, no excitement, no incontinence, no vomiting, no nothing. A quick introspection had me calling myself a stupid shit for being disappointed at not being nearly killed. I was really starting to worry myself. In no time we settled back into our funk. The thrill was gone.

During the subsequent quiet time, Roiger explained the inner workings of the 34 and showed me how to John Wayne it by holding the barrel sleeve with my left hand and draping a belt of ammo over my left arm. I spent nearly a thousand rounds just farting around. Then I got out my Luger and shot at Nahle's canteen for a while. Roiger and Sutton came over and shot a bit, too. Sutton used a .45. Roiger had a Luger too; but then, what else would he have had? After ten minutes we left Nahle's sieve alone and had supper. The evening and night passed without alarm, as did the next two days.

The vacuum-tube deity spoke again on July 30, and this time it relayed a message of salvation. We were pulling out at noon. We were to save what we could get on two choppers and blow the rest.

No one was ever going back to that shit hole. Everyone was ready when the bus came. We were aboard in minutes and away quickly. A half-mile out, the top of the mesa erupted. We never heard the explosion, but we could see the column of black smoke until it disappeared over the horizon. I dozed but woke when Wolkert gently kicked me and yelled that this was our stop. We dropped off our gear at the hut and made a beeline for the beer and showers.

On my penultimate Vietnamese morning, I woke up with a half-consumed can of beer in my right hand resting on my chest. None had been spilled. I must not have moved at all in my sleep. After breakfast, we were called to the briefing hut and told that THOR-COG was history. We were going home tomorrow. Was that a twinge of disappointment I felt?

The Agency had decided that THOR-COG was too risky and would soon yield American casualties that would be difficult to explain. This would draw unwanted attention from the news media and subsequently from the American public, who, up to now, were under the impression that the United States was only involved in Vietnam in an advisory role. We were to be paid and sent home. Roiger said the story was a lot of bullshit and that the Agency only canceled an act if there was a better one in the wings. It was his impression that things were about to take a sudden turn. I personally didn't give a shit. I was out of it, a deal is a deal. We had to sign some separation papers, one of which was an agreement not to talk about this operation with anyone for twenty years; that would be 1983. The next was a list of dos and don'ts: do not try to contact any member of the team; don't bank the money. Another paper listed a phone number to call if there were any "difficulties." Finally, there was a card for us to fill out if we were interested in future work with the Agency. We were told we would get the money when we got to Fort Hood just prior to separation.

The flight out was scheduled for the next morning, August 1. I changed into fatigues without insignia, and I looked up the Army chaplain who visited this dump on Wednesdays. I made a general confession and told him the whole story. I explained I wasn't sure what to ask forgiveness for. He said I had it, so I shouldn't dwell on it. Simple as that. Kill more people in one month than Al Capone did in a lifetime, get absolution and go back to school. I was sure glad I wasn't a Protestant. The black-and-white outlook bestowed by a Jesuit education made these sorts of issues a lot easier to deal with. I hate to think of what would have happened to me if my faith had faltered. After another five seconds of philosophical pud-pulling, I needed a beer, several beers. Wolkert and I spent the rest of the day getting shitfaced. Around dark, the conversation, as it often did, turned to women. After we had swapped multiple lies, we thought about hiking into Tam Ky for some real action. I declined to go on the grounds that I could handle my killing of the natives more easily if I could keep from thinking of them as real people. A valid argument, but not the whole truth. I had enough to feel uneasy about as it was. I had another beer and hit the sheets; I had a very important bus to catch in the morning.

The miscreants who had gone to Tam Ky were dragged in about 2:00 a.m., and then all was quiet until about 3:00. Wolkert had another nightmare and scared the shit out of everyone. He would not be getting home too soon.

The morning came quickly, and after our last breakfast in the tropical paradise of South Vietnam, Nahle handed out Zippo lighters he had had made in town. Each had a naval-code pennant letter on it. Put together, they spelled *DUNG Lo*. Nahle took *N*, Wolkert took *D*, I got *U*, and Roiger got *Lo*. The *G* would have been for Hoehnfeld, but he was gone. We got into a truck and headed south to the airfield. Here Nahle had another idea; two in one day was real good for a marine. Just before boarding the plane, we all whipped out our wands and took a final piss on Southeast Asia. This must have appeared strange to the civilians getting off the commercial airliner across the way.

Our route put us back in Fort Hood at exactly 11:16 p.m., August 1. Only when those wheels touched that Texas dirt did I know for sure I was delivered. We were taken by bus to the same goddamned barracks as we had been in before. We cleaned up and sacked out. The next morning, in the briefing room, there was that son of a bitch Rhaspberry. In front of him on the desk were nineteen small gray plastic briefcases. Hadn't we started with twenty-five? Each had a paper tag with a name on it. He passed them out, and when we opened them we found ten thousand dollars in old, used twenty-dollar bills. It looked like a ransom. Rhaspberry reiterated the admonition not to bank the money. When someone suggested that carrying this kind of money around was dangerous, he replied that he couldn't think of anyone who could take it from us. Tall talk for a little fuck in a blue suit.

I looked up the quartermaster and asked him if I could buy the rifle I had been using. He said five hundred dollars would cover it and put it in a box with some kind of voucher on the outside, which he signed. I returned to the barracks with my prize, changed into my civvies, and had a beer. I was examining the Luger that Roiger had swapped for mine on the last day in Vietnam when Wolkert came running in saying that the bus was here. We said a few brief good-byes to those staying behind and boarded for a short trip to the airfield.

On the way north, Wolkert and I were accompanied by one of the boys from Omaha and the ubiquitous Rhaspberry. The guy from Omaha looked about ten years older and twenty pounds lighter than he had on the trip down. He said not a word. Wolkert and I probably didn't look too great either. I got a little choked up when we let Wolkert off in Little Rock. He had been the only one I could have called a "Kamerad," as Roiger put it. Kameraden have a special bond. People who have been together in real combat have a union unlike any other. Words like *trust, devotion,* and *love* are inadequate to describe it. Once we had willingly shared the possibility of imminent death, ours was a oneness that no other relationship could duplicate. Now I wouldn't see Wolkert again, ever.

After we were airborne again, I talked with Rhaspberry for a while. I asked what this shit was really all about, as if he would tell me. His answer was that we truly had been sent to disrupt the flow of supplies into South Vietnam, and we had done a damned good job. He said that THOR-COG had accounted for an estimated fifty-four tons of arms and supplies, not to mention the lives of some eight hundred Viet Cong. I asked why, if things had been going so well, the operation was halted. He said that there were going to be some political changes in the south and after that, there would be a heavy escalation in the military confrontation with the Communists and no need for this type of penny-ante operation. It was also his impression that I had made a very good deal; soon there would be those doing a lot more for a lot less. Who knew if he were telling the truth? My parting comment to him was that the enemy shouldn't be called Victor Charlie. Victor Charlie had a bad ring to it.

When the plane landed in Columbia, the landlady was waiting with my car, and she drove me back to the house. In a few minutes we were there. As I went up to the third floor, I could see that people were moving into the other rooms. The padlock on my door was still in place, and as I opened it, a hot gust of stale air fell out of the room. For just a second I was back in Tam Ky. I opened a window, but that only let in more hot air. It was definitely August. I dumped all my junk and relocked the room. It was time for some supper.

As I drove down the main street, I noticed that *PT 109* was still showing. Jesus, that was weird. I picked up a paper and drove to the Wigwam Cafe. I ordered french toast again and perused the news. There was absolutely nothing in the paper about Vietnam. I felt like I was in the Twilight Zone. I had blinked my eyes and two months had passed, but the world had not changed. After I ate, I went for a walk around the campus. All these people going about their business had no goddamned idea of what was going on over there. Well, it wasn't my job to tell them. It was probably too late anyway.

It was also too late to apply for graduate school, and it was very difficult to explain a return home. I had time and I had money. I'd audit some classes, drink some beer, and go to graduate school next year. Dung lo!

As Bev finished reading the first chapter, the clock downstairs let out a solitary *bong*. Looking at her watch, she noted that it was 5:30 p.m. She wanted to press on, but she was getting hungry and had a number of chores to do.

"I'll get some supper and finish it tomorrow," she thought. That night, the multiple cups of tea and the imagery of the account she had read made for a very uneasy sleep dotted with disturbing dreams. When she arose, she felt little better than when she had gone to sleep. It was daylight and she had never been able to lie around and go back to sleep, so Bev faced the day. While in the shower she remembered the part about taking such things as showers for granted. A jet of water stung her right nipple and reminded her that Connie had not been home for two days now. She decided against what she had been considering doing; it would just be better when Connie got back.

Some thirty minutes later, Bev had dressed and went down for breakfast. After a few cups of coffee and an English muffin, she was as good as new. Finishing her third cup, she walked out onto the back porch. It was going to be one of those summer days that held the threat of impending storm. The sky to the southwest was dark, and she imagined more than heard very distant thunder. "Well, I'll not be able to get anything done today, so I might as well read the diary," she mumbled to herself. The temperature was rising and she had acquired a mild glow in just a few minutes, so she went back inside.

With the air conditioner set at seventy-two degrees and a fresh pot of coffee at hand, she took up the manuscript again.

CHAPTER THIRTEEN

RHASPBERRY AND WITTMOND FOLLOWED Wolkert into his basement. Wolkert had constructed his cabin on top of a bunker that he explained was left over from the Cold War. The bunker walls were constructed of poured concrete and the ceiling was flexicore, reinforced concrete panels. There were no windows, just a steel door. The room had cots, food and water, a well, a propane-powered generator, and a ventilator system.

"What were you expecting, Wolkert?" Wittmond asked as he gazed around.

"What the hell do you think?" Wolkert shot back. "Tell me you don't have one."

"Well …" Wittmond paused. "Mine had a flush toilet, not like that chemical thing over there."

Wolkert shook his head and took hold of Wittmond's arm to usher him to the table. "This is my wife, Elise," Wolkert said. An attractive blond woman with short hair and crystal blue eyes forced a smile onto a face tense with apprehension.

"At the risk of sounding trite, I've heard so much about you, and I'm glad to finally meet you," she offered.

"This is my daughter, Erika," Wolkert went on. The thirteen-year-old copy of Wolkert's wife also managed a smile.

"Over here is Christopher Conrad." The sixteen-year-old did not change his somber expression but nodded.

"They all know what's going on," Wolkert added. Everyone looked both angry and scared. The children went over to a group of bunks and Wolkert's wife busied herself with preparing some food.

"I've got to get back outside. You guys get dressed and eat. I'll be back in a little bit," Wolkert said.

Rhaspberry and Wittmond ate with Wolkert's family. As they were finishing the meal, Wolkert reappeared. He sat down as

Elise poured more coffee. Looking very haggard, he proceeded to describe the layout of the property on a legal pad.

"The cabin is on a knoll that overlooks the dirt road some two hundred meters south. That's the road you came up. The drive way comes up in an arc on the west side of the cabin and ends up in front of it. I have installed seismic intrusion detectors here and there along the road and in the woods behind the road and the cabin—here, here, and here. They're numbered one through five so you can see on the monitor which one has been triggered."

Wittmond nodded. "Okay. What else?" he said.

"I have two claymores, but I waited until you guys got here to arm them. One is taped to the inside of the cabin door, about balls high, and the other is in the bushes about ten feet from the bunker door, facing it. The first will fire if anyone opens the cabin door; the second is triggered from in here. "

There were a few seconds of silence as Wittmond and Rhaspberry pondered the situation.

"We really need one of them alive," remarked Rhaspberry. "We have to find the old man or it'll never stop. He'll just keep sending new ones."

The other two men nodded in agreement. Wittmond glanced around and saw Wolkert's family in the corner and realized it could be his. He thought of the kids and the plastic bags. "Yeah, we definitely have to get to the old man," he seconded.

Rhaspberry took control. "Here's what we have to do. We'll set up a rotation. One sleeps, one watches the seismic intrusion detector, and one sits stands guard in the woods."

"Chris could watch the monitor," Wolkert offered.

"No, goddamn it!" Rhaspberry shot back. "Don't get your family involved. This is too important to trust to a teenager. No offense, Chris." He glanced at the boy.

"He's right," Wittmond confirmed. "If anything went awry, the boy would blame himself forever, no matter how insignificant his part."

Rhaspberry reached into his bag and produced a Ruger .22 semiautomatic with a silencer. "The guy outside will use this pistol, and we'll keep the big guns for backup.

"There will be three bad guys. They're very good, and they're merciless—they plan to kill Wolkert and his family. Keep that in mind if you start to harbor any caring-and-sharing Christian thoughts. There is no honor, no valor here. The only thing that counts is survival. If we can take one of them alive, it'll make life easier, but take no unnecessary risks."

"I'll take the first outside shift," Wittmond volunteered. "Wolkert needs sleep badly, and you can sleep next."

He picked up the Ruger and checked the chamber. It was loaded. Wolkert let him out quickly.

"If you want back in, the password is 'Dung Lo,'" he whispered with a smile before securing the door.

Outside the bugs were buzzing and the humidity was building. It was going to be a hot mother. Wittmond slipped into the bush and gradually made his way down to the curved in the road. He took perhaps thirty minutes to cover the fifty yards to the spot where the number-two sensor was supposed to be. He sat against a tree and carefully scanned the ground and road in front of him, inch by inch. Wolkert had done an excellent job of hiding it; he couldn't see the sensor even though he knew where it was.

The seismic sensor, a metal tube about six inches long and one inch in diameter, was pointed at one end and had a screw-off cap on the other. The piezoelectric device inside, powered by a nine-volt battery, could detect the slightest vibration. The sensor also contained a small radio transmitter sent a signal at a specific frequency to the monitor when tripped, which, in this case, would light up the indicator for number two. The sensor could pick up human footsteps within about fifty feet and passing automobiles within about one hundred feet.

Every fifteen minutes, Wittmond would stomp his foot to let Rhaspberry know he was okay. His four-hour shift passed very slowly and without incident. At eleven thirty, he stomped and proceeded back to the bunker very slowly and cautiously. Wittmond gave the password, handed Rhaspberry the .22, and took up his position by the monitor. It was good to be away from the bugs and in the coolness of the bunker. Wolkert was still sawing logs, the kids were watching TV.

Elise brought in some lunch and sat down next to Wittmond. "I can't tell you how grateful I am that you're helping us," she said. "I know you two have been though some wild times together, and your being here must have something to do with male bonding, but I want to thank you anyway."

"You know he'd do the same for me," Wittmond replied, feeling a little guilty about not having said much—okay, anything to Bev about Wolkert and his experiences.

"I'm scared, and my kids are scared. Are you scared?" Elise asked.

"Yes, I'm scared," Wittmond admitted, "but there are a few things you have to hold on to. These guys are coming to us, and we should have a three-to-one advantage over them just by being the defenders. They think they're up against one man, but they aren't. They're city hoods, and this is the jungle. They're in this for money or reputation, but our lives are on the line. And they think their ruthlessness will brush us away. They can't imagine the malevolence they're about to deal with."

Elise caught her breath and glanced at her children.

Wittmond stared at her and added, "We will prevail. You believe that."

"I ... I do believe it," she answered, shifting her gaze to the floor. "But I'm still scared to death. You're so like Larry. I don't know how you can turn it on and off. I mean, law-abiding citizen, loving father, dutiful husband on one hand, and ... well, you know, on the other."

"I can't answer that. I have asked myself the same question at least a million times, and the obvious answers are too unpalatable to consider. When your analysis of your behavior conjures up words like 'compensated sociopath,' you stop analyzing it," he replied.

Elise deftly changed. "I'd like to meet your wife someday."

"I think that is a great idea. We'll do it as soon as this mess is cleared up," agreed Wittmond.

She gave him a wistful smile, rose, and took the dishes to the sink. Wolkert was still asleep, the kids were still watching TV, and Rhaspberry had just given his second fifteen-minute stomp.

Eventually, it was 4:00 p.m. and Rhaspberry was at the door.

Wolkert had been up, had eaten, and was ready for his turn at the stand. Wittmond took another turn at the monitor and Rhaspberry ate and went to sleep.

The men repeated some variation of this cycle for the next two days without interruption. Wittmond began wondering whether Sherlock's information was inaccurate.

"Maybe those guys are too stupid to find Wolkert's place," Wittmond offered.

"Maybe they're too smart to rush," countered Wolkert.

"Maybe you had better get your ass on the stand, Wittmond," said Rhaspberry, ending the conversation.

That evening when Rhaspberry was on watch, Wittmond and Wolkert talked about the old days in Vietnam. Christopher listened with rapt attention. "We got out pretty clean from THOR-COG," Wittmond said. "I don't know why you needed to go back there"

"Yeah, maybe not my smartest move," Wolkert said wryly, "but I missed the action. I decided that dying of boredom was worse than dying by bullet." Wittmond then pressed Wolkert to tell about his extraction from Vietnam in the war's final days. Wolkert had promised to do this some time ago and now the time was right, so he closed his eyes and slowly began, careful not to omit any detail.

"We were flying over some goddamned ten-shack village when heavy machine-gun fire riddled the cockpit, cargo compartment, and engine of our chopper. Without power, the dying pilot autorotated the chopper into a clump of trees. It hung like a dead insect in a spiderweb.

"I frantically checked myself and found that I had no extra holes or broken bones. The other three passengers and the pilot were dead or dying. We had come down about two kilometers northeast of the hostile village. No doubt a search party would come after us. I had to get away.

"There was a lot of stuff in the chopper, and I had to fight panic and force myself to make choose the right things to take. I had my .45 and took the extra clips of ammo from those who wouldn't be needing them. No rifle. It would be too cumbersome. I wasn't going to fight, I was going to run. I took an extra knife and a machete; indispensable items in the jungle. There were two usable canteens.

A third had a hole in it. I also took a coil of rope, an extra poncho, and the dead guys' cigarettes and lighters. Feeling like a grave robber, I pulled the ring on a satchel charge and jumped to the ground ten feet below. I quickly gathered up the stuff I had dropped in the fall and ran for cover. When the charge detonated, it blew the chopper in half.

"I later thought about why I blew the chopper; I came up with three reasons. First, if anyone inside had a spark of life left, this kept him from capture; second, it kept any useful material from falling into the hands of the enemy; and third, it covered any trace that a fifth person had escaped. With a pang of guilt about the first reason, I headed northeast, away from the village. The enemy would be on his way.

"I had run headlong for about ten minutes when I realized that I was leaving an obvious trail. Some of the survival training was seeping back into my fear-wracked consciousness. I doubled back on the trail for about fifty yards. I really dreaded going back toward the enemy. I then took off at a forty-five degree angle to my old path, almost due north. I was very careful not to disturb any vegetation. I even ducked under a large spiderweb. I was a shifty mother. After about an hour, I repeated this evasive maneuver, and this put me back on a northeasterly course. As I asked myself why northeast was the preferred course, I realized I had no map. Goddamnit! There had been one in the chopper. This was big mistake number two; number one, as you know, was being in Southeast Asia.

"I squint and squeezed the bridge of my nose, trying to remember what the map of this area looked like. We had been flying northeast out of Bu Prang for a good half-hour before we went down. As I pictured the map in my mind, I realized that I was in the middle of miles of solid jungle. If there were a way out, it would be due east. Hopefully, I could find a road or a river that would take me to the coast, which was at least a hundred kilometers away. This depressing thought was followed by another. The whole war was going badly. Would the coast be in friendly hands when I got there? This trip was going to take awhile.

"An out-of-place noise brought me back to my present predicament; it was an F-4 flying over, several hundred feet up. Lucky bastard. It was getting dark. I had to find a place to sleep.

"When I woke up, I jumped, startled, When I looked down a twenty-foot drop. My then mind engaged, and I felt for the rope that secured me to the tree. I undid the rope and carefully descended to the ground. My paltry possessions were still at the base of the tree. Grabbing the canteens, I determined that I had about one and a half quarts of water left. I took a long drink; I deserved it. Breakfast took the form of a stick of Juicy Fruit gum and a Pall Mall. At least there were no dishes to wash. I sat on a fallen tree, determined to get my shit together.

"My first concern was clean water. If I got sick, I was dead meat. Rainwater was relatively clean, but stream water was teeming with disease. Fortunately, it rained a lot where I was. My second problem was getting food. I had plants and animals to choose from. The plant life was alien to me. I might have poisoned myself. If I were going to eat animals they had to be slow enough and small enough for me to hunt quietly and safely with a machete. This constraint pretty much limited me to frogs, snakes, and lizards. I would have to cook all the meat because of possible parasites. This, of course, required a fire.

"Problem three was capture, or rather, evasion from capture. I was definitely not going to be captured, no matter what. I knew what happened to the captured.

"That meant I couldn't risk the smoke from a fire, so I wouldn't be able to eat. I had no choice but to move east at a slow, energy-conserving pace. If I made no enemy contact in two days, I'd build a fire and cook the first unfortunate beast I came across.

"The next two days exhausted me. I probably had not gone more than three kilometers. The only positive event was the rain. When it started, I took off my shirt and spread it and my poncho to collect the water. I then filled the canteens and drank my fill. My thirst was slaked, but God, was I hungry.

"I had wrung out my shirt and was putting it back on when I heard a thrashing in the undergrowth a few yards away. My first thought was of the enemy, and I froze. No one emerged from the bush in the following five minutes, so I adjusted my grip on my .45

and investigated. I found a four-foot-long black snake with two feet of a green snake hanging out of its mouth. I terminated their *danse macabre* with the machete. It was suppertime. After beheading and skinning both snakes, I washed the meat with a little of my precious water. Dry wood was scarce, but I found enough for a fire under a fallen tree. I got everything ready but waited until dark to light the fire. I figured that smoke in daylight would be more visible than a small fire at night. I got it lit and, as I had anticipated, it really smoked. I wrapped the snakes around a green stick and roasted the hell out of them. Jesus, that tasted good. There was actually more than I could eat. With a full belly, I slept.

"The next morning I was hungry again. Funny how that happens. The leftover snake was good but did not give me that pleasant full feeling. I had to move on. I erased every vestige of my presence and gathered my gear. With the compass, I determined due east, picked out a tree in that direction and walked to it. Then I repeated the process. Naturally, as I plodded along, I kept an eye out for potential meals. By nightfall I had collected two lizards, one small snake, and a truly tiny frog. Beggars can't be choosers. I also had a hat full of berries. I had noticed the birds eating them, and I supposed if they were okay for birds, they were okay for me. I ate the berries while roasting the reptiles. A little confidence was my dessert. I wasn't going to die of thirst or hunger. I did, however, need to conserve my fire-making devices, so I decided to cook meat every other day and fill the gaps in my diet with plants. I would watch monkeys and birds to determine what was safe to eat.

"Around noon of the sixth day, I climbed a tree to get an idea of what kind of terrain lay ahead of me. As high up in the branches as I dared to go, I could see mountains to the east. To the north, the jungle gave way to foothills about halfway to the horizon. To the south and the west, there was solid jungle as far as I could see. I peered back to the east and saw a thin column of smoke. It was rising nearly vertical from a spot in the jungle about five kilometers away. Numerous questions ran through my mind. What should I do? Does the smoke represent safety or danger? Is it a village thriving or a village burning?

"I took a compass reading on the smoke; 47 degrees northeast.

I decided to approach the source of the smoke very cautiously, and I set out.

"Near the end of the day, I climbed up to get another bearing on the smoke. There was not a goddamned wisp to be seen. I would try again in the morning. I descended to a branch about twenty feet off the ground—biting insects are seldom found more than five meters above the ground—and tied myself to the tree for the night.

At dawn, the jungle was very misty. There was no way I could tell smoke from fog. With hope, I continued on the 47-degree-northeast course. I would get my bearings again around noon.

"In the crotch of a tree, I was lunching on a pomegranate-like fruit when I again spied the smoke. A compass fix had it at 42 degrees northeast. Depressingly, it seemed about as far away as it had before. But I pressed on.

"That night was supposed to be a meat night, but I had been unable to catch anything. As I was getting close to the source of the smoke, I decided not to build any fire until I identified the source of the smoke.

"Well into the next day, I came upon a path. It generally ran southwest to northeast, toward the smoke. Walking it was a lot easier than going through the jungle, but was it safe? Was it mined? Was it patrolled?

"It was just too tempting to ignore. I drew the .45, cocked it, and locked it. With the gun at the ready, I slowly proceeded."

CHAPTER FOURTEEN

CHRIS SAT SPELLBOUND AT his father's story of survival. "So what happened next, Dad?" he asked with urgency. "Well, just be patient and I'll tell you," Wolkert said, smiling.

"It was very easy traveling compared to what I had been doing for the last eight days," Wolkert began. "I peered ahead with my eyes fixed on the most distant part of the trail. I was ready to jump into the bush at the least suspicious sight or sound. After thirty minutes or so, I felt I was getting close to the objective, so I went off the trail and climbed up for a look-see. I could now see part of a village about three hundred meters away. I found that the column of smoke was coming from three or four separate cooking fires. I decided that that night, I would take a closer look.

"I dozed in the tree but was awakened after only a few minutes by shouting. I slowly put the trunk between me and the noise and then carefully peered around it. Down the trail, thirty meters away, three armed men were searching an ox cart. Their AK-47s were proof enough for me that they were hostile. I pressed myself closer to the tree. After a few long minutes, they let the cart proceed on its way southwest. Where had the soldiers come from? Had they come up behind me? Did they have a guard post I had just missed?

"As I speculated, they walked to the village, and I remained in the tree to contemplate my next move. The village was out. I still had to go east, and it was likely that there was a path in that direction on the other side of the village. I planned to circle around the village to the north and try to pick up the trail on the other side. I would execute my plan at first light. I told the tree good night and tried to sleep.

"First light took its time coming. I woke up around 3:00 and could sleep no more, so I climbed down and waited at the base of the tree. At around 5:30, I could see ten to fifteen feet in front of me, so I set out. Giving the village a wide berth, I traveled north for a solid hour. Sure that I would clear the village's limits, I turned due east and prayed that I would find a path. Traversing the jungle was exhausting. By noon, though I had cleared the village and its dangers, my confidence was wavering. My water was low, and I had no food. I was very tired and very alone.

"The remainder of the day proved to be no better than the beginning. Nightfall found me hungrier, more tired, and more depressed. I went up a tree to sleep the hunger pangs away.

"When I woke up and looked about the next morning, I made a discovery that induced harsh self-recrimination. From the tree I saw that my course had run parallel to a road, with only about a hundred feet of jungle between it and me. At least the walking would be easier from then on. As though to balance the scales, fate gave me a break later that morning. I was proceeding extremely cautiously east on the road. I sighted an unusual shape ahead of me and quickly took to the bush. After watching it for several minutes, I hadn't detected any hostile intent or even any movement. I approached the shape through the jungle parallel to the road. As I got closer, I saw that the shape was an abandoned cart. The cart had a broken axle. The driver had evidently taken the oxen and gone for help. I quickly searched the cart and found several treasures. A ten-pound bag of rice, a small bag of salt, some old clothes, and a straw hat. I grabbed them and made a run for it. I put several hours between me and the cart before I took to the jungle to rest. It was amazing what a change that dollar's worth of groceries made in my outlook. I was sitting on a log examining the clothes when I heard the squeal of an animal in the bush. I slowly made my way toward the squeal. Some type of constrictor was in the processing of crushing a very small deer. The gods were not smiling on me that day, but they were grinning a little.

"After dispatching the deer and the snake with the machete, I had to cook it. I had to cross the road so it would be upwind of a fire. I moved about a hundred meters into the bush and cleared a spot for the fire between the roots of a tree trunk. Using a lighter and some military script, I got my fire started. I lit a cigarette and I cleaned the game. Putting about one inch of water in an empty canteen, I then added a handful of the rice and placed it in the fire.

I roasted the deer first, and while I ate deer and rice, I smoked the snake. It was big. I was going to have meat for days.

"It took most of the night to smoke and salt the leftover meat, and when it was finished I took it up in the tree with me. Nobody and no thing was getting my food.

"The usual muscle cramps and stiffness greeted me in the morning, but they couldn't dampen my confidence now. I carefully loaded up my belongings, made my way to the road, readied the .45, and was off to see the wizard.

"Over the next nine days, I had occasion to dodge civilian traffic six times. That was not particularly frightening; I always saw them before they saw me, and I was in the bush in an instant. Because I was wearing camo, I had only to be still until they passed. On the twenty-second day of the ordeal, I witnessed a truly disturbing event. I had been off the road to let some civilians pass and was gathering my stuff to resume my trek. I heard shouts. I flattened against the ground, facedown, holding my breath. After a few anxious moments, I chanced a look up. There was a squad of armed men escorting six prisoners. These captives were Americans, and their flight suits indicated that they were pilots. Their hands were bound to short poles that lay across their shoulders. One was staggering so badly I could tell the poor bastard wasn't going to make it. The group was headed in the same direction I was, so I had to give them a good lead before I followed. I had to remind myself to look back as well as ahead.

"The next day I came across the body of the staggering pilot. I was amazed that he had made it as far as he had. He was off on the side of the road and had been bayoneted in the back. His hands were still tied. I dragged him into the jungle and untied him. Reluctantly, I removed his boots, socks, and flight suit. Taking his dog tags, I discovered he was Harold P. Rogers, Captain, USAF. I asked God for mercy for both of us. Using Harry's pole and bonds, I carried my booty. Night had me asking what the point of this fugue was. The slit in the back of Harry's flight suit was my answer.

"At daybreak I was back on the trail. I ate some of my snake. It was already starting to go bad. I didn't want to waste it, so I stuffed myself until I almost puked and then threw away the rest.

If I hadn't, I would have been tempted to eat it later and may have been poisoned. As I said before, if I got sick, I was dead. Anyway, the rice would feed me for some time.

"Around 2:00 p.m., I came across the remains of the night camp of the group I had followed. The fire was cold, but the undisturbed ash on the end of some small twigs told me it was theirs. The only other evidence was a silver wrapper that still smelled of Juicy Fruit gum. The captors had no doubt taken it from the airmen. Maybe it had been Harry's. The implications of the fire were that the enemy was at least nine hours in front of me, and they were pulling away. I wouldn't have to worry about bumping into them. But I still didn't know where they, and I, were headed. Their goal was probably a little more concrete than "east."

I didn't come upon their next camp until dusk the following day. Now they were a full twenty-four hours ahead. That camp was situated on the trail about fifty meters before the path forked. Try as I might, I couldn't tell which way they had gone. After a night's sleep, I again tried to determine their course. With no better luck than the day before, I took the path that headed more eastward. Over the next five days, I didn't come across any campsites; I guessed that they had gone the other way. Actually, after I had made my choice at the fork, I had seen no one.

"For the twenty-ninth time, I was bedding down in a tree when I caught a glimpse of the mountains through the foliage. Goddamn! I was getting close. That night it rained. As a matter of fact, it rained for the better part of the next four days. My canteens were full, and so were my boots. I didn't even try to build a fire; I just ate uncooked rice. I kept trudging along, sure that no one else would be on the trail. I wore the straw hat in an attempt to keep the water out of my eyes and spent most of my time watching where I was stepping.

"On one terrifying occasion, I looked up and saw three human forms coming at me out of the downpour. It was too late to hide. I couldn't even get to my gun. It was under all my clothing to protect it from the rain. I could hear my heart pounding as I looked down and walked right past them. All the time I was mentally chanting, "Don't look at my boots! Don't look at my boots!" After I was about ten paces beyond them, I took a quick glance back. They had disappeared into the mist. What kind of fools were they, out in that kind of weather? The thought crossed my mind that I hadn't looked at their footwear either. I cursed at myself for being careless and got off the road to rest. After that I had to have a cigarette. Examining the pack, I saw that I had smoked only five in the last thirty days. Hell, I thought I might even be able to quit.

"I spent the thirty-third day of my odyssey in the bush. There was a veritable flood of civilization moving hurriedly down the path in the opposite direction. Evidently, something disastrous had occurred up ahead. Those folks were carrying as much as they could on their backs. They were mostly women and children, but there was an old man here and there.

"The next morning the road was clear, and I pushed on. Around every bend in the road was something I had to investigate carefully. A large pot, a bundle of rags, a wooden stool. They all caused me anxiety until I identified them. The worst was the dead body of an old man leaning up against a tree trunk. It took over a half-hour to get past that obstacle.

"The junk in the road thinned out, and I figured that I was getting close to where the debacle happened. The jungle was thinning out too. The mature trees were about as thick as before, but the undergrowth was definitely diminishing.

"After a few hundred meters of travel, I saw a thatch hut on the left hand side of the road. After I patiently observed and inspected it, I found it uninhabited. Further up the road there were more huts, and those were empty too. As it turned out, those were the suburbs of a rather good-sized village. As I walked toward a denser concentration of housing, I caught the stench of rotting flesh. At that instant I knew what I was going to find. There, in what passed for the town square, was the pile of bodies. I approached it. I started to count the bodies and stopped at twenty. There were at least five times that number. It looked like they had all been shot. Each body showed multiple wounds all lined up, which indicated automatic weapons. A spent shell casing told me the massacre had been committed with AK-47s.

"I went through each hut looking for useful items and found very little. I restocked my rice bag with some that I found spilled on the floor mats of a few of the huts. I found two bodies in the community well. Someone had been trying to erase that place. I had little reason to hang around, so I left.

"The sun was setting as I reached the outskirts of the village, so I decided to spend the night in the second-to-last hut. That one had a woven pallet to sleep on and a piece of cloth to pull across the doorway. I cooked a little rice, ate it, and then went to sleep on my back for the first time in thirty-four nights. It was ecstasy to be able to roll over and move my arms and legs, all comforts denied you if you sleep in trees.

"I was awakened at dawn by a rooster's crowing. He had not crowed twice before I pictured him on a spit over a low fire. Catching him wasn't much of a hunt; he came over to me when I exited the hut.

"As I was cleaning off a drumstick, it occurred to me that these people probably had gardens. I went behind the huts and there before me were row upon row of various vegetables. I couldn't identify most of them, but they certainly were safe to eat. No doubt they had fertilized the garden with manure, so I was going to have to prepared the food carefully. I picked a good variety and returned to the hut. With my bundle on Harry's pole over my left shoulder, and the remaining drumstick in my right hand, I took the most eastward of the three roads out of town. I no doubt looked like a Vietnamese Charlie Chaplin.

"Several kilometers out of the village the road became hilly. The jungle was really thinning out and cover was hard to come by. About midafternoon, my dirt path intersected a paved road. The road ran north and south, and a crude sign indicated that a place called Buon Blech was nine kilometers to the south. I hid and watched the road for fifteen minutes. Most of the traffic was headed toward Buon Blech. The travelers were mostly pedestrians and an occasional animal-drawn cart. On two occasions, though, ancient cars headed south carrying military personnel, not ours. This observation convinced me to continue east on the path.

"I crossed quickly at dusk and had gone but half a kilometer when I came upon a very dilapidated footbridge. That bridge spanned a small river about twenty meters across. It was getting dark, and I thought it wiser to wait until light to attempt to cross it. I walked off the path toward a gully, where I planned to spend the night. In the darkness, I fell and tumbled headlong into a sleeping family of four. I must have scared the hell out of them, as they did me. We stared at each other for about five seconds. I had lost the .45 in the fall and felt around for it. They finally recognized me for what I was and shouted, 'Friends! Friends!' Everyone's fear subsided a little then, when we all realized we were not trying to kill each other.

"Over a little food they offered me, I told them my tale. The man of the family, in turn, told me theirs. He had been a minor official in a village to the northwest. It had been rumored that the North Vietnamese were sweeping through the area, so he and his family had pulled out. A day later they saw the smoke of the burning village behind them. They had been on the run since, and that had been nine days ago. They were headed southeast toward some relatives. He had been using the paved road but had gotten off it at night to avoid bandits. I told him about the soldiers I had seen going south. He said his strategy was to mingle in with all the other refugees. I would have had difficulty doing that. I had to continue east. The next morning, I found the .45 and said my good-byes. The family gave me a little dried meat of unknown origin and some rice. They headed for the road and I, for the bridge.

"At the bridgehead, I tied all my belonging into a bundle and secured it with the rope. I then tied the end of the rope to my wrist. That way, if I fell in, at least I wouldn't lose everything. The crossing was tedious and speckled with near falls. I reached the opposite side without mishap, and I sat down for a smoke. Harry's dog tags fell out of the cigarette pack, and as I drew on the Pall Mall I wondered who he had been. After a few minutes of musing my eyes fell on the bridge, and then I had a very selfish but practical thought. With just a few whacks of the machete, I severed the ropes of the bridge and the east end fell into the river. I then put Harry's tags back in my pocket and snuffed out my butt. So much for followers.

"For the next four days I was in hilly terrain doing my impression of a giant Vietnamese ragpicker. My beard was now full and shaggy. I had made every effort to hide my fatigues with native garb and the woven hat. The true test of my disguise came on the fifth day beyond the bridge. I was traversing a barren area when I heard the rotor of a chopper coming up behind me. As I turned I saw that it was an American gunship. I also saw that it was about to commit a very hostile act. For a second I thought about waving and shouting, but I quickly dismissed that thought and dove into a clump of rocks just ahead of a string of M-60 bullets. The occupants of the chopper must have been in a hurry because they kept on instead of turning and easily finishing me off. As I gathered my junk, I heard a more sustained burst of fire up the trail. The assholes were shooting at everything they saw. I adjusted my rags and proceeded.

"About half a klik on, I spotted victims of the chopper gunner. I approached with the .45 ready. I hunched over so I looked smaller. When I was twenty feet away, I saw rifles lying on the ground beside a form administering to three bodies. Fear jumped into my throat, and I eased the safety off the .45. As I slowly closed the distance between us, I could see that two of the men in the group were dead. The one being helped was groaning. The one giving aid evidently sensed my presence and quickly turned. I could tell by her face that for a split second she did not recognize me as an American. In the next second she did and turned her head to find a weapon. She was a second behind, and a shot from the .45 caught her full in the chest. The man she had been attending to saw all this and made a move for a weapon as well. He suffered a similar fate. After I was sure all four people were dead, I looked around for other witnesses. I was doing a very poor job of keeping a low profile. That place looked like the OK Corral. I quickly picked over the bodies, taking their food, the largest pair of sandals I could find, and the first aid kit that was lying open next to the body of the last one to die. With my booty, I quick-marched on my way. I was trusting that the whole mess would be blamed on the gunship.

"Several days later, as the trail was heading in generally downhill, I saw that I was coming into the jungle again. Nearly an hour later, I came upon a sign that said Hau Bon. I wasn't sure what a Hau Bon was, but I presumed it was a village and had to be avoided. As the trail that I had been on was running northeast, I decided to skirt the village the south end in hope of linking up with a more easterly trail. I had forgotten how difficult it was to travel in the bush. I tired quickly and had to drink frequently. That night I had to sleep in a goddamned tree again. It bothered me that not only was I getting good at this survival stuff, but that I was also getting used to it. I couldn't remember what sheets felt like. The veneer of civilization had rubbed off."

CHAPTER FIFTEEN

WOLKERT GOT UP AND poured himself a cup of coffee. Everyone else remained seated. "Don't stop now, Dad," Chris said. "What happened next?"

Wolkert returned to the group and continued his story. "At midmorning the next day, the gods smirked again. I happened onto a trail leading east southeast, toward more mountainous regions.

"As soon as the road came out of the jungle, it began to parallel the south shore of a river. It ran east for quite some distance and turned gently southeast. The terrain became a series of steep ups and downs. I was less cautious than I should have been because I had seen no one in several days. Shortly after noon of the forty-seventh day, I spied several caves on the cliff face to my right. The mouths of the caves faced northwest. It was not yet dusk. The idea of a rest in the relative safety of a cave was irresistible. I had to climb up a sixty-degree grade for about fifty feet to get to the second most accessible cave. The opening was six feet across, and it went back about fifteen feet. There were remnants of a fire in the middle of the floor, but these appeared very old. A few flat rusted cans also littered the cave. These were from GIs and indicated that some long-range patrol had briefly used this place for shelter.

"The sky signaled an impending storm, and soon lightning lit up the cave. A half-hour later, the rains started, but I was dry and felt safe for the first time in a long time.

"With what little light was left before nightfall, I decided to conduct an inventory of my ever-increasing possessions. There was nothing else to do while my rags and clothes soaked up water for my canteens. I still had the two knives and machete. As I examined the .45, I remembered that I had expended two bullets. I replaced them. The shoe department was in good shape. I had been wearing the sandals I had found in the ox cart and still had Harry's and my boots in reserve. The contents of the first-aid kit were scanty—a few bandages, some sulfa powder, and scissors. The scissors afforded me something close to a shave as I used them to cut my beard back to stubble. I bathed in the rain, wrung out my clothes, and set them up to dry. After eating the last of the food from the OK Corral shootout, I slept. It rained all night, and the sound of the downpour was very soothing.

"The rain continued into the next day, leaving me rested and bored. I made a crude calendar out of Harry's pole, notching it for each day since the beginning of the march east. I made special marks next to certain days to commemorate notable events. When it was complete, the marks took up about nine inches of the four-foot-long pole. I hoped I wouldn't use all of it. I really had no idea how far I'd come or how far I had to go.

"Depression set in rapidly. Prior to finding that cave, I had been so intent on survival, so busy with chores, so uncomfortable that I had not had time to really reflect on my situation. Now I did. I thought about Vietnam and how I had come to be here again.

"By the end of 1972, there were fewer than forty thousand Americans left. As in the early '60s, these were "advisors." By the spring of 1973, the NVA were all over the south. The whole thing was coming loose. There were massive enemy-troop movements toward the south from the north and west. The South Vietnamese were not equal to the task, even with a fairly large covert air force.

"Whenever native agents on our side seemed to be in danger, we made every effort to extricate them because trustworthy people were scarce, and morale among the locals would drop if we abandoned them.

"My unit was on an extraction mission the day before we crashed. We had received word that the NVA were going to overrun a place called Bu Prang, a town near the Cambodian border. In that town, there were three agents who had to be pulled out fast. At dawn the next morning, a pilot and I flew in a Huey to Bu Prang. By noon, we had collected the agents, and we were on our way back to base when we were hit. I stopped thinking about the past and tried to focus on the present, and, hopefully, my future.

"I knew I was in a race to get to the friendlies to the coast before U.S. forces left, leaving me to fend for myself in a country totally controlled by the enemy. The more I analyzed my predicament, the more hopeless it appeared. So I stopped.

"After a long time, the rains ended and I resumed my solitary trek. During my time in the cave I had put together a fair disguise and felt that I could pass for Vietnamese if seen from more than fifty meters away. The path I traveled on paralleled the river for many hours before a bridge took me to the other side. On the north side, the path went but a few hundred yards before it branched out to the east and southeast. True to form, I selected the eastward route. I had been picking my way along for about thirty minutes when I crested a small rise and spied a single NVA soldier three hundred yards down the trail, making his way toward me. The terrain was rocky and he was watching his footing. At first I thought this was going to be a minor problem, but within two minutes it became clear that he was the point man for a group of at least thirty.

"There was no place to go except back, and I had to go quickly. When the NVA crested the rise, they would be able to see quite a distance too. I shifted my ass into high gear and tore out. Running generally downhill had me back to the junction in less than ten minutes. Without hesitation I took a sharp left turn and continued headlong down the southeast fork I had previously rejected. A few minutes later I was spent. Taking shelter in a rock pile, I allowed my heaving chest, gasping lungs, and pounding heart to return to near normal. The running, the fear, and breathing through my mouth had made my mouth so dry that my tongue stuck to the roof and wouldn't come loose without water. As soon as the water hit my stomach, I puked. How did those guys who went out into the bush every day handle this shit? I prayed that the soldiers behind me were going for the bridge. The possibility that they weren't had me quickly on the road again.

"Several hours later, I spotted the smoke of a small village. I approached to within two hundred meters to observe it. The road ran right through the center of town. I could see eleven huts from where I was; there were probably more beyond my field of view. I couldn't skirt this one. With the few hours left before nightfall, I memorized the way to and through the village. After the populace had gone inside for the night, I adjusted my disguise and proceeded.

It had gotten dark rapidly, but I could still just make out the path. I tried to stay in the middle of the road and walk slowly enough to not arouse any suspicion. I had a few tense moments when I heard dogs barking and a family squabbling, but I gained the opposite edge of town without incident. A short time later, I was in the jungle again. I got off the path and found a safe-looking place to spend the night.

"Halfway through the following day, I came across another hapless reptile and hid in the jungle to eat. That was the first meat I had had in many days. It was great. Back on the trail, I had to dodge a little pedestrian traffic. As I was getting underway for the fourth time, I noticed a sign that read Phu Tuc. No doubt another settlement. If it had a sign, it was probably of fair size. Populated areas were getting closer together. I hoped that this meant I was getting closer to the coast.

"I chose to try to skirt this town by following the riverbank on the south side. This gave me the best chance of picking up the trail again on the other side of town. I waited until dusk and went down to the river. There was a four-foot dropoff about ten feet from the water's edge. This minor cliff paralleled the river. I planned to stay next to the bank and quietly bypass the town. Ten minutes later, I saw the first buildings. Some of them were concrete block. A little further on, I saw an airstrip and a small control tower. A single wrecked helicopter sat on the runway. A bit further on there were more buildings. It was a pretty big place.

"I felt a wire across my shin. I froze. I looked down, but it was too dark to see anything. Slowly I reached down with my right hand and felt for the line. Finding it, I gently traced it toward the riverbank to a stake. I then followed it in the other direction toward the water. Half expecting it to be a booby trap, I was surprised to find it went into the water. I pulled on it slowly and pulled out a fishnet. I confiscated the three fish inside and returned the net to the water.

"A half-kilometer south of the town's last building, I left the river and headed east into the bush. I smoked the fish over a low fire and retired for the night.

"At dawn, I took a compass reading and set my course due east.

I had to find the trail again. For once, things worked out, and by nine o'clock I was on the path and headed southeast. There was jungle on both sides, which provided me with things to eat and drink over the next two and a half days.

"As my course came around to the east, the countryside was turning into foothills. The foothills became mountainous. At midmorning on the fifty-sixth day, I came up over the edge of a mesa. The flat top had been a firebase. There were pits, sandbag bunkers, concertina wire, and shell casings all over. Some hut remnants led me to believe that this had been a village at one time. Everything was old and corroded. Nothing had happened here for a long time. The obscenities scrawled here and there made me smile. It reminded me who I was and where I wanted to be. A little lighter at heart, I crossed the mesa and faltered down the other side.

"Around 4:00 p.m. the same day, I was confronted by another fork in the road. A weathered sign indicated that Cung Son lay to the south. There was no indication of what lay to the east. By nightfall, I was in jungle again on the eastward path. This path showed no signs of use. There were branches across it as well as large spiderwebs. I wondered whether I had really gotten lucky.

"The next three days were uneventful, bordering on boring. I didn't see, hear, or smell any evidence of people. The next day, the jungle thinned out again. Around noon, the foliage overhead had diminished, and I saw the mountain that lay before me. It was a big mother.

"I decided to spend the rest of the day gathering food for the barren days ahead. That night and the next morning I really tanked up on calories. With what I had eaten and what I was carrying, I could last a week. The sun had not yet peaked when I came across a bridge of logs that spanned a small river flowing some ten feet below. I crossed it and left the jungle behind and began the ascent. The incline seemed to be about thirty degrees, and I got tired fast. I was resting fifteen minutes out of every hour. At midafternoon, I could look back and see that I had come a fair distance. Looking ahead, the spot where the path crossed the mountain's crest didn't seem any nearer.

"At the end of my third day on the mountain, I was within four hundred meters of the top. I had wanted to be there then, but my body said it would have to wait until tomorrow. I took shelter in the rocks, ate, and imagined what was over the crest.

"I rose the next morning determined to have breakfast on the ridge. It took only fifteen minutes to get there. As I peered out near the horizon, I swore I could see the ocean. I was sure of it. I figured the ocean couldn't be more than twenty miles away. Goddamn, I was going to make it! As I looked below me, I saw a very large river. I could see that my path was going to divide at the base of the mountain and that one branch would continue on the north bank, headed east. From where I was, the northern path seemed easier going. My enthusiasm was rekindled, and I began the descent. The angle down was steep and the travel was faster but more dangerous. It took most of the day to get to the intersection I had seen from the top that morning.

"After an hour or so, the path diverged from the river bank. This was good because even though I hadn't seen any boats, there certainly would be some on the river. I made a fireless camp, munched on some fruit, and tried to calculate the number of days to deliverance. I went to sleep convinced that it would be four at the most.

"Day sixty-four was the worst of my life. I had overslept, and in the daylight I was spotted by a group of six Vietnamese soldiers. They were in the process of robbing me when they discovered I was an American. About the same time, I realized that they were South Vietnamese. They were openly hostile, which really surprised me. As they were examining my watch, I asked them what the problem was. They finally said that all the Americans were gone and that they were from Tuy Hoa and heading for the mountains. They took what they wanted and left me trying to comprehend what they had said. 'All the Americans are gone.' Goddamn! All this way for nothing. All the pain, the bug bites, the hunger, the exhaustion, for nothing. The assholes left me behind. What the hell was I going to do!

After a half hour of alternate swearing and crying, I had calmed down a little. I wasn't thinking straight and had to get to shelter until I figured this goddamned thing out. Ahead lay the coast, civilization, and capture. The last deep jungle was several hours behind me. I had to get back in the bush. I began to retrace my steps from the previous day slowly. I didn't want to catch up with the bandits. By noon I was back at the intersection where the southern path crossed the river. I crossed the bridge, took the path south for a few hundred meters, and then entered the jungle. I searched for and found a large tree. I made a temporary camp at its base and sat down to think.

"If all the Americans were gone, it meant that the South Vietnamese had lost, or were rapidly losing, their country. The North Vietnamese would surely round up any supporters of the south. People would try to buy their lives with information, and several of them knew I was about. Cover in the deep jungle was the only answer. Maybe after things cooled down there would be a prisoner exchange, but I'd be goddamned if I'd surrender. The U.S. couldn't just leave me there. There were probably others like me who had been stranded in the pullout. They would have to come and get us. I had stayed alive for over two months, and I could probably go on indefinitely.

"Fortunately, I didn't have to. A few days after I had resigned myself to oblivion, the gods grinned again.

"I was drying my only pair of socks when I picked up on a distant hum. At first I thought it was a plane. I frantically searched for my signal mirror, but while tearing through my stuff I realized the frequency of the noise was closer to a boat. Abandoning the mirror idea, I grabbed the .45 and ran to the river's edge and hid in the bush. The whirr of the motor grew closer. That guy was going like a bat out of hell. As it came into view, I saw the shielded twin .50 calibers on the front and I knew it was one of ours. I jumped into the water at the river's edge and yelled and waved my arms. I yelled, 'American! American! Don't shoot! American!'

The engine cut back, and the barrels of the .50s followed me as the boat slowed so the skipper could take a cautious look.

"'American! I'm an American!' I yelled.

"'Well, get your ass over here,' was the skipper's reply.

"They weren't coming close to the bank, so I had to swim for it. I swam for my life.

"As soon as I was aboard, the skipper had the throttle wide open in an instant. We shot hell-bent for the coast. The skipper, the four crewmembers, and I were getting the hell out of Dodge.

"There was no problem until we had to pass the docks at the village at the river's mouth. The motherfuckers heard us coming and were lined up to extend their greeting. The skipper correctly read the ploy and yelled, 'Guns left!' With this, he took us as close to the right bank as our speed allowed. The crew raked the docks with an M-60 and the twin .50s while I did an imitation of deck paint. We had to be doing forty miles an hour as we passed them. They weren't hitting us much, but the docks were taking heavy damage. With death and destruction in our wake, we headed straight out to sea. When we were out of sight of the mainland, the skipper shut the engine down and started to check the radio. The crew left their stations and came over to inspect me.

"One asked where the fuck I'd been.

"Another said I looked like shit. This was no doubt true. I gave them a brief rendition of what I had been through, and they agreed I was one lucky son of a bitch. I asked what came next.

"They said a destroyer was supposed to pick them up that night, so we waited. They explained that they were supposed to pick up an ARVN officer and his family, but he hadn't show up on time. They gave him his two extra hours and then split. Then they found me.

"The big boat showed up, and I rode back to Guam in comfort. I was mustered out, paid off, and sent home."

Chris said, "Dad! You *were* one lucky son of a gun. What happened when you got home?"

Wolkert took another sip of coffee and cleared his throat. "I farted around in engineering for a while and finally made up my mind to go to medical school. I graduated in 1977. I completed my residency in surgery in 1981 and have been in private practice since."

"The parallels between us are pretty spooky," Wittmond said.

"Damned spooky," Wolkert agreed as he refilled his cup.

CHAPTER SIXTEEN

CAREFUL NOT TO DISTURB the sequence of the papers in Connie's journal, Bev found the place where she had left off and resumed reading.

Rhaspberry and I crossed paths again twenty-five years later in 1988. Another mission came calling. My account of this mission is more exact than the last, as I recorded my thoughts only a few weeks after its conclusion, whereas my account of the first mission was gleaned from memory and a twenty-year-old diary.

I remember that Mrs. Gardner was the last patient on the medical call list that day. My good cheer had been pretty well used up by the previous fourteen hospital patients I had seen, and only she stood between me and Saturday afternoon.

The previous week she had been in the office with a complaint of weakness and a weight loss of twenty-two pounds over the last two months. A chest X-ray showed a four-centimeter mass in her left lung, and a subsequent CT scan of her chest indicated that the mass had a high probability for malignancy. It also showed an additional half-centimeter mass in the right lung. She had a fifty-year history of smoking, so I was fairly sure that this was going to be the end of the line for her.

I did the usual sputum culture and cytology studies, but these, as usual, did not yield a definite diagnosis. Pathologists who read these studies had to keep their thesauruses open to the word *inconclusive*; there were so many ways to say it. Without receiving a definite answer using the easy methods, it became necessary for me to consult a thoracic surgeon. The surgeon, Dr. Charles Tate, two radiologists, and I sat down and discussed the case. We decided to needle biopsy the lesion in the right lung under fluoroscopy.

The needle biopsy, to everyone's surprise, showed tuberculosis. We put Mrs. Gardner on the appropriate antitubercular drugs, and she was recovering well. I would say she was a very lucky woman.

I made my way to the doctors' lounge for coffee. I was on call for the group two weeks early because I had an elk hunt in Colorado planned, and naturally, the season coincided with my call weekend. One of the other five internists had been kind enough to trade weekends. No doubt I would repay the good deed when ski season arrived.

As I poured coffee into a cup, the odor signaled that I would need at least three sugars and two nondairy creamers to make it tolerable. With the mixture in hand, I sat down to read the newspaper. As if an electrical circuit had been completed, my beeper went off the second my butt touched the chair. Then, after three seconds of high-frequency noise, "Doctor Wittmond, please call the exchange," came through the device with a whine that could curdle milk. Dutifully, I called the exchange for the ninth (or was it the tenth?) time that morning. This time I was requested to call a Dr. Sherlock at hospital extension 520.

"Who the hell is Dr. Sherlock?" I pondered as I dialed. A number of new doctors had come to town last July, and I had not met many of them. I was hoping this wasn't someone wanting an infectious disease consult; I wanted to get home for lunch. The man who answered identified himself as Jay Sherlock, and he requested a meeting. I told him I was in the doctors' lounge and invited him down. Several minutes later, the door opened. Sherlock was a white male, approximately forty years old. He stood about five feet ten inches tall and weighed about one hundred eighty pounds. He displayed no obvious deformities and appeared in good health. It was a bad habit, but after fifteen years of practicing medicine, I evaluated every new person I met like a patient. I shook Dr. Sherlock's hand, and we sat across the table from each other. I warned him about the potentially lethal coffee and he wisely decided against having any.

I cautiously sipped my acrid brew.

"I think we have a mutual acquaintance, a Mr. Jerome Rhaspberry," he said. He waited for the reaction.

The mention of the name brought back a flood of memories over twenty-five years old. I paused to partially regain my breath and composure and warily asked how he knew Rhaspberry. He openly stated that he worked for him.

I knew from my previous encounter with Rhaspberry that it was best to get right to the point, but Mr. Sherlock was not going to do that. He had a spiel, and I cautiously listened.

"We have a problem," he said.

There was always a problem. He went on to say that there was a group of "freedom fighters" in an unnamed country that seem afflicted with some sort of ailment. This guy was so vague he could have been a pathologist. He must have read the "what the hell are you talking about?" expression on my face and reluctantly attempted to clarify what the problem was.

It seemed that over the last eight months, the freedom fighters had been plagued by a definite lack of aggressiveness. They had become listless and tired all the time.

I wished I had a dime for every time I heard "tired all the time."

Except for a slight cough, the men showed no other symptoms. The Agency sent blood samples back to the United States, but they revealed nothing. Now Jerome Rhaspberry wanted a doctor, and not just any doctor, to go in and evaluate.

Actually, I had not been Rhaspberry's first choice, or even his second. But after the others suffered an untimely accident and a heart attack, respectively, Rhaspberry was calling in third string. Sherlock said he had been given my file, which had been kept up-to-date since the early '60s, and was told to do everything reasonable to recruit me for this task. It seemed that Rhaspberry thought I was, well, dependable. All I could think of were the words of Yogi Berra: "This is déjà vu all over again."

Almost with resignation, I asked what the deal was. Sherlock proceeded to lay his cards on the table.

If I agreed, I was to proceed with my elk hunting plans. When I landed in Denver, Colorado, a man would take my place on the hunt, and I would board a plane that would take me to a staging area. I would be taken to the problem area to investigate, and I would be brought home. Naturally, I was to say nothing to anyone for the customary twenty-year period, and I would receive thirty thousands dollars in gold for my trouble, ten now and twenty later.

They knew about the hunt. They even knew which flight I had booked to Colorado. By now I shouldn't have been amazed, but I was.

Sherlock then stated that he needed an answer in forty-eight hours. He said that this operation probably would be a lot safer than the last one, but he could not provide any more details. Giving me a card with an address and phone number on the back, he got up and said, "You guys must have been something." He shook my hand and left.

I moved to the sofa. I had to think. This time there was no sword over my head, no disguised threats, just an overt deal. The thirty thousand dollars wasn't the bait but the sweetener. The Agency wanted my help, and no doubt were confident of my cooperation. They knew everything. They knew I had three children, sons ages fourteen and eighteen, and a daughter aged twenty-two. Caring for them was a lot of responsibility, but less than it had been a few years before. The Agency knew I was the senior partner in a seven-man medical group. That was a lot of financial security. Yeah, they were confident of my cooperation, but even they couldn't know the real reason I'd probably do this, could they?

Rhaspberry no doubt pictured me as a forty-nine-year-old fat-cat doctor with all the baggage of success who was now watching himself turn into his father. He probably figured that the time would be ripe to bring a little excitement into my maturing life. Certainly I would welcome the opportunity to ditty-bop one more time. After all, weren't big-game hunts just surrogates for the most dangerous game?

All of this was true. I had been in practice for fifteen years, and although the first five had been exciting and challenging, the last ten had been much less so. Fundamental changes in health care were making medicine progressively less gratifying to practice. HMOs had come to the fore, and while they had promised much, they delivered much less, and this left patients irritated and difficult to deal with. Each year, Medicare had cut back on its benefits while increasing the deductible, much to the chagrin of older patients.

All in all, it seemed that forces were at work to get the American public so aggravated that they and their doctors would welcome a national health care plan. In addition to that, I guess I was just getting tired of hearing people complain.

In truth, over the past several years, I had caught myself daydreaming about the days when the solutions to problems were much more, shall we say, direct. I had, as I believed anyone else my age had, longed to be free of being so goddamned responsible and had felt a desperate need to do something dangerous. I had often wondered what I would do if the Agency called. Subconsciously I knew the answer; I had kept myself in shape and had kept certain potentially useful skills well polished. As sure as they had me the first time, they had me now. They were masters at manipulation. They found out what I needed and played me. They had what I needed, but I don't think they knew exactly what it was. What I needed thirty years ago was a lot different than it was now.

I called Sherlock the next day from the office and told him it was a go.

He enthusiastically replied, "Excellent." It was almost as though he thought I might have said no.

Sherlock then instructed me to make a small list of equipment I'd need for the investigation and mail it to him tomorrow at the address on the card. When I asked why they didn't bring the patients to the United States for treatment, he said they couldn't risk bringing an unknown ailment into the country, and the expense of security and running a specialized medical facility would far exceed what I cost. Once again, I was the economical solution. At my request, the lab data on the samples would be made available in Denver. I think I definitely detected a note of excitement in Sherlock's voice as he said, "I'll see you on the twenty-ninth." He hung up. This little coup would probably get him major points with Rhaspberry. I wondered if he knew he was on the way to becoming a Rhaspberry.

The next ten days were so normal that I wondered if I had imagined the events of that weekend. Things stayed normal until Thursday, when a small cylindrical package addressed to me arrived at the office. I removed the brown paper wrapping to reveal a plastic cylinder containing twenty-five Krugerrands. I guess I hadn't imagined the events of the weekend after all.

With the elk hunt three days away, I began to pack. Somehow I managed ten days of gear and clothing into two duffle bags. I would have to pack my rifle in a hard case for the airline. It only took a few hours to assemble all my hunting gear; I had done this once or twice a year for the last five years. In the bottom of the bags I secreted five medical books: *Medical Microbiology*, by Jawetz, Melnick, and Adelberg; *Textbook of Pulmonary Disease*, by Baum; *Antimicrobial Therapy*, by Kagan; *Infectious Diseases*, by Hoprich; and *A Diagnostic Microbiology*, by Bailey and Scott. It would not do for someone to see these in my luggage on an elk hunt.

I rose early on the October 29, eager to get underway. I had loaded all the gear in the Plymouth Voyager the night before because Kurt had to be dropped off at the high school by 8:00 and my flight was at 9:17. Bev dropped me and all my gear off in front of the terminal a little before nine—I had plenty of time. At the check-in counter, I picked up my ticket and a clerk took the baggage. One clerk plastered a big UNLOADED GUN sticker on my gun case, and it disappeared down the conveyor belt. I hoped I would see it again.

In Denver, I had to switch to a local flight to the small town of Silverthorn seventy-five miles farther west. The original plan for the hunt had the guide meeting me at the airport and driving me to a ranch just east of Kremmling. Here we would hunt from the base camp consisting of several large tents. Now, someone would assuming my name and go on the hunt while I played Marcus Welby to freedom fighters instead.

As I deplaned, I heard, "Wittmond! Over here!" A smiling Sherlock deftly guided me to the men's room, where we met my surrogate. I was directed to give him my wallet and baggage-claim check. He took these and left. I hoped he enjoyed the—*my* hunt.

Sherlock then gave me a new wallet containing an ID and a passport. I was surprised that these documents used my real name. After pocketing the wallet, I was briskly ushered to another concourse. In short order we were aboard a small plane and airborne.

With the sun coming in the window on the left, I could tell we were headed south. On the seat next to me were my books and shaving kit. After we had achieved the desired altitude, everyone except the two pilots—Sherlock, another passenger, and I—took off their seatbelts and settled down for the flight. I asked Sherlock who the other man was. He replied that he didn't know and smoothly changed the subject by presenting me with the lab data I had requested.

I thumbed through the extremely thorough lab workup on the blood samples of the afflicted. The data had been tabulated by computer so that the tests were listed down the page and the nine patients' ID numbers were listed across the top. The other doctors who had examined the data had not found the cause of the problem. It was unlikely that I would be able to succeed where they had failed, but the investigative process had to begin somewhere.

The most basic lab tests were listed at the top, and as I read down the page, the data became more esoteric. The row for CBC, or complete blood count, gave a rundown on the count of each patient's red and white blood cells and platelets. All nine subjects had plenty of red blood cells, so they weren't anemic.

I then checked the white blood cell counts for signs of an active infection, indicated by an elevated count, or suppressed immune system or infection so massive the white blood cells were depleted, indicated by a low count. Seven of the nine subjects had white blood cell counts between eleven and thirteen thousand, mildly elevated above the normal range of seven to ten thousand per cubic millimeter, but hardly alarming, and certainly not the sixteen to eighteen thousand that would indicate a massive infection like appendicitis. I made a red check in the margin to highlight this abnormality and moved on.

The next parameter in the CBC was the differential count, or the percentages of the various kinds of white cells. The diff counts were almost normal but showed an increase in "segs," bacterial infection–fighting cells. The cell sizes and platelets count were within normal limits, so I next examined the SMA-26.

The SMA-26, a panel of twenty-six tests that evaluated most of the function of the internal organs, some four or five times, showed normal levels of blood sugar, sodium, potassium, and chloride in most cases. The creatinine and BUN, both measures of kidney function, were slightly elevated, however. This could have meant early kidney failure, but more likely meant dehydration. I made another red check mark there. The subjects' thyroid, cholesterol, triglyceride, calcium, phosphorus, and uric acid values were all normal. Bilirubin and the three liver enzymes were all normal except LDH, which was elevated, possibly indicating mild cellular damage but not in the liver, considering the normal counts of the other enzymes. LDH was also produced in lung tissue, so I made a note. The last test on the SMA-26 checked a pancreatic enzyme, and it was normal.

The plane ride was a little bumpy, and the motion combined with reading the small numbers was making me sick. I put the papers aside and asked Sherlock how he was doing. He had been sitting quietly while I was reading but became animated by my question.

When I asked where he was going to drop me off he replied that he was going to be with me the whole way in, and hopefully out. Rhaspberry had specifically told him that if anything happened to me, he didn't need to come back. I told him that Rhaspberry was kidding; he wasn't reassured.

In an attempt to alleviate his anxiety, I asked how long he had been in the Agency. "Seems like forever," he replied. Now, at the age of thirty-three, he was engaged in his first foreign assignment. He then asked me, "Did you know you were Rhaspberry's first foreign assignment?" After a telling pause, all I could say to that was, "I hope you do as well as he did." He laughed and I went back to the lab data.

CHAPTER SEVENTEEN

BEV FROWNED. SHE KNEW there was something funny about that elk hunting trip. Connie had been acting strangely before he left. Now she knew the truth. She turned the page and continued reading.

The next tests, urinalyses, were normal but showing a high specific gravity. This confirmed my dehydration hypothesis and ruled out renal failure. After this, the data showed a run of completely normal tests; even the Coombs and cold agglutinins were okay.

The next slightly positive test was the erythrocyte sedimentation rate, a very old test of the rate at which red cells in the whole blood settled to the bottom of a glass tube. The elevated rate only told me that these subjects had an inflammatory process going on somewhere.

With the information I had so far, I was hopeful that the upcoming bacterial and viral cultures would yield pay dirt. The little positive data that I had pointed to a low-grade infectious process, perhaps located in the lungs. As I read on, I found that the urine, blood, and stool cultures were completely negative. The sputum cultures had grown only the normal flora. found in the upper respiratory tracts of healthy people. I dismissed the lines showing two of the nine sputum samples were positive for *Serratia* and *Aerobacter*. Those organisms were found on rotting vegetation and were probably contaminants acquired in the sample collection process. The viral studies were absolutely negative.

That was the end of the data. There were no obvious answers, so it was obvious why the Agency were calling in an onsite observer with infectious disease expertise.

As I flipped over the last page, Sherlock asked if I wanted some coffee. I said yes, and he poured some out of a thermos, apologizing for the lack of cream and sugar. After my first sip, I asked about our destination.

"I thought you'd have it figured out by now," he said.

"It's either El Salvador or Nicaragua," I guessed.

"You're good," he answered with a smile. "Uh, it's not El Salvador."

"Oh, Christ, not the jungle," I thought.

In an effort to make light conversation, he asked what I'd done since my last experience with the Agency. Though I was sure he knew all about that, I gave him a thumbnail sketch. I told him that after Rhaspberry and I parted company in late '63, I stayed at the University of Missouri until the summer of 1964. I audited some classes, drank some beer, and gained back the twenty-three pounds I had lost in Vietnam. I started graduate school at Saint Louis University's Department of Chemistry in the fall of '64 and graduated with a PhD in physical chemistry in '67. That fall, I moved to Huntsville, Alabama, to start a job with Boeing-NASA and met my future wife. After three and a half years in the thermal analysis group of the aerophysics division, we saw that the public interest in space was waning, as was congressional funding, so I decided to be my own boss. I took the prerequisites for medical school at the University of Alabama at night, then chose Saint Louis University because of its reputation and proximity to home. I received my MD the spring of '74, and I completed my residency in internal medicine in 1977. Not long afterward, a classmate and I opened an office, and that was more or less it. It had been a peaceful existence until he showed up.

He asked why I agreed to come and I told him that it was probably a combination of things—an attempt to prove I wasn't getting old, a desire for a little excitement to lighten up a dull profession, a chance to help the country, maybe some other stuff.

He looked puzzled. He couldn't know about the Feeling, I thought. Changing the subject, I asked about our itinerary. Sherlock said we would first land at Fort Hood and pick up our gear. We would then fly to Honduras and approach the Nicaraguan border on foot. I wondered if the fort had changed much since my last visit.

Sherlock and I arrived at the Fort Hood airstrip about 3:00 p.m. We boarded a jeep and we were whisked away to a hangar with a row of lockers lined up against the wall and several piles of equipment. Sherlock talked to the guard and determined that the smallest of the piles was ours. He picked up a checklist and began an inventory of our gear. When he finished, he gave me a bundle and a key and directed me to locker 174. I was instructed to change clothes and store all my personal gear in the locker. After I did that, I returned to our pile. Sherlock was already in fatigues and continuing his inspection. I interrupted his audit to tell him I wanted a barracks hat. I was not going to wear a jungle boonie hat. Just putting it on lowered a person's IQ by thirty points. Even Clint Eastwood would look dumb in a boonie hat. Sherlock laughed and said, "No problem." After he finished his duties, he came over to where I was waiting, still trying to get my boots to feel comfortable.

He asked what kind of sidearm I preferred. I said I didn't prefer sidearms; I wanted a rifle, preferably an H-K 91, a semiautomatic version of the G-3 used by the West Germans with a twenty-round magazine. It fired a full-house .308 NATO cartridge, not the puny .223 varmint round of the M-16. It was fairly light, had minimal the recoil, and had one minute of angle accuracy out of the box. Sherlock was gone for about twenty minutes and returned with a rifle, a belt of four twenty-round magazines, and a carton of a hundred cartridges. We had an hour and a half until the flight out, so he allowed me to try that baby out on the range.

On the way, we picked up some sandwiches and soda; we ate as we walked. On the range, I loaded one full magazine, and as I slipped it into the rifle I noticed the selector switch had a full-auto position. It was actually a G-3, not an H-K 91. I looked at Sherlock and he shrugged. It was all he could get. I'd just have to keep the switch on single fire.

I dropped to the prone position and slipped the sling around my arm. With my left thumb, I pulled down the cocking lever just forward of the magazine. The bolt slammed home loudly and carried a round into the chamber. Sherlock flinched at the sound. I rechecked the selector switch to make sure it was at single fire and then adjusted the turret rear sight to full open. I aimed at the top of three twelve-inch black bull's-eyes one hundred yards downrange, placing the front post sight just under the bull's-eye and even with the first notch on the rear sight. I slowly took up the slack in the trigger until it set. I took a deep breath, let about half of it out, and touched off the trigger. The trigger was very mushy, like most military rifles. I repeated the aiming and firing procedure four more times and then looked at the target through the spotting scope. All five rounds had hit the paper, but only two were in the black. I glanced over at Sherlock and he stared stoically into space. The son of a bitch wanted to laugh.

I moved the sights down to the middle target. I paused for a few seconds to compose myself and fired five more shots. This time, four of the five shots were in the twelve-inch circle. I could feel it coming back. Moving down to the bottom bull's-eye, I fired another five shots. These felt pretty good, and all five had landed in a four-inch grouping in the right upper quadrant of the black. With the small screwdriver that came with the gun, I made the slightest of adjustments to the rear sight and then fired the last five rounds at the bottom target. These felt really good. They landed in a two-and-half-inch group almost dead center.

"There, you little shit," I thought. I came up to sitting, removed the empty magazine, and then refilled it and three others with the remaining rounds.

As I was putting the now-full magazines into their belts, Sherlock said, "That was pretty good shooting for iron sights."

"It was pretty good shooting for any kind of sights," I smugly replied.

We then packed up and returned to the hangar. Our pile of gear was gone. "It's on the plane and we should be too," Sherlock said, reading my mind. When we exited the hangar through a door opposite the one we had been using, I beheld a ancient C-47. Sherlock saw the look of misgiving on my face and said that it was a real dependable craft.

"Well, at least it has a door," I mumbled.

After setting into the webbing seatbelts, I asked Sherlock about our next landing site. He said we would be setting down on a "special" landing strip just south of Yuscaran, Honduras.

"Where the hell is that?" I asked.

He flatly replied, "About thirty minutes southeast of Tegucigalpa, the capital."

"That really pinpoints it for me," I said. He lowered his voice and said that it was about fifteen miles northwest of the Nicaraguan border.

He went back to his papers. I took a nap. I hadn't lost my ability to sleep anywhere anytime.

After a brown-bag supper, I settled back with a Styrofoam cup of Sherlock's coffee. The sun had set and all I could see through the starboard window was a thin orange gash on the horizon. By now, Sherlock had put his papers aside and was sipping coffee as well. My knowledge of the contra–Sandinista fracas had come from the network news, so I took this opportunity to get an insider's opinion.

Sherlock started explaining by asking what I already knew. I said I thought I remembered that the Sandinistas had overthrown Somoza and the national guard in about 1981. After taking power, they had been rather ineffective at governing until the election of Daniel Ortega in 1985. Since then, he had moved the country toward socialism and cultivated a friendship with Cuba. The contras, generally ex-national guard soldiers and Somoza supporters, had been waging a bush war with the government for years with only minimal success. The U.S. Congress had cut off all lethal aid to the contras last year, and various elements in the western hemisphere had been calling for the dissolution of the contras since then. That was about all I knew.

What I said was true, up to 1985. Sherlock brought me up-to-date on the rest. The election that installed Ortega was a well-orchestrated sham to give the impression of democracy, which the press swallowed hook, line, and sinker. Ortega was a very articulate man. In public, he was the very voice of democratic reason; he simply couldn't understand why the United States was opposed to him. In truth, he was a calculating Communist disciple who was providing a foothold for the spread of that doctrine in Central America.

The man was ruthless under the facade of being the concerned leader of an oppressed people. In opposition to him and his plans for Central America, the United States had imposed a total economic embargo, which had probably done more to weaken his government than the contras had.

The contras had been ineffective in fighting the enemy troops but had greater success in destroying economic targets. The Sandinistas knew the economy was their Achilles heel and were quite aggressive in trying to prevent the contras from damaging it further. They had even launched raids into Honduras to seek out the contras. The CIA, under direct order of President Reagan, was covertly helping the contras inflict maximal damage on the Nicaraguan economy without ruffling U.S. Congressional feathers. In other words, we helped them destroy crops, mining, logging, and other operations while trying to avoid direct confrontation with armed forces.

Little by little, it was working. Ortega was getting help from Cuba, but Cuba had its own problems, and both countries were a big economic drain on the Russians. Like Communists before them, when things went poorly, they wanted to negotiate. The previous year, there had been a big to-do with Cardinal Obando y Bravo mediating discussions between the contras and Sandinistas. After the United States reduced its aid package and deleted lethal aid, the negotiations fell apart. Big surprise. Now, the contras were back disrupting the economy, and the CIA was helping them. The news media still showed the masses supporting Ortega, but these staged demonstrations did not reflect the true situation. Ortega was gradually losing support, and when he got desperate, there would be reports of contra atrocities and even larger staged demonstrations by his supporters. This escalation would signal the beginning of the end.

"How long will it take?" I asked.

"Probably years. Who knows?" Sherlock replied. "One must be patient. We learned that lesson in Vietnam."

"One of the many lessons, I hope," I commented.

"Yeah," he replied thoughtfully. I leaned back and opened the infectious disease book to the chapter on mycoplasma. I was asleep two minutes later.

The sixteen-hundred-mile trip took fourteen hours, counting the fuel stop somewhere in Mexico. This placed us in Yuscaran around 7:00 a.m. Saint Louis time, 8:00 a.m. local time. This landing was a little bumpy—the runway was only smoothed dirt. As the plane rolled to a stop, a half-dozen shacks with corrugated metal roofs came into view. There was no welcoming party. We deplaned, and the crew unloaded our gear next to the runway. Sherlock told the pilot it was okay to go, and he did. The plane faded into a tiny black dot in the sky. Sherlock and I sat perched on our crates like two buzzards on a dead goat.

I asked if someone was supposed to meet us, and Sherlock said that they'd come.

By God, he was right. Forty minutes and two gallons of sweat later, a small train of five donkeys and eight men slowly wound its way from the forest edge toward us. I was excited; Sherlock seemed tense. Picking up on his signal, I also tensed. I flicked the safety off the G-3. He spread the fingers of his left hand, advising caution.

"Easy, Rambo," he muttered. Easy, shit! I was taking my cue from him. He said he just wanted to be sure they were our people before they got too close. The lead man held up his left fist and pumped it up and down four times. A smile spread over Sherlock's face and he said it was okay. The distance between us and the convoy closed, and I could see that the leader was an American in his twenties. The other seven were very dark skinned and had the facial features of American Indians. They were all armed to the teeth. Sherlock told me to stay put, and he walked over to confer with the other American. They mumbled in low voices, staring at the ground. Two or three times the pack leader shook his head and flailed his arms. Sherlock said something else to him, and the leader jerked his head up, and as he faced me, I could read his lips saying, "No shit." The pair now moved toward me, and as they got close, Sherlock said, "Jack, I'd like you to meet Dr. Conrad Wittmond; Doc, this is Jack Coburn. He'll be taking us into the badlands."

I replied that it was nice to meet him but still wondered what Sherlock had said to elicit the "No shit."

Jack explained that we had about twenty-five hard miles ahead of us that would take about ten hours. We'd set up camp that night just inside Nicaragua and complete the trek to Ocotal in the morning.

Just then I heard the distant hum of a propeller-driven aircraft. I asked, "Who's that?"

"It's a Nicaraguan recon plane patrolling the border about fifteen miles away," Jack said. "They fly over two or three times a day, rain or shine." Jack then made a motion to his companions, and they carefully loaded the gear onto the donkeys … or burros or whatever the hell they're called. When they had finished, we headed south, single file, with Sherlock and me bringing up the rear. As we plodded along, I asked Sherlock what he had said to Jack. He said that Jack was, to put it mildly, skeptical about taking a middle-aged doctor on this trek. I put on my best irate expression, and Sherlock said, "Calm down. I told him you were one of the veterans of THOR-COG."

"And that changed his mind?"

"Oh, yeah," explained Sherlock. "Like I said before, THOR-COG was Rhaspberry's first field excursion, and it went quite well. It brought him to prominence in the Agency and, as you know, the victor writes the history books. The rest of his circle regarded the participants of that operation highly. Now you're heroes. In ten years, you'll be legends.

I asked if he knew the real story behind the operation, and he said, "What's it matter?" I thought I detected a wisp of envy in his voice.

"It matters to me," I said. "THOR-COG wasn't any legendary operation; it was a bunch of dumb kids with more luck than sense playing bullet tag with Charlie. Everyone was constantly scared shitless and anybody who says different is a fucking liar."

Sherlock raised an eyebrow. "Well, Rhaspberry's version tells of a highly trained cadre of steel-nerved marksmen terrorizing the VC from one end of Nam to the other. Hell, according to him, another three months of operation and you guys would have been in North Vietnam."

"Rhaspberry is as full of shit as a Woodstock Porta-Potty. He wasn't even there," I replied.

Sherlock almost nodded in agreement but caught himself and only smiled.

The column halted at about three in the afternoon. So far the terrain had been a series of lightly forested hills, and the going had been relatively easy. We were about a mile from the border and would wait for dark to cross it. We hid as well as we could under the vegetation to avoid recon flights. Several hours later dusk arrived, and we took up the trail. Sherlock tapped me on the shoulder about an hour later and pointed to a small pile of stones.

"Welcome to the badlands," he whispered, and then he pointed for me to go ahead. Suddenly the G-3 wasn't so heavy anymore. About thirty minutes later it was quite dark, and we had reached cover heavy enough to hide us for the night. The crew unloaded and hobbled the pack animals. We had some MREs and settled down to sleep. I dozed off thinking about the distinct advantages of Hueys over burros.

CHAPTER EIGHTEEN

BEV PUT DOWN THE journal and flexed her fingers. They were getting cramped after holding the manuscript for so long. Connie was really something, she decided. There was more to this guy than she had ever imagined. After a minute or two, she picked up the journal again.

The first morning in Nicaragua, I was awakened by unintelligible jabbering between Jack and one of the Indians. It seemed that there were two government soldiers on a cliff overlooking the trail we were to use. As Jack explained it, we could either go around the mountain and add two extra days to the trip or have the Indian creep up the cliff tonight and take out the soldiers. Sherlock wanted a personal look, so he and Jack went forward to observe them. On his return, Sherlock gave us the full picture. There were two soldiers perched on a ledge some three hundred feet above the trail. The cliff extended above them another two hundred feet. The path from the ledge sloped down the cliff and away from where we had planned to approach but afforded the soldiers a view of our route all the way down to the trail. The men were equipped with rifles, binoculars, and a radio, so if they spotted anything, they could call in support of some kind. The closest we could approach them without detection in daylight would be about two hundred fifty meters. Sherlock considered his options. I kept my eyes on him, wondering when he would think of the obvious. In less than thirty seconds, his eyes came up from the ground, and he looked directly at me.

"Do you—"

"Yeah," I interrupted. "But first, I have to have your assurance that these men are minions of the Prince of Darkness and pose a direct threat to the free world." He instantly replied that he had it on excellent authority that they were and that they did.

"Fine," I said. "I don't want to hear that they're just peasants earning two dollars a month in the army because it's more than they can make farming."

"Definitely not the case," he added, salving my conscience.

Approaching as close as we dared, Sherlock determined that we were exactly two hundred forty meters away from them—his binoculars had a range-finder reticle.

Figuring that that the average Nicaraguan male was five feet six inches tall and that angle from the horizon was a little less than thirty degrees, I calculated that for a little less than thirty degrees, the cosine was about 0.90.

With a line of sight of two hundred forty yards, I then calculated the effective range of the bullet to be two hundred sixteen yards. The two-hundred-meter sight on my G-3 would be just about right. I turned the turret sight until I saw the yellow 2.

After a few minutes of discussion, Sherlock and I decided on a following plan. I would take out the man on the left, who was sitting next to the radio. Then I would direct fire at the radio. I would probably miss it, but the remaining man would see the effect of the incoming rounds and, if he had any sense at all, would go in the opposite direction, down the trail. Sherlock would keep an eye on him through the binoculars so I could find him after he moved away from the radio. With the plan in place, I went back into the forest and found two large rocks to use as a solid cradle for the rifle. I carefully positioned them, put a blanket over them, and then lay down behind them. The G-3 fit snugly in the V, and I bunched up the blanket until the elevation was right. I then established the sight picture. The man only took up about a fourth of the width of the front sight blade. This shot would have been so much simpler with a good telescopic sight. I bowed my head for a full minute to allow my breathing and heart rate to slow. I realigned the sight, held it, and took up the slack on the trigger.

"What are you waiting for?" Sherlock whispered

I turned my head and replied, "Will you shut the fuck up and let me do this?"

He winced. He had no understanding of the ritual I was

performing. I had to start over again, and he didn't interrupt this time. I fired, but the target stood up instead of falling over. Quickly, I followed up with a second shot, and he crumpled. I then fired four shots in the direction of the radio.

"He's coming down the path," Sherlock whispered cautiously. I moved my body a few inches to the left and to align myself with the fleeing man. I directed Sherlock to spot for me.

He called the next shot. "Three feet behind, elevation okay." I extended the lead a few feet and fired again. The man fell but got up again.

"It seems on target!" Sherlock exclaimed. I fired again, and the man fell again, this time off the path and over the edge of the cliff. He landed on the rocks about one hundred fifty feet below his launch point.

"Unbelievable!" Sherlock laughed.

"Yeah," I said. "Unbelievable." Ten minutes later, we passed the second victim's body on the trail and found that he had not been hit by any bullet. He had fallen to his death.

I wondered if my marksmanship were the reason I had been selected and why just any doctor wouldn't do. I couldn't put anything past Rhaspberry.

When Cheech and Chong back there failed to report in, the area would definitely warm up, so we had to get away. We walked quickly but quietly for several miles. Over the next eight miles on our way to the outskirts of Ocotal, we had to seek cover at least six times to avoid detection by air.

The camp near Ocotal was a mess. It consisted of thirty big tents, a few tables, benches, and some water barrels. There were about twenty-five men there when we arrived and probably five or six sentries posted in the bush around the camp. According to Sherlock, Ocotal had been chosen for this operation because it was the camp nearest to the border that had been afflicted by the plague. Sherlock and I set up residence in a tent next to Jack's. We unpacked our gear and the medical equipment I had brought along, such as it was.

I told Sherlock that I wanted to see two or three representative patients in the morning. He said that patients listed as numbers five, six, and seven on the lab data had come to the camp, but number six had been killed the previous week.

"Do you think I could see numbers five and seven before they're killed too?"

"They'll be in after breakfast," he replied, detached.

The thin foam-rubber pad I slept on did not really make the ground comfortable. Even with the sides rolled up, the temperature in the tent must have been about ninety degrees. But the bugs were only moderately vicious, so I could sleep fitfully.

The next morning after a breakfast that tasted like a mixture of Velveeta and cat food, we got down to business. I first interviewed and examined patient number five, using Jack as an interpreter. My notes from that interview follow.

Number Five is a 24-year-old Hispanic who appeared chronically ill.

Chief complaint: Weakness and shortness of breath on exertion for at least ten weeks.

History of present illness: The patient states that he was well until about two and one-half to three months ago. The illness started with a generalized malaise and mild weight loss. After a few weeks, he developed a cough and would occasionally have sweats. He denied having fevers and said the cough produced white phlegm with an occasional blood streak. He denied any pain whatsoever but admitted that his neck was tender off and on. He said that the malaise leveled off after a few weeks, as did the cough. It didn't get much better or worse on the whole over the last four weeks but did seem to get a little worse when the weather was bad. A few days after that, the symptoms would return to a lesser degree of severity.

Past history: The patient denies any serious illness in the past. He had a wrist fracture at age twelve.

Family and social history: The patient states that the place he was born has no name. He was the fourth of seven children. Both parents are alive and well. His father is a 45-year-old farmer. His mother is a 35-year-old housewife. He knows nothing of the health of his grandparents; they are apparently alive.

Positive Findings of Review of Symptoms:
Ears: Bad earache at age nine.
Throat: Sore to touch lately.
Chest: Shortness of breath on exertion over the last few months. Patient specifically denies that he or any member of his family has been exposed to tuberculosis.

Physical Exam:
Vital Signs:
Blood pressure, 124/78
Heart rate, 82 bpm and regular
Respiratory rate, 24/min
Temperature, 99.2 °F
Weight, 159 pounds
Height, 5' 7"

Skin: Free of jaundice, petechiae, and eruptions. Had three café au lait spots on back.
Head: Free of scars, tenderness, and bruits.
Eyes: Pupils equal, round, and reactive to light and accommodation. Disc sharp and A/V ratios normal. Visual fields are within normal limits.
Ears: Tympanic membranes visualized. The

left is normal; the right bears a scar from previous infection.

Nose, mouth, and throat: Mucosa of the nose and throat are red rather than pink. I note no exudates on the tonsils, but they appear slightly enlarged.

Neck: Supple. Thyroid normal size without nodules. Lymph nodes mildly enlarged and mildly tender to palpitation. Carotid arteries have full pulses without bruits.

Back: Mild scoliosis to the left. There is no vertebral point tenderness, paravertebral muscle spasm, or CVA tenderness.

Lungs: Clear to auscultation and percussion. Mild large airway sounds present on expiration.

Heart: Rhythm regular. There is a grade III/IV systolic murmur present. There are no S3 or S4 heart sounds. No gallops or rubs detected.

Abdomen: Belly is scaphoid with mild wrinkling of skin indicating recent weight loss. Bowel sounds are active; no bruits noted. There is no organomegaly. The liver, spleen, and kidneys appear to be normal size. No hernias or abdominal masses detected. There is mild epigastric tenderness but no guarding or rebound.

Extremities: Pulses were full in the brachial, radial, femoral, popliteal, and dorsal pedal areas. No joint abnormalities noted except for the left wrist, which has decreased range of motion. No edema, cyanosis, erythema, clubbing, or abnormal pigmentation.

Rectum: The sphincter has good tone and is free of hemorrhoids. There are no masses in the rectal vault, the prostate was 1+ in size, symmetrical, and free of tenderness. The stool was negative for blood.

Neurological: The patient is alert and oriented with respect to person, place, and time. The motor and sensory components of the neurological system are intact. The reflexes are 2+ and symmetrical in the biceps, triceps, knees, and ankles. Patient demonstrates good coordination and normal gait. He tires easily with repeated exercise of any muscle group.

Diagnostic Impressions:

1. Malaise, shortness of breath on exertion, cough, and an increased respiratory rate about two and a half months' duration; cause undetermined. Suspect chronic infectious process involving upper respiratory tract.
2. Grade III/IV systolic heart murmur. Suspect functional (harmless).
3. Healed fracture of left wrist.

When I had completed Number Five's exam, I proceeded to Number Seven's.

The patient designated Number Seven is an 18-year-old Hispanic male who appears chronically ill.

Chief complaint: Weakness and shortness of breath for six weeks with some weight loss.

History of present illness: The patient states he was last well about two months ago. His problem with weakness and shortness of breath started a few days after he left his village in the northeastern corner of Nicaragua to join the contras. He says that the symptoms are always present but have periods of exacerbation. When asked directly, he did not tie these periods to the weather, though he did recall that everyone's symptoms seemed to get worse at the same time. The last spell started ten days ago, and that was a day or two after a rainy spell. But, he adds, it rains a lot here.

Past history: Patient denies any serious illness in the past. He has had no operation and takes no medication.

Social and family history: The patient is the third-born of 5 children. He was born in the village of Bilwascarma and has lived there with his maternal grandparents and mother after his father was killed by the Sandinistas. He is aware of no chronic diseases, such as tuberculosis, in his family.

His physical exam was almost identical to Number Five's and just as unrevealing.

CHAPTER NINETEEN

BEV LOOKED UP FROM her reading when she heard the dog barking. "Probably a squirrel," she thought. "He'll be quiet in a minute." She wasn't going to let anything disturb her reading of the journal. His medical notes were fascinating. She turned the page and continued.

After I had completed the histories and physicals for both men, I carefully reviewed my notes to pull out the common threads. I was now convinced that the problem we were dealing with was a bacterial infection. If so, why didn't it show up in the lab data? There were several possibilities. The organism might not survive long outside the host. The medium for each culture may have been inadequate. Whatever the reason, I had to reculture the urine, blood, and most important, the throats and sputa of both men. I collected the samples under sterile conditions. From there, I initially plated all samples in triplicate on carefully labeled blood agar plates because virtually all pathogens will grow on blood agar. I placed one set of plates in a black box in the sun, the second in a tent, and the third in the shade outside to give the organism a range of temperatures, in case one would be more conducive to growth than the others. On the outside chance that the organism did not grow in the presence of oxygen, I prepared a complete set of cultures in airtight bottles containing the culture medium. With all this done, I had to sit and wait for forty-eight hours. There was no way I could accelerate the growth.

I took a stroll around the camp. I noticed that perhaps two-thirds of the men had some sign of the disease I was investigating. I asked, using Jack as a middle man, if anyone in the village had the problem, and they said no. The village was only about a kilometer away and was disease free, which told me that the infection was not contagious because the contras from this camp went into the village all the time. What was the organism? What was the mode of infection? And what was the cure?

While I pondered this on my walk, I passed a tent in which three men—boys, really—were recovering from wounds. A local lady acting as a nurse asked me to take a look at their injuries. The first two had only superficial wounds that would heal nicely with topical antibiotics and regular dressing changes. The third was a different matter. This gentleman had been shot through the outer left thigh, about ten inches above the knee. The entry and exit wounds were both draining green pus. When I asked him what happened, he said that the injury had occurred four days ago. He had been taking oral antibiotics and cleaning the wound with peroxide every day, but the pus persisted. It was obvious to me that something was embedded deep in the wound, which was at least six inches long from entry to exit. I told Jack that incision and drainage was absolutely necessary if the wound were ever to heal. He explained this to the man in Spanish, and a look of understanding and apprehension spread over the man's face. When I acted out the procedure with my hands, I could see his apprehension grow. After a little jawboning from Jack, the man agreed to treatment.

Two rather impressive first aid kits held all the equipment I needed. With two long swigs of whiskey in the man's belly and ten milligrams of morphine sulphate in his right buttock, we were ready to operate on him. Two of the soldiers in the camp placed the patient on his right side on a picnic table, leaving the entire left leg exposed. The nurse washed the wound with soap and water, patted it dry, and then doused it with alcohol. My inspection at this point indicated that the bullet had entered the outer thigh from the back and exited the front about four inches lower. It appeared that this guy had been leaving the scene when he was hit. I introduced a sterile probe into the entrance wound and slowly advanced it along the wound channel. It met little resistance, and the probe tip emerged from the exit wound coated with blood-streaked pus. The smell of rotting flesh intensified. I planned to leave the probe in place and dissect the tissue down to it; this would ensure that the wound channel would be completely open. Fortunately, the man's vital structures—the femoral artery, vein, and nerve—all descend on the inside and middle of the thigh, so all I could damage with my dissection were a few minor blood vessels and cutaneous nerves.

I made the initial cut from entrance to exit wound, fifteen centimeters long and about a half centimeter deep. This exposed the fat layer between the skin and underlying muscle. I clamped off the small cutaneous bleeders with tiny mosquito clamps. After a few minutes, I could remove the clamps and the vessels would have clotted off and not require ligature. My victim was skinny, so the intermediate fat layer was very thin. In a few seconds, I was down to the muscle. Using the probe as a guide, I cut the muscle from the entrance wound to the exit wound, pausing only to tie off any aggressively bleeding vessels. Finally, I exposed the wound and tediously cleaned it. The debridement process removed copious amounts of pus along with a few cloth fibers and some hair. The last two were no doubt pushed into the wound by the bullet passing through his pants and skin. I cut back all grayish tissue until I noted minor bleeding. Fortunately for the patient, I did not need to completely transect the entire vastus lateralis muscle, so he would retain partial use of it. Because of the extent of the wound and the degree of infection, I couldn't suture the wound closed and instead left it to heal from the inside out. I packed the wound with sterile gauze and bandaged it. Healing would be a slow process, requiring weeks of daily dressing changes and antibiotics.

Popping off my gloves, I looked up from my work to see that only the nurse holding the patient's hand, the patient, and I remained. The rest of these folks had clearly never spent any time in the Saint Louis City Hospital on a Saturday night.

I mimed instructions to the nurse for the daily care of the wound, slapped the patient on the face a few times to make sure he would wake up, and left for a cup of coffee. I found Jack and told him that the patient was doing okay but would take a few weeks of care. He said he'd move him across the border tomorrow. There were some folks in Honduras who would help him. I told him I'd like to send written instructions along to make sure they understood his postop care well. Jack had no objection.

Soon it was suppertime, and I told Jack I couldn't stand the food and asked if he had any MREs. He replied he had a lot of them; the natives didn't care for them at all. He left the tent for a few minutes and came back with a small green metal case. He opened the top and presented it to me. All just for me and none of it over two years old.

I rummaged through the food and found a packet of pork chops, a packet of mixed vegetables, and a packet of spice-nut bread. I poured hot water over the meat and veggies and ate the bread while waiting for the main entree to rehydrate. The food was good; very good. Rations had come a long way in twenty-five years. With modification, my sleeping accommodations that night were much, much more comfortable, and my second night's sleep was considerably more restful.

The night passed without incident, and on arising, I washed and shaved in a metal pan of scalding water. Now it was time to hit the MRE box for breakfast. Gathering up ham, fruit, and tapioca pudding, I patiently set about reconstituting them. I took it outside to eat at the picnic table. The morning was very humid and gray. It had drizzled on and off during the night and everything was damp. A thin mist hung in the air, and it threatened to rain again at any time. I pulled the lids over the fruit and tapioca to keep any water out while I ate the ham. Jesus, it was better than the pork chops I had had the previous night.

As I picked up the fruit container, I heard the drone of a propeller driven aircraft. After the second bite, I decided the plane was coming my way and concluded that the best place for me was in the tent. There, I finished the fruit as the plane passed slowly overhead and then went on its way. Jack entered the tent with Sherlock. They were talking about the plane, and Jack reassured him that it was just another recon flight. Sherlock wanted to know how long it would take the bad guys to respond if they had seen anything. Jack replied that it would take about a day for them to get here, but it was unlikely that there would be any trouble, as the planes had flown over numerous times before without consequence.

Relying on them to do what they did best, I proceeded to set up the equipment to identify any organisms the agar plates might grow. To begin with, I would do a Gram stain—I'd smear samples of the organism on glass plates and dye each one differently and examine them with a microscope to establish the morphology of the bug. I would then note whether they were cocci (spheres) or bacilli (rods) and note the color. If they were dark purple, they were called Gram positive. If red, Gram negative. This would be very useful in identifying what pathogen caused the illness.

I would then examine the structure and grouping of the bacteria. Are the cocci clustered in pairs, for instance? Are the bacilli long or short? Do the bacteria have flagella? These observations would allow me to narrow the field of organisms that could cause the illness markedly and would direct how I would conduct the next step, to observe the organisms' behavior.

Because different bacteria utilize various nutrients differently, I would subject each culture to different sugars and other chemicals and observe its reaction. If the cultures grew or shrank, that narrowed possibilities even further, to the point that could pinpoint and name the specific bug.

I impatiently checked the plates, though I knew full well it was too early to see growth. The anaerobic bottles were clear, so nothing was growing; the substrate would be milky if there were growth. The agar plates in the tent were clear as well. Outside, the plates in the shade were also devoid of growth, but I could barely perceive colonies growing in the plates in the black hot box. Excited, I looked for Sherlock and told him that I thought we had something in the black box and that we'd probably be able to start an ID in about six more hours. By my watch, that would have been about four in the afternoon. I somewhat cheerfully took a deck of cards and went to the picnic table to play a little solitaire until lunch. My breakfast refuse was still on the table. As I cleared it off, I noticed that the tapioca had a quarter inch of water on top, while the ham container was dry and empty. I poured off the water and found that the pudding was not flat on top but sloped. For a second, I considered eating it but then discarded it and the ham container.

I thought this odd but put it aside and I dealt the first game of cards. After twenty or thirty minutes, Jack and a contra named David strolled up to me.

Jack said David wanted to see my rifle. "Yeah, sure," I answered. Jack got the rifle from the tent, removed the magazine and round in the chamber, and handed it to David. David examined it thoroughly.

He had been with us when I shot those two guards, and apparently he was impressed.

After looking the rifle over and examining the loose round that Jack had handed him, he looked at me and grinned. He pointed to the rifle and then the cartridge and shrugged, unimpressed. Pausing for a few seconds, he then pointed to me and then to his right eye and nodded. Handing Jack the rifle, he smiled.

I told Jack that David was an astute son of a bitch and dealt myself a new game.

David hung around us as though he wanted something but was reluctant to say anything. Motioning David to come closer, I asked Jack to find out what he wanted. After a bit of prying, Jack turned to me and said he wanted me to show him how to shoot. I asked what Jack had been telling him.

Sherlock and Jack had exchanged information about THOR-COG while David was around, and apparently he picked up on some of it.

I told David it takes a long time to learn to be a good shot. He persisted.

"Let's go, David," I said, motioning for him to follow me as I got up. I noted that Jack was trailing along, too. Taking the G-3 from David, I led the group down the trail toward Honduras for a few hundred yards to an open spot that afforded a view of the base of a mud cliff some seventy-five yards away.

Jack could translate if things got sticky, but David seemed to have a fair grasp of English; he just didn't talk much.

"We have to begin at the beginning," I said. "First, you have to learn the difference between precision and accuracy. Precision is a property of the gun that allows it to place multiple bullets in or near the same hole. Accuracy is the ability of the marksman to put the hole where he wants it. The precision of most military weapons exceeds the accuracy of their owners, with the possible exception of that M-1 carbine you have, David.

"The G-3 has the precision to place five shots in a circle of less than one inch in diameter at one hundred meters, if the gun is resting on a solid surface. A log, a stone, anything will do."

With the gun on a solid rest and David in the prone position, I introduced him to the formidable four: sight picture, breathing, heartbeat, and trigger pull.

I explained that the sight picture is the placement of the weapon's sight on the target after distance, wind, and elevation were taken into account. Most military rifles had preset sight marks that corresponded with military ammunition. The wind and elevation made little difference at the fighting distances possible in the jungle.

I explained how David could control his breathing to prevent moving the gun off the sight picture. I had him take a few deep breaths and let the last one out halfway and hold it; this would give him at least thirty seconds to pull the trigger.

I then explained that David would just have to learn to shoot between heartbeats. Like breathing, I said, the rate is usually rapid and intense in a firefight, but that the increased force of the pounding would make it easy to time the beats.

I then moved on to the trigger pull. David's military weapon, unlike a target rifle, had a quarter inch or so of slack in the trigger that he would have to take up before the sear would start to move. So I broke the trigger pull into two stages: slack uptake and sear let-off. The first is quick—the shooter just pulls back gently until he meets resistance. Then the shooter gently squeezes until the rifle fires. If done properly, David should not know exactly when the shot had gone off.

All this was easy to say in a few minutes but would take David months, if not years, of practice to get it perfect.

The shooting technique explained, I positioned David on the ground properly, adjusted the position of his rifle, and had him dry fire it a few times while I observed the motion of the barrel. He got the breathing part right, but not much else. What the hell was I expecting anyway? I then loaded the magazine into the rifle and had him fire at a Styrofoam cup about fifty meters away. The results were fair; the shot landed within a foot of the cup. Toward the end of the twenty-round magazine, he was coming within six inches of it. The man showed promise. I didn't want to waste any more of my ammo, so I ended the lesson after twenty rounds. David was all smiles; I mused briefly about what I had just created.

After lunch, I was nursing a second cup of coffee when Sherlock told me that Jack's radio contact had said that the Sandinistas were staging an afternoon move about thirty miles from us. "We don't know which way they'll go, but if they move in our direction, we'll have to bug out," Sherlock said.

"What's your best guess as to how much time we have if they do come our way?" I asked.

"They won't move during the night, so if they're headed our way, it'd take them about fifteen hours to reach us," he replied. "They're not about to make contact in the dark either, so they'd have to stop for the night, so it'd be the morning after next before we could expect contact. Of course, we'd have to be out well before then."

I tried to compute the time I needed to complete my bacterial analysis. If I could get the inocula into the sugars by around 4:00 p.m., I could start identification by 8:00 the next morning. While waiting on the samples in the sugars, I would smear some plates for antibiotic sensitivity tests. I could have those ready in about twenty-four hours. If all went well, it'd take until tomorrow evening for the drug sensitivity tests to show results. Using my fingers, I figured out that that gave us ten hours before the bad guys arrived.

"No sweat," I muttered to myself.

"Wanna bet?" myself muttered back.

CHAPTER TWENTY

BEV GOT UP TO grab a Diet Pepsi out of the fridge and hurried back. The suspense was killing her; she wanted to know what would happen next.

At exactly 4:00 p.m., I gathered all the cultures and began going through them. None of the anaerobic cultures showed any growth, so I set them aside. On all of the culture plates that had been in the tent, there were only a few scattered colonies. Contaminants, no doubt. These, too, I set aside.

The throat and sputa cultures from the hot box were dotted with colonies, as I had expected, although the blood and the urine cultures were negative. Each throat culture had at least four different types of colonies. One sputum culture had two types, the other had one. There were gray-white groups of colonies spreading on both the sputum and the throat cultures. Was this the culprit? Without wasting any time, I proceeded to Gram stain each of the eleven colonies. After about thirty minutes, I had slides ready for viewing. I set up a flashlight to direct its beam into the illuminator stage of the Leitz-Wetzler binocular scope.

I examined the throat culture of Number Five first. Two of the cultures were Gram-positive cocci, normal flora of the throat, one was a Gram-negative bacillus, which was not normal. Next, I checked Number Five's sputum. His had grown out a single organism, and it too, was a Gram-negative bacillus. It seemed identical to the one in his throat. I moved on to Number Seven's cultures. His throat cultures were identical to Number Five's. His sputum held a small surprise: though the culture plate showed two types of colonies, a very sparse red colony and a prolific gray-white group, the Gram-stain of each seemed identical—both were Gram-negative bacilli. Now I had a gray-white colony of Gram-negative bacilli in all the throat and sputum cultures grown in the hot box and a single red colony that only appeared in the sputum of Number Seven.

I couldn't take any chances, so I decided to identify and do drug sensitivities on both the gray-white and the red colonies. I placed one milliliter of sterile water each in five sterile test tubes. I then placed a wire with a loop in the end into the flame of a Coleman stove. After the wire became red-hot, I removed it and let it cool. I then used the wire's loop to scoop up the largest gray-white colony from Number Five's sputum plate and put it into one of the test tubes, swishing the wire in the water. I repeated this flaming-and-inoculating process for each of the three remaining gray-white cultures and the red one. After I inoculated each tube, I poured a few drops of the infected water onto five new six-inch agar plates, making sure the inoculated water covered the surface of the plate. Last, I placed fifteen five-millimeter paper discs containing various antibiotics approximately one-half inch apart on each of the plates. I covered each plate and put it back into the hot box to incubate. The bacteria would grow everywhere on the plate except around any disc containing an antibiotic that inhibited their growth.

Now that the sensitivity plates were cooking, I turned my attention to identifying the culprit. For this job, I had brought a special device: a clear plastic tube about eight inches long and three-fourths of an inch in diameter containing nine compartments, each about three-quarters of an inch long. In each compartment was a culture medium containing a different sugar or nutrient. Written on a label below each chamber was the name of the substance and what constituted a positive test. I inoculated all the compartments by threading a wire dipped in innoculum through the tube, capped off both ends of the tube, keeping the wire in place, and placed the whole thing in the hot box. I repeated the process until I had four tubes, one for the red colony and three for the gray-white colonies, labeled "For Identification of Gram Negative Bacilli" in the box. Now I had to wait.

I eased back on my bunk and closed my eyes. I could only hear the humming of the insects and smell the acrid, moldy odor of the jungle mixed with the exhaust of the lantern. If I opened my eyes, I was sure Roiger would be standing there.

Around 10:00 a.m. the next day, Jack informed us that the Sandinistas were definitely headed our way. Sherlock was visibly upset, his eyes wide with apprehension. He asked pointedly how long it would be before I had an answer. I told him 6:00 or 7:00 p.m. at the earliest.

He exclaimed, "That's going to be cutting it close! Are you sure they won't come in until dawn, Jack?"

Jack replied that he wasn't sure of anything. He was taking the contras to set up an ambush south of Ocotal on Highway 4 this afternoon and said that we had better have our asses out of there by dawn. He would leave us a guide to get us back to Honduran border. After that, we'd be on our own. The ambush the contras were planning may slow them down a little, but we knew it would be a feeble effort; the contras were not supposed to engage in combat unless they could really clean the enemy's clock.

"You make it a good fight, goddamnit!" yelled Sherlock. "If we don't get the answer to this problem, your men are dead meat and so is your project."

Over lunch, everyone was in very pensive. Jack left the table and returned ten minutes later with David.

Jack said that David would be our guide back to Honduras. He knew the way and was very dependable.

Jack shook hands with Sherlock and wished him luck. He shook my hand with both of his. "Glad to have met you," he said. "Try to get the cure back to us quickly." He turned and led his pathetic little column southwest out of the camp. We watched them until they were out of sight. Suddenly the camp was very quiet. The afternoon passed slowly. A little after four o'clock, a recon plane passed overhead again.

With time on my hands, I ambled through the camp, smoking the first cigarette I had had in twenty years. The camp was a quasiorganized collection of about thirty tents. A few stored supplies and the rest were barracks, each housing four men. Only a handful of men remained in camp, and they only to collect the usable gear before bugging out.

The interiors of the barracks tents were typically decorated with macho slogans and *Playboy* fold outs. I nosed around the supply tents and saw that the dates on the food and ammunition were about a year old. Some damaged weapons were piled in one corner; they'd probably stay there. The characteristic buttstock of an MG-34 protruded from the bottom of the pile. Fondly remembering my last association with this venerable warhorse, I took it out to a picnic table and disassembled it. The barrel, receiver, bolt, and trigger group all seemed okay. The feed plate and cover were functional as well. Puzzled, I asked why it was in the pile. David said, "It just won't shoot." I took the answer as a personal challenge. I asked David to get some ammunition. After a few minutes, he returned with a belt of fifty rounds. I examined the cartridges. They were Portuguese-manufactured 7.92 mm rounds and seemed in perfect condition.

Moving off to a safe area, I removed four rounds from the beginning of the belt and fed it into the opening on the left side of the gun. When the tab appeared on the right side, I pulled it firmly, seating the first round on the plate. I squeezed the trigger, and the gun fired one round. Working the action manually, I reset the mechanism. Again I pulled the trigger and only one round fired. Nothing had jammed; the bolt just didn't go back far enough to pick up the next cartridge. I could tell when I worked the action manually that the recoil spring was functional, so I reasoned that the problem had to be in the front end.

I remembered from the old days that a chamber on the MG-34 just in front of the end of the barrel collected the propellant gases and that these gases pushed back against the barrel face, causing the whole barrel to move backward and unlock the breech. If the gases didn't exert enough force, the barrel wouldn't push the bolt back far enough, and no second shot would fire. I didn't see a problem with the chamber, situated between the flash suppressor and the barrel face revealed no problem, so I surmised that the ammunition was probably a little weak. To fix the problem, I screwed the flash suppressor out as far as it would go to increase the size of the chamber and, therefore, increase the pressure of the recoil blow. I pulled the trigger, and a quick string of ten shots rewarded me. I wondered how many conflicts this gun had been in and how many lives it had taken since its manufacture in 1936. I wished I could take it home, but alas …

As dusk settled in, Sherlock and I returned to our tent. David stood guard down the trail to the east; everyone else had gone. At six, I took a good look at the culture plates. Nothing.

We had supper, and afterward Sherlock took some food to David. I readied my books for the time when I would interpret the data. Now I had to wait anxiously. At eight o'clock, I took the cultures and held them up to the light of the Coleman lantern. Still no growth.

"Goddamnit!" I yelled. I put the cultures back in the box. I told Sherlock I'd recheck them around ten o'clock. He and I counted the hours until five o'clock, the time we had to be out. Seven hours— plenty of time. I moved the hot box close to the lit Coleman stove. I hoped the extra heat would speed up the process a little and not screw it up completely.

The ten o'clock check yielded good news and bad news. The good news was that I could read the identification tubes; the bad news was that I could not yet interpret the more important sensitivities. The sensitivity plates went back into the box, and I busied myself with the ID tubes. I made up a crude table of the nine tests and the four cultures.

	Culture I	Culture II	Culture III	Culture IV (red)
	P-5 Throat	P-5 Sputum	P-7 Sputum	P-7 Sputum
Indole	-	-	-	-
Methyl red	-	-	-	-
Sucrose	+	+	+	+
Mannitol	+	+	+	+
Urease	-	-	-	-
Citrate	+	+	+	+
Lysine-D	+	+	+	+
TSJ	-	-	-	-
Inositol	-	-	-	-

With this fingerprint, I could draw two conclusions: all the cultures, including the red culture, were identical, and the organism was either an *Aerobacter* or *Serratia*. Because the red colony was identical to the rest and because *Serratia* could produce red-pigmented colonies in addition to those of other colors, *Serratia* was a good bet as the culprit. The evidence pointing to *Serratia* raised another question. Members of the genus *Serratia* are saprophytic and so are found all over, especially in rotting vegetation. It would be prevalent in a forest or jungle, but it was not a known pathogen. It didn't make any sense. We had a nonpathogen causing disease in normally healthy people but that didn't spread just half a kilometer away. I went over this information with Sherlock, but he gave no indication that he knew what I was talking about. I refilled my coffee cup and sat back to let the information roll around in my mind.

I dozed off, and Sherlock woke me at midnight to check the cultures. I held them up to the light and saw that they were definitely starting to grow, but it was too early to tell if any of the antibiotic discs were inhibiting the growth. Five hours to go. Things were getting tense. I sensed Sherlock's impatience and told him that if I could make the fucking things grow faster, I would. He grunted and lay down on his bedroll. I was setting the alarm for 2:00 a.m. when David burst into the tent yelling, "Sandinistas!" and pointing to the east.

Sherlock yelled, "Holy shit! We gotta get out of here!"

I went to the black box and retrieved four plates. I taped them together and put them in my left breast pocket and buttoned it. We had to take the books and the microscope or they'd know what we were up to.

Sherlock stacked the plastic microbiology gear in the middle of the tent and poured white gas over it. I slung my rifle, grabbed the microscope with my left hand, and grabbed the books with my right. David made for the trail north, and I followed right behind him. Sherlock set fire to our tent and a few others and joined us at the edge of the camp. He took the books from me, and we melted into the darkness.

The fire let them know the camp was not deserted but we

couldn't carry everything out, we couldn't let them find any microbiology gear.

We stumbled after David for hours, fearing to stop. We had to move slowly, as we could use no lights. Our pursuers could use lights, and looking back from a rise, we saw the white dots of flashlights jerking along the trail we had trod only minutes before. As I threw the books and microscope down a ravine, I asked Sherlock how far away he thought those lights were. He thought it was about four hundred yards. That was close to what I thought, so I took the G-3 and set the turret at 4. I found a comfortable spot on the rocks, aligned the sights with the moving white dots, and squeezed off five rounds. The dots stopped moving. I fired two shots at the brightest dot. Within seconds, all the dots were extinguished. We moved on.

When the moon rose, we could quicken our pace, but the enemy's flashlights were following us again, and they were gaining on us. It became obvious that within an hour they would close in on us. At the next rest stop, I brought up the idea of an ambush. We clearly weren't going to outrun them. Sherlock was apprehensive; the number of flashlights indicated about ten pursuers, and we were but three men with two rifles and a pistol. I laid out a plan.

I suggested we go ahead until the trail started uphill in an area with thin cover on the hillside. Then the man with the pistol would go to the ridge top and take cover. The other two would take cover at the bottom, one on each side of the trail but far back enough that our pursuers couldn't see us and would pass us. When the point man crested the hill, the guy with the pistol would shoot him and keep firing down the hill to draw their attention. We at the bottom would shoot at their backs. With any luck, they wouldn't even realize it until they were dead.

In theory it sounded good. I was proud of the Roigeresque feel it had. Sherlock was still apprehensive but could think of no alternative, and we had to do something or be caught.

We pressed on, and perhaps twenty minutes passed before we came to a spot suitable for the ambush. I looked at Sherlock.

"Here?" I proposed.

"Yeah, I guess," he relented, panting.

I cautioned that, everyone should remain absolutely still for thirty minutes by the clock after the shooting stopped. That way we would know that anything that moved was them and not us. We didn't want to shoot each other. (Another Roiger touch.)

"Thirty minutes after the last shot," David repeated in broken English. I nodded and added that he would take the people nearest us and I'd start at the head of the column and work my way back. That way we wouldn't be shooting the same guys. Sherlock just had to distract them.

As planned, Sherlock proceeded up the hill and disappeared over the ridge. I faded into the undergrowth on the left side of the trail; David did the same on the right. I found a comfortable spot behind a good thick tree that gave me a clear view of the trail almost to the top of the hill. I looked across the way to where David had gone and could see nothing. We had to wait less than five minutes before the muffled noise of someone on the trail attracted our attention.

The enemy's point man was moving pretty fast, and his followers were only a few steps behind. I held my breath as they passed scarcely thirty feet away, hoping they wouldn't hear my heartbeat. These guys weren't very good. The point man was careless, and the squad of eleven behind him was following too close. They were all bunched up. My insides were starting to quiver and my stomach was ready to blow supper. Fortunately, events were moving too rapidly to dwell on intestinal rumblings.

As the point man topped the hill, I heard a single shot ring out and saw the man fall straight onto his back, feet pointing uphill. The squad froze for a second and then each man hunched down and started firing blindly at the ridge of the hill. The bad guys' fire was answered by a few shots at the top, and they started backing away from Sherlock towards us.

The time was ripe for David and me to enter the fray. We opened up when they were about twenty meters away. Six of them were down before they even realized they were being ambushed. Three more turned around to face us and dropped. The last two went into the bush. All was quiet. We waited. Ten, fifteen, twenty minutes passed. My every sense was attuned to pick up the slightest stimulus. I was drenched with sweat; I could hear it drip off my chin onto the leaves below. I bowed my head, straining to detect any sound of movement.

Then I heard a whisper, "Juan. Juan!"

Barely moving my head, I zeroed my ears onto the sound of the voice. I could see nothing, but I knew where he was. He received no answer to his call. I waited. A faint rustle in the undergrowth had me peering even more intently at the spot from which the voice had come, just twenty feet away in the brush. A second later I picked him up in my sights. He was on his belly, pointed toward the trail, gun ready. He was very still as I brought the rifle into alignment. I set my sights just about where his ears should have been if I could have seen more clearly.

As I was taking up the slack in the trigger, my target let off a burst of four shots and someone across the trail screamed. I pulled the trigger and sent a single round into the side of his head. I remained motionless. The screaming across the way was terminated by a single shot. All was quiet again.

The next thirty minutes passed very slowly. Why hadn't we arranged a signal? I heard no further indications of enemy movement. I didn't know what David's condition was, but after the mandatory thirty minutes, I yelled, "David!" and rolled away to the right. After a few seconds, a voice that seemed familiar answered, "Here I am." I ventured to ask what his last name was. He answered with about six appellations and came out of the bush to stand at the edge of the trail.

I really didn't know David's last name, but he didn't know that. Anyway, convinced he was who he said he was, I too emerged from the bush. We cautiously examined the bodies to make sure they were really dead.

CHAPTER TWENTY-ONE

BEV SIGHED. HER HUSBAND had to be the dumbest, luckiest man in the world. Or the smartest. She wasn't sure which. She kept on reading.

In the aftermath of the ambush, we found that Sherlock had shot the first victim in the chest, below the larynx, and he died instantly. The rest of the bodies on the trail had two or three holes each. One guy on my side of the trail had shot and wounded his buddy just before I shot him, and David had then finished off the wounded man.

Sherlock was shaking. David seemed elated. I was mildly disappointed. It had been okay, but I didn't get the Feeling.

We continued on our way at a more leisurely pace. Danny Ortega was going to be pissed when he heard about this.

At dawn we reached the spot where we had waylaid Cheech and Chong on our way in. Their bodies were gone, and no one had taken their place. We passed the place cautiously and reentered the cover of the forest. Now we were but two miles from the Honduran border.

Without warning, a bullet tore a chunk of bark from a tree about eighteen inches from Sherlock's head.

He shouted, "What the fuck?" as he hit the ground.

David pointed back up into the rocks. It seems that Cheech and Chong did have replacements, but they hadn't noticed us until we had passed. They had probably been asleep. Another bullet whined over us. David's M-1 carbine and Sherlock's Colt.45 pistol were certainly worthless at this range. I turned the sight on the G-3 back to 2 and charged it with a new magazine.

I volunteered to keep their heads down till those two got out of there, then I'd follow. "Go!" I said. I fired ten rounds, one about every half second.

I stopped shooting and looked back. Sherlock and David were gone. A few seconds later, the enemy, now up in the rocks, cut loose with a few more rounds. I answered with ten more and then ran like hell. I was long gone before they looked up again. I joined David and Sherlock about a hundred meters up the trail. Both looked at me expectantly. "I didn't kill them," I said, anticipating their question. Sherlock raised an eyebrow, but David was positively disappointed.

At exactly seven minutes to eight, we passed the rock pile marking the Nicaragua–Honduras border. David stopped and told Sherlock we'd have no trouble finding the airstrip some fifteen miles up the trail. All we had to do was head northeast. Sherlock nodded in agreement and shook David's hand. David came back to me, smiled, and shook my hand.

I told David to give me his gun. He complied, somewhat confused. I took the M-1 carbine and traded him the G-3 with the remaining magazines.

I told him that a man of his promise needed a good weapon, not a piece of crap. I admonished him to go back and make every shot count.

He gave me a hug, and for a second I thought he was going to kiss me. He regained his composure, to my relief, and started back, turning and waving intermittently until he was out of sight. His hug reminded me that I had the four plates in my shirt pocket. I carefully removed them and opened the first. There was a single spot of inhibition on the plate, but all the discs had fallen from the plate surface and were bunched at the edge. The second plate showed the same thing; definite spot of inhibition, but the goddamned disc was gone. Without the disc on the spot, there was no way I could identify the antibiotic. I held my breath when I opened the third plate. Some of the discs had fallen off, but disc number 14 was still clinging to the agar, and it had the clear halo of inhibition around it.

"Number 14, what the hell was it?" I muttered, trying to remember. It really made no difference; knowing the number, I could easily learn the name when we got back.

"Sherlock!" I yelled. "Remember number fourteen!"

We had no water or food, so all we had for lunch was rest. I took the plates and hid them under a large rock. I then checked out the M-1 carbine. No wonder David did not object too much to the exchange; he had only two cartridges left in the magazine. Well, he needed the G-3 more than I did.

"I need to talk directly to Rhaspberry when we get back to Fort Hood," I told Sherlock.

"Hey, I can tell him about the antibiotic," he replied.

"No. There's more to it than that," I said. And I suspected much more, but I could only tell Rhaspberry of my suspicion, and I was sure he would want it that way. Sherlock looked quite confused and perhaps a little annoyed.

We made the airfield at about four thirty in the afternoon. Slow, I know, but we got lost twice, and I was an old fart. The field was deserted—no plane, nothing. I followed Sherlock the length of the field and into the woods. Here was a small shack with an antenna sticking out of it. He waved to a guard in the bush and then knocked on the door, paused for a second, and then went in. I waited outside. In a few minutes, Sherlock emerged from the hut.

Good news! There was a plane coming in about forty minutes, and we could take it out. The man in the radio shack had encoded my request to meet with Rhaspberry and would send it directly.

"This had better be good," Sherlock said. "You don't know how he is."

I told him I knew exactly how he was and this was exactly how he would want it played. I added that Sherlock himself had done well.

By dark, we were airborne, heading back to hot food and a hot shower. I had been away from home for six days, and I was really getting tired. The crew shared a few pieces of fruit and a Twinkie with us after we told them we hadn't eaten in twenty-four hours. I dozed on and off during the flight. We arrived at Fort Hood very early in the morning. An MP took the firearms and drove us to a barracks in a jeep.

"Shower, shave, and sleep here tonight," he said and left.

The barracks, which could easily accommodate forty men, was empty. The room was spotless. I showered for a half hour. God, it felt good. The issue razor was a little rough on my face, but the six-day growth gave way eventually. I donned clean underwear and crawled into the bunk. I was out like a light.

Someone was poking my shoulder. I woke with a start.

"What the hell—" I said, staring at Sherlock's face a foot from mine.

His head went back and his eyes went up to focus on something behind me. I rolled over, and there was a middle-aged man sitting on the bunk next to mine. I squinted.

"Rhaspberry? Is that you?"

He nodded.

"By God, it is you!" I said.

"You have something for me," he replied.

"As gracious as ever," I thought. "Yes, I do, and I think you'll want it to be for your ears only," I said, glancing up at Sherlock. Rhaspberry looked up and asked Sherlock to excuse us.

Sherlock left. When I heard the door shut, I began.

"Suppose you were the charismatic leader of the only Communist government in Central America. You had these old-guard rebels in the north who were more than a minor annoyance. You had to deal with them, but you also had to maintain an image of the benevolent leader of a very small country being hounded by the United States. Wholesale violence such as bombs and napalm kill indiscriminately, and dead or wounded villagers are bad press. If you use too much power, then the rebels become the little guys and get the sympathy. A real quandary."

"Where are you headed with this Wittmond?" Rhaspberry interrupted.

Annoyed, I said, "Do you want to hear me out or not?"

"Continue," Rhaspberry said, sighing.

"Okay, well, as I was saying, a real quandary. This guy from East Germany who has been vacationing in Cuba comes to visit you. He knows of your dilemma and offers a possible solution. His solution is a tailored microorganism. It is resistant to all common antibiotics. It does not kill the host; it merely makes him ill. It is a variant of a ubiquitous organism, so detection is very difficult, and if it is isolated, there is no proof it wasn't just a natural mutation. It has been bred to be fastidious, it will not live long at temperatures less than or greater than ninety-eight degrees. The man from East Germany tells you that you can spray the organism over rebel camps without detection if you do it right after a rain so the victims don't notice the mist. The dusting plane never shoots, so the rebels think it's a recon plane and stay hidden. The pilot can get very close and not endanger villagers. All very neat and tidy. The rebels get sick and weaken. Your ground forces easily overcome them if they offer any resistance."

"What's the bug?" Rhaspberry asked.

"A *Serratia* variant," I answered.

"What's the antibiotic?" he continued.

"Cefoxitin," I replied. "It can only be given IM or IV, but not by mouth."

He wanted to know the basis for my theory.

"A cup of tapioca." I paused.

"Well?" he asked, irritated.

I recounted the story of how I had left one empty ham packet and full tapioca container on a picnic table in the camp just before a plane flew over. Three or four hours later, I noticed that the tapioca container had about a quarter inch of water in it, but the ham packet next to it was empty and dry. I could not explain it at the time, but the incident came back to me two days later when I was trying to identify the organism. After running tests, I had narrowed the field down to *Serratia* and *Aerobacter*. According to one of my books, *Serratia* liquefied gelatin much more readily than *Aerobacter*. I was wishing I had some gelatin when a light came on and everything fell into place.

Rhaspberry wanted to know if anyone else knew about this.

I told him he was the only person I had told. I knew he would have wanted it that way.

"Very good, Wittmond," he replied. " I have something here for you." He took two cylinders from his pocket. Twenty thousand dollars in Krugerrands, as agreed.

"The situation is not unlike that of the Montagnards, you know," I said. "We gave them weapons and guidance and let them exterminate themselves."

"Sometimes we win, sometimes we lose," Rhaspberry countered. He got up to leave but turned. "Did you find what you were looking for?"

"No," I replied. "Not really. It was close, but our pursuers really weren't very good."

"Didn't wet your pants, huh? We'll have to try again. I'll keep in touch," he said.

"I'm sure you will," I responded. He left. Sherlock reentered a few minutes later.

"You sure made his day. He was actually smiling."

We dressed and left for a late breakfast at the mess hall.

After breakfast, I went back and slept until three in the afternoon. Sherlock woke me by poking my shoulder.

The flight to Colorado was departing at 4:00 p.m. I had time to shower again, dress, and get a snack before we boarded. The flight was uneventful. Sherlock gave me a key and said all my gear would be in a locker at the airport. He was not getting off at Silverthorn, so I shook his hand as I left the plane and offered him some advice.

"Rhaspberry puts his pants on one leg at a time just like you and I do. You'd do better if you just did your job and took no shit," I told him.

His eyes got a little larger, but I couldn't tell if I was getting through. I just wished him good luck and deplaned. As I walked across the runway apron, it began snowing. Inside the terminal, I found the locker, took my clothes bag from it, and went to the men's room to change out of the BDUs. Everything in the bag was too neat, so I mussed up the clothes to make them look as though they had been worn. I shoved the BDUs on the bottom and zipped the bag. Checking the mirror as I left, the face looking back told me that I was definitely too old for this shit.

I took my tickets to Denver and Saint Louis dated for two days from now and exchanged them for earlier flights. At Denver, between flights, I called Bev to tell her I was coming home early and to pick me up at Lambert Field. She asked how I did on the hunt. I replied I hadn't seen one elk, and with the weather turning bad, I wanted to get out before I got snowed in. She noticed that I sounded a little hoarse and said she hoped I wasn't catching cold. I hoped that I was.

"That son of a gun!" Bev muttered.

She remembered that hunt and how reticent he had been. She thought it was just disappointment, and perhaps to a certain extent it was. The weather outside was really brewing up now, so she took a break to check the windows and fix a little lunch. As she ate, the phone rang. Her sister-in-law, Marilyn, wanted to go out to dinner that evening. Bev explained that Connie was gone for a few days, and Marilyn asked, "What's he hunting now?" Bev responded with great sincerity, "I really don't know."

"Well, to hell with him," she returned. "Vince and I'll be over about seven and pick you up. We'll just go out without him. Okay?"

"Why not," Bev said. "It'll be fun. I'll see you at seven."

She figured she had about five hours before she had to get ready to leave and figured that would be plenty of time to read the next portion of the diary. Bev took her Diet Pepsi and sat next to the windows in the music room on the sofa. She could read and still keep tabs on the storm.

CHAPTER TWENTY-TWO

IT WAS 1992 WHEN I was contacted again. This scenario was even stranger than the last.

I was in the office as usual, just finishing up the day. Looking at the appointment book, I could see that I had only four patients left to see. I'd be out of there in an hour. The chart on the door was crisp and thin; this indicated a new patient. The stamp SANUS on the outside indicated that what I had was a new HMO enrollee. I opened the chart and scanned the preexam history sheet. Mrs. Schmidt was a thirty-nine-year-old bank teller who, according to the sheet, had enjoyed excellent health.

I mumbled to myself that it was probably the flu as I entered the room. Everyone had the goddamned flu.

As I closed the door behind me, I saw Mrs. Schmidt sitting next to the small desk. She did not appear ill. I introduced myself and shook her hand. As I sat down, I gave the stock line, "What's going on that I might be able to help you with?"

She asked if I were Dr. Conrad C. Wittmond.

"Yes, I am," I replied. Hers had not been the usual answer to my stock line.

"Do you have some form of identification?" she asked.

"I have my driver's license," I said. I must have looked annoyed because she asked me to humor her for a minute or two and said it'd all be clear.

I produced my license. She looked at it intently for about ten seconds, looked at me, and then looked back at the license. After another few seconds, she handed the card back to me.

She was obviously looking for a positive identification, but why? I stiffened a little as my body went to DEFCON 2. I had done a few unpleasant things in the past; was this payback time? I couldn't see a weapon, and her purse was on the floor. She smiled reassuringly and said, "It's okay, Doctor. Relax. I'm not here to harm you."

"What do you want?" I replied, still tense.

"Rhaspberry wants to talk to you."

Goddamnit, I might have known. Didn't he have a phone?

"There will be no phone, nothing written down, no intermediaries. No trail or trace at all. He sent me to find out if you were interested in a job. If you are, he will talk to you personally," she explained.

"Why does he trust you?" I inquired cautiously.

"I'm his daughter," she said flatly.

As she leaned to the left to get her purse, I stood up and told her to wait and just hand it to me.

She cocked her head up at me and smiled. She mockingly held up her purse between her index finger and thumb. I took it and walked to the far side of the exam room, putting the exam table was between us. I emptied the contents onto the table and asked her what I should look at. She pointed to a maroon pocketbook. I opened it to the card section and found her driver's license.

It didn't help. It said she was Cheryl Becker.

"Look behind it," she said.

I slipped my index finger behind the top card and pulled out a second card. This was a West Virginia driver's license that had expired in 1979. It was a photo of a younger Mrs. Schmidt, Becker, or whatever, but the name on it was Cheryl T. Rhaspberry.

I checked one last time for weapons and put her purse back in order. I handed it back to her.

"This all sounds very ominous," I said.

She said, "I don't know. I was just contacting you to find out if you were interested in listening. If you are, a meeting is already set up."

"Listening doesn't obligate me?" I asked.

"That is correct," she answered.

"Well, I'll listen," I said.

She instructed me to be at the 10:05 p.m. showing of *War of the Roses* at the Halls Ferry Cine the following Sunday. She got up to leave, but I stopped her.

I had to put something on her chart. I told her she had a sore throat with fever and chills that had lasted four days and a cough that produced yellow sputum. I added that her exam showed a red throat with exudates and swollen neck glands. I diagnosed an upper respiratory infection, and like anyone else, she wanted an antibiotic. So I gave her a prescription for Amoxil 250, four times a day, and Tussi-Organdin DM, two teaspoons every four hours. Then I showed her out.

I easily dealt with the last three patients, and Friday office hours came to a close. I passed the call baton to the unfortunate soul who had to cover the group for the weekend, and everyone but me had cleared out of the office by 5:05 p.m.

I leaned back in my chair, propped my feet up on the desk, and sipped a Pepsi, pondering the possibilities of my meeting with Rhaspberry.

Democracy was breaking out all over. Certainly no one would want to do anything to screw that up. Of course, Nicaragua and Cuba were notable exceptions. These seemed too small-potatoes for all the security I'd deal with. China? Let's not get ridiculous.

It had been four years since I had last been in contact with Rhaspberry. He always had something interesting.

I was never one to wish away a weekend, but the idea was tantalizing, and only Sunday night would bring answers to my questions.

On Sunday at 9:59 p.m., I arrived at the theater, bought a ticket for *War of the Roses*, and waited inside the lobby. The theater was one of those fourteen-screen jobs showing every movie made in the last six months. The lobby was far from crowded; perhaps fifteen people milled about. When I entered, the theater was absolutely empty. I sat about midway down on the right, next to the wall. Settling in, I patted my coat pocket and felt the reassuring form of the .45 automatic. Maybe Rhaspberry would come, but maybe not. Why take any chances?

I took a few sips of my Pepsi, and the lights dimmed and the trailers commenced. About halfway through a schizophrenic sneaker commercial, my peripheral vision caught a black form slowly padding down the aisle. He sat in the first seat across the aisle in my row and casually munched some popcorn.

I eased the .45 out of my pocket and let it rest beside my right thigh. A white light shone down the aisle as a few latecomers entered the theater. With this light, I could see that the dark figure was Rhaspberry. I engaged the safety on the .45 and repocketed it.

I had watched him for a few minutes when he got up and moved one seat to the left. I took this as a signal to join him. I left the theater for the refreshment stand, purchased some Milk Duds, and went back in and sat next to Rhaspberry. We were at least fifteen rows from anyone, so we could talk freely.

Rhaspberry, in his usual businesslike manner, immediately began to unfold his plan. "Everything I say here is absolutely secret. Understood?"

I nodded attentively.

It seemed that a gentlemen at the *highest* level had personally instructed him to execute this mission. No more than twelve people would ever know about it, period. As on the last two missions, I had several unique qualities that were desirable—necessary— for the job. I was a doctor, a helicopter pilot, and I could shoot. Perhaps he should have said I *would* shoot. But before he would tell me how we were going to execute the plan, he'd tell me what we were planning to do, and then I could tell him if I were in or out.

He explained that a few leaders of a drug cartel had to be dealt with in permanent way.

"You want me to kill a few drug dealers?" I asked. The boldness of the idea surprised me. "I have no problem with that," I said after momentary reflection. "What kind of a time frame are we talking about?" I added.

He indicated it would be about two months, one in training, one on the road. Being away from home only one month was workable. I told him I was in.

I suspected that having just come off ER call two weeks ago and having seen five overdoses of illicit drugs made me answer a little more quickly. As Danny DeVito counseled the Roses, Rhaspberry gave me some of the details.

One month would be spent honing my marksmanship and flying skills. I'd be given five thousand dollars to purchase the rifle and scope of my choice as well as flying time. I'd have to arrange all that. On May 20, I'd meet him in the same theater at the same time, and he'd tell me more.

He offered an envelope, which I assumed held the money. I took it and slipped it into my pocket next to the .45.

He had to go, he said, he had others to contact.

After he left, I watched some of the movie but found the gratuitous violence too unsettling, so I left too.

Before office hours the next day, I prepared a budget for the five grand. I selected a Winchester Model 70 Laredo in 7 mm Remington magnum. That would run about thirteen hundred dollars.

A Mark IV Leopold twenty-power scope would cost another fifteen hundred dollars. The rest of the money would buy about fifteen hours of helicopter time.

I placed the order for the gun and accessories by phone and was assured they would be in by Friday. My next call reserved a Bell 47G helicopter at Bill's Chopper Service for two hours every Thursday and Sunday up to and including May 20.

On my way home that evening I stopped at Kevin's for Guns and bought two twenty-round boxes of 7mm commercial ammo, a hundred Winchester-Western 7mm mag shell cases and a hundred 162-grain Hornady A-Max boattail bullets.

As promised, the gun arrived Friday by UPS. Saturday morning, I headed for the rifle range.

On the bench seat, I used up the forty rounds of commercial ammunition sighting in the scope. The recoil arrestor subdued the mighty 7 mm mag to the point where its recoil was equivalent to a .223.

The scope sight was crystal clear and free of parallax. Out of the box, the gun held a 1.4 inch group for the first thirty rounds, then this started to shrink to about 1.1 inches after the fortieth round. Not bad for commercial ammo, but I was going for better performance with hand reloads. So I gathered the empty brass and went home.

When working up a very accurate load for a particular gun, I had to keep the number of variables to a minimum. I weighed the bullets I had remaining and set aside those differing by more than a grain. Hornady had excellent quality control, and only two out of the hundred bullets I had bought exhibited this much difference. I primed the brass and divided forty cases into eight groups of five, loading each group with IMR 4350 powder. I loaded the first group lightly, with 58.5 grains, and I increased that by one-half grain for each successive group. After the powder, each casing received a bullet, which I seated just deeply enough to barely engage the rifling when chambered.

The next afternoon I took my forty hand-loaded cartridges to the range and proceeded to determine which group was most accurate. After the smoke cleared and the noise died away, the group loaded with 60.5 grains held a 0.52-inch group of five rounds at one hundred yards. This was excellent.

Back home again, I loaded four groups of five at one-tenth grain intervals on both sides of 60.5.

The targets from these loads showed that the 60.8 grain load gave the best grouping, 0.44 inches. Considering that a 7 mm bullet is about a quarter of an inch in diameter, this means that the five bullets in the group were essentially in the same hole.

With ten of the forty cases loaded with the most accurate load, I headed for the five-hundred-meter range to make sure the one-half minute of angle load held on at greater distances. With the rifle securely bench rested and allowing one minute between shots for cooling, all ten rounds fell within a four-inch circle. The fact that the group wasn't tighter was probably more my fault than the rifle's. Nonetheless, this would do very nicely.

I spent my helicopter time practicing high-performance takeoffs, steep approach landings, and nap-of-the-earth flying. The Bell 47G, just like the ones on M*A*S*H, was smaller, quieter, and had a lesser infrared signature than any of the larger turbine-powered craft.

On the downside, it was also slower, had only a two-person payload, and had a only a two-hour flying time without extra tanks.

Each Thursday and Sunday I flew, and each Saturday I

shot. In between, I exercised a little more strenuously to fine-tune my body.

On the night of May 20, I returned to the theater and, in a replay of the first meeting, joined Rhaspberry.

I was as ready as I could be knowing what I knew.

He handed me a thin manila envelope and said that the packet would explain it all.

Inside, I found some more money for expenses.

"The papers inside are in a code, two numbers per word. The first number is a page number and the second is a line number. The word is the first on that line. All you need to know now is the name of the book it is based on. The final decision will be made in two days. If the mission is go, you'll receive the name of the book," he explained.

This deal of Rhaspberry's was so surreptitious that it was unnerving. His parting words were, "If all goes well, I'll see you in a short time."

After I got home, I opened the packet. Within was a small envelope containing fifty one-hundred dollar bills and four sheets of paper covered with numbers. Naturally, these made no sense and could never be interpreted unless the master book was known. I put the money and papers in my desk drawer, covered them with some other stuff, and went to bed.

On Wednesday morning, with the mail on my desk was a letter informing me that my hardcover copy of Tom Clancy's *Clear and Present Danger* had arrived at Walden Books.

I went home for lunch, dug out my copy of the book, and proceeded to decode the message:

79-14	with
138-25	weapons
167-22	come
348-32	to
535-26	your
303-21	airstrip
627-3	on
312-32	six
484-23	fifteen

57-41	at
154-6	zero
533-26	six
369-28	hundred.

I continued the decoding process.

"Cover will be medical aid team. Will perform as such for three weeks prior. Other has map and timetable. Burn this note. ARE."

CHAPTER TWENTY-THREE

BEV HEARD THE CLOCK chime. Looking up, she saw she still had a couple of hours before Marilyn and Vince would pick her up for dinner. She decided to forgo a snack and press on with the journal.

Dutifully, on June 15 at 6:00 a.m., I was at the north practice area. This was a grassy strip just north of and parallel to the hard runway at Spirit of St. Louis Airport used exclusively by helicopters to fly patterns below and inside the patterns of the fixed-wing aircraft using the adjacent runway. I had parked my car in the Millionaire Flight Service lot and carried my knapsack and gun over to the strip. Long before I could see it, my ears picked up the *whup whup whup* of an incoming chopper. As the sound grew louder, I saw a small speck in the eastern sky. This speck gradually took the form of a UH-1H. As it cleared the last hundred yards, the noise and air turbulence had me trying to protect my ears and eyes simultaneously. After the craft landed and the engine slowed, I was able to approach it, stuff my gear inside, and climb aboard. I sat in the back alone. The copilot seat was empty. As soon as I had slid the side door shut, the pilot was powering up, and in ten seconds we were away.

A slow 180-degree turn pointed us back to the east. The pilot cleared us through Lambert TCA, and we pressed forward, over the Saint Louis Arch into Illinois. Within ten minutes of crossing the river, we landed at Scott Air Force Base.

The pilot pointed to a small executive jet fifty yards away. I grabbed my equipment and trotted across the runway to it. The side door was already down, waiting for me. The helicopter departed as I climbed the stairs.

Inside, I stored my gear and sat in the leftmost front seat across from a lone figure asleep with a hat over his face. My stirring seemed to wake him.

With a hand on each side of the brim, he pulled the hat up to reveal his smiling face.

It was Wolkert, an older, grayer Wolkert. The past thirty years had carved a few lines on his ugly mug. I was almost in shock. I had thought about him many times since our Tam Ky days. I hardly knew where to start, there was so much I wanted to know. I could see he was having the same problem.

"I had no idea ..." I stammered.

"I only found out yesterday," he said.

Rhaspberry must really have been hurting to fall back on the two of us. We sat in silence for a moment.

"You go first," Wolkert said.

I proceeded to relate my life story since 1963—graduate school, my job with NASA, medical school, and my practice.

As we talked, he asked if I had done any work for Rhaspberry, and I told him of the little episode in Nicaragua. We had some coffee, and then it was his turn to bring me up-to-date.

He had returned to school and attained his degree in engineering as he had planned. His first job was with McDonnell-Douglas in Saint Louis, where he rose up the ladder. By 1969, he was a lead engineer on a titanium-honeycomb project and terminally bored with the work and its political infighting. For months he toyed with the idea of calling the number on the card Rhaspberry had given him, and he finally did. Within a month, he was back in Vietnam. Initially he was used to train SOG people in long-range ambush. Gradually, his administrative and organizational skills became more important to the Agency, and he became involved in gathering intelligence from a network of local inhabitants. Over a period of several years, his network became very successful because each agent report directly to him. He kept no names lists; he dealt only with numbers and faces. This process kept him hopping from place to place, constantly making contacts and gathering information. He became quite fluent in French and Vietnamese. Life was pleasant until President Nixon began the Vietnamization of the war.

As American troops withdrew, it became more difficult for him to blend in and maintain his low profile. Here and there, his agents were made and dealt with. Toward the end, he was told to abandon intelligence gathering and try to get his people out. He claimed the story of his last extraction was amazing and that he would tell me about it sometime when we had more time. The jet gained altitude and headed south.

Our plane landed somewhere in the desert southwest, as usual. Wolkert and I waited patiently as the plane was refueled. Then the door creaked and opened. A man entered, head down, watching his step. When he was through the portal, he looked up, and we saw none other than Rhaspberry.

"Well, if it isn't Doctors Death and Demento," he greeted us.

We stared at him in silence. I was sure he sensed a certain degree of reticence.

It wasn't that we didn't trust him implicitly, but a little more detail about what we were doing would have been reassuring.

And that was why he was here.

He sat down across from us and opened an inch-thick manila envelope.

First, he gave us passports and plane tickets. Wolkert would be a Dr. Colin Taylor, and I would be Dr. Edward Green. Rhaspberry said these were names of real doctors who had training nearly identical to our own in case anybody checked. We two would fly to Lima by commercial airline and then travel to Piura, where we would serve as doctors at the aid station under the auspices of the Latin American Aid Organization, a hole-in-the-wall operation that provided primary health care to the indigent. We were to go about this task for the subsequent two weeks. A meeting of the cartel big boys was to start the last Saturday of the month at a hacienda near Cata Caos.

He held up a picture of the hacienda from the ground and another from the air. He also showed us a floor plan. We would have to do recon on the place and pick our own time and opportunity to go in. The road to the house came in from the south and was guarded. He indicated that our best approach would be from a trail along the river south from Castilla. It came to within a thousand meters of the house and was probably unknown to the current occupants. Afterward, we had to go back down the trail to Castilla and from there head east to a barn. With a nicotine-stained finger,

Rhaspberry pointed out the barn, a little red dot on the map. He told us a chopper would be in the barn, fueled up and ready to go. He then gave us the maps. Taking them from his hand, I asked him why we were using a helicopter.

He explained that the bad guys were going to be really upset and would have everyone looking for us, so commercial travel wouldn't be safe. The courses were plotted on the maps. Basically, we would leave Castilla for Pasto, Colombia, then go on to Panama, where we'd ditch the chopper, fly to Mexico City, and catch a bus to Laredo. He promised to meet us in the Laredo Motel 8, room 213.

I asked how we'd get our weapons in, and he explained that the weapons would be in a crate marked "Generator Parts" and would be shipped to the Aid Station. When we were finished with them, we were to wipe our prints and ditch them.

He gave us pictures of the three targets. We were to be sure we got them and *made sure they were dead*. Not probably, not wounded, *DEAD*. As an aside, he informed us that we wouldn't want to leave any witnesses. He wouldn't tell us any more about the why so if we got caught, we'd know nothing. He did promise to tell us everything if, or should I say when, we got to Laredo.

"Nail those bastards good," he said. Then he turned and exited. Wolkert and I stared at each other for a few seconds and then laughed.

"As gracious as ever," commented Wolkert.

I felt a little uneasy about this whole thing.

Rhaspberry seemed to have such an active role in this, which seemed unusual for someone so high up. What if this were one of those "renegade" operations like I had heard about in the sixties?

Wolkert thought Rhaspberry was too much the bureaucrat for such original thinking, but he agreed that it did seem a little unusual.

We were still mulling over the situation when the engines revved up and we started to taxi. After a three-and-a-half hour wait at Dallas, we were aboard the L-1011 bound for Lima, Peru.

With a single stopover in Mexico City, we arrived in Lima. It was hotter than the hubs of hell. In the off-loading area, a little man paced up and down holding a sign reading "Drs. Green and Taylor." I whistled and motioned him over to us. He was all smiles. In broken English, he introduced himself as Lupe and conveyed the idea that he was from the Latin American Aid Organization. We gathered our belongings and accompanied him to his ancient truck.

"This thing is going to take us the five hundred miles to Piura?" Wolkert asked, surprised.

"It might make it, but I doubt if we will," I offered.

Our baggage stowed in the back, we sat three across on the front seat. Lupe ground a few gears and we leapt forward toward Piura. A mixture of pavement heat and engine gases rolled up through the holes in the floorboard. A montage of empty cigarette packages and candy wrappers completed the decor. The plastic dash was split in several places, but a glow-in-the-dark statue of Jesus was firmly affixed a relatively pristine area. I was suddenly distracted from my visual inventory by olfactory input that told me that Lupe had not bathed in a while. Or was it Wolkert?

As I shifted my gaze from the shrine to Wolkert's face, his gray-green color told me he was tolerating this miasma about as well as I—and we hadn't yet left the city limits of Lima.

The trip was uneventful and somehow reminded me of the vacations I had taken with my parents as a kid. With the heat, the bumps, and the itchy upholstery, all I needed was a stick of Juicy Fruit gum and I'd puke up my socks.

It took nineteen hours to reach Piura—we averaged about twenty-six miles per hour. The aid station was a group of tin buildings to the east of Piura. The main building bore an emblem of a white circle with a red cross in the center on three sides.

Judging from the well-trodden path to the door, the organization must have taken care of quite a few folks there.

Lupe said he would stow our gear while we met the head honcho. Inside the weather-beaten door was a weather-beaten desk occupied by a weather-beaten man. He looked up, and we introduced ourselves. He said he was happy to have us aboard but realized that the trip was quite tiring and that we had best rest. We would talk tomorrow.

Lupe appeared behind us, and the man directed him to show us to our quarters. Crossing the compound, Wolkert asked if this place smelled familiar.

"I was just about to mention that," I said.

The magical combination of the smell of diesel fuel and excrement seemed to be a common denominator of all hellholes. The accommodations were crude but a little cleaner that what I had expected. Maybe that was a trick my brain played to allow my body to flop on the bunk and leap into unconsciousness. The last thing I remembered was the white pillow heading for my face.

The next morning we had breakfast with the entire crew of the aid station. We were given a very brief introduction by the administrator as "two new doctors who will be with us for a while."

The staff was composed of six native nurses' aides, four American RNs, and the native doctor-administrator we had met last night. Lupe and two others who composed the maintenance squad rounded out the party.

After the meal, the head nurse, Karen, came over and announced that it was time to go to work. We followed her out of the mess area to the clinic building. Lines of patients had already formed outside; there must have been twenty people waiting at the door.

Karen was big, maybe five feet eleven and solidly built. She had a ready smile but a look into her eyes told me that this castle had a substantial moat. I could only speculate about the series of events that had brought her there.

The clinic was well stocked. It was Wolkert's opinion that some fairly decent surgery could be done here. I, on the other hand, was more interested in the medicine chest.

We donned our white coats as Batman dons his cape and set to work. The parade of patients reminded me of the clinic at Saint Louis City Hospital during my medical school days. There were fevers, coughs, wounds, belly pain, and on and on. At noon, when we stopped for lunch, the line was still twenty people long. As we ate, Lupe's squad restocked the meds, got rid of the used bandages and other disposable equipment, and cleaned the floor. When we reopened the shop at one o'clock, all was ready for another round.

When the day was over, Wolkert and I sat with Karen at supper. "How do you handle all this with only one doctor?" I asked her.

"We just do it more slowly," Karen replied. Without stopping, she asked, "Do either of you gentlemen know anything about generators? The new parts have just come in."

Wolkert looked at me and I at him. We both turned to Karen and she returned the gaze with an almost imperceptible smile.

I volunteered that I knew a little about machinery. I'd take a look at it for her.

According to Karen, the last pilgrim that had come through had taken it apart, found the problem, and ordered the parts but didn't stay to reassemble the damn thing.

I got the feeling that she was being very cautious while trying not to give that impression.

My suspicions were confirmed when I entered the generator shed. She flipped on the light and proceeded to search the entire building. I waited, not knowing what she was looking for.

She finally told me that at least one of the nurses' aides and one of the maintenance men worked for the opposition.

I asked her who the opposition was, exactly.

"Either the Sendero Luminoso, or Shining Path, the Communist terrorist group, or the drug cartel, or both," was her answer.

Satisfied that the area was secure, we approached the desk-sized crate marked "Generator Parts." After a brief clumsy struggle with the fasteners, I revealed its contents. Karen sifted through the excelsior, removing the actual generator parts. She made one neat pile of packing material on one side of the crate and another pile of parts on the other. About eighteen inches into the crate there was a hinged divider. Very tidily, she swept the top clean with her hands and then raised the divider. The light reflections off the plastic wrapping inside obscured the contents until Karen's small knife slit it. Rhaspberry had been thorough, if not generous. In addition to our rifles and ammunition, there were BDUs, boots, binoculars, MREs, .45s, ten Mexican gold pieces, and a packet of papers.

"What are you old boys going to do with all these young boy toys?" The karate chop to my ego's groin had barely registered before Karen added, "Never mind. I'm not supposed to know."

Everything seemed to be in order. I placed the long weapons on the bottom of the crate. We wouldn't need them for a while. I packed the BDUs and recon stuff conveniently on top and closed the box.

We collected the generator parts and went to repair the machine.

"Old boys, huh?" repeated Wolkert after I recounted what had just happened.

I quietly emphasized that there were some unfriendlies around us, so we had better play everything close to the chest.

The moon would be near full in ten days, so we would begin our reconnaissance then; for now, we'd just play our parts.

That meant we'd have two nights for recon and to pick our spot considering the meeting was only twelve days away.

CHAPTER TWENTY-FOUR

BEV AGAIN GLANCED AT her watch. She knew Marilyn and Vince would be there soon to pick her up, but she couldn't put Connie's journal down. She turned the page.

On the night of the first recon mission, Wolkert and I met in the machine shed. Here we changed into the BDUs and slipped away from the compound toward the river. We crossed it and picked up a trail that paralleled the river. Rhaspberry's map was quite accurate, so we could easily find the landmarks along the way, even by moonlight.

It took us a little over three hours to get to the area across from the hacienda. The trail continued south from there, but we had to go east and pick our way through the undergrowth to gain the crest of a knoll that overlooked the hacienda. We then moved south along the ridge to find a spot that gave us a full view of the courtyard. With the range finder in the binoculars, Wolkert determined that the distance to the patio table was 630 meters. That's where they'd be having breakfast.

Rhaspberry had been right so far, but that was going to be a hell of a shot.

"Nothing we haven't done before," Wolkert reassured me.

We retraced our steps and were back at the compound in less than two and a half hours. We changed clothes, repacked the crate, and got to bed for an hour's sleep before reveille.

The clinic was busy the next day and I sorely felt the lack of sleep. We decided not to go out the second night, as we needed to be rested for the following one. We were "old boys," after all.

Clinic duty the following day was much easier after a night's sleep. Karen commented that we looked a little better and added that the Peruvian night life would get us if we weren't careful.

When Karen and I were alone, I asked if anything unusual was going on. She answered that things were pretty calm. There was no indication that anyone had picked up on anything.

"We'll be going tonight, and I want to thank you for all of your help," I said.

"I hope you have good luck," she said. "This is the only time I haven't been fully briefed on an operation, so it must be pretty sticky."

"That's why they've sent in the old boys," I said, smiling.

She laughed and shook her head and walked away.

Supper, nightfall, and lights-out slipped by. Around 1:00 a.m., Wolkert and I adjourned to the machine shed. We changed into BDUs and put our clothes in backpacks. With all the equipment hanging from various parts of our bodies, the parts crate was empty when we refastened the top. After one last look around to be sure we had left no traces, we departed. By the light of the moon, we again made our way south. Landmarks, one after another, slid by. The load slowed us, but by 4:30, we were at the base of the hill where we turned east.

We carefully made our way up the hill as we had on our recon mission before. We cautiously approached the area we had chosen to fire from, keeping below the ridgeline. We settled in and then crawled up to the ridgeline to survey the courtyard. Wolkert confirmed his 630-meter reading. The table and chairs were empty, but soon the inhabitants would rise and breakfast out there. We waited.

Ever so slowly, the sun made its way over the trees on the ridge across from us, and the shadow of the ridge crawled down the hillside. By 8:30, the whole house was exposed by the sunlight. One man came out and arranged the table and chairs; another set the table. They both went back inside. In a few minutes, four men emerged and sat down. Four other men deployed for guard duty, two on the roof and two in the garden between us and the patio. The view through the telescopic sight contained two Caucasians and two Latinos having a leisurely breakfast. I quickly checked the photo cards Rhaspberry had given us and confirmed that they were very probably the intended victims. Six hundred yards was a long way.

The cards were numbered one through four, in order of priority. Wolkert would take Number One and I, Number Two; then I would take Three, and he, Number Four. We had to hurry our preparations if we wanted to shoot while they were still seated. With the guns well-situated and sight pictures procured, we began to count down from ten to allow us to get in synch. We wanted to fire the first round simultaneously to maximize the chances of killing Numbers One and Two. When Wolkert said, "Zero," we both fired. Quickly working the bolt, I reloaded and caught Number Three in my sights as he cowered behind a flower planter. I could almost see the look of apprehension on his face as I touched off the trigger. The guards fired in our general direction. I took the men on the roof, Wolkert the men in the garden.

The guards on the roof went down easily. As I was admiring my handiwork, two more men came out of the house with small automatic weapons. Before I could shoot, Wolkert had dropped the one I had my sights on, so I had to switch to the other. In a second, he was down.

The echoes of gunfire died out, and it was very quiet.

With the binoculars, we surveyed the damage. Nothing was moving. We then advanced on the house, using the bounding overwatch approach: I went ahead fifty yards to cover while Wolkert watched, then I watched while he went a hundred yards to take up a position fifty yards in front of me, and so on until we were at the edge of the garden. We saw no motion on the patio. We discarded our rifles and took out our .45s. I examined each body for life while Wolkert watched with his weapon ready. No one was alive. We had really made a mess.

We picked our way through each room of the two-story hacienda expecting a firefight at each threshold. We found nothing but a little cocaine, a few guns, and a couple of thousand dollars.

"No broads," remarked Wolkert.

The goings-on at the hacienda were probably too incriminating to have "broads" around. We adjourned to the patio to ID the bodies. I counted only nine bodies; there had been ten men here. We hoped the missing one wouldn't be important. Going through the photos, we tried to identify the four important targets. Wolkert found Number Three. I announced I had found Number Four and Number One.

Comparing the bodies to the photos, we couldn't find Number Two among the remaining six bodies. "Goddamn it! You might know the one that got away would be important," Wolkert exclaimed. "Rhaspberry isn't going to like this. We have got to find him!"

We started in the center of the courtyard and walked in ever widening circles, peering at the ground to find a clue of which way the tenth man had gone. There was blood spattered all over the concrete; it was hard to tell which pool belonged to which body. As our circle widened beyond the bodies, Wolkert spotted a solitary drop of blood about the size of a pencil eraser on a flagstone that gave us direction.

We paused and scanned the garden toward where we thought he went and saw about one hundred yards of open area, then jungle.

"I wonder if he's got a gun," Wolkert said. Several of the others had, so it was a safe bet that he did too.

We decided that because I had hunting and tracking experience, I would lead out and Wolkert would follow about twenty yards behind to cover my back. It was only 9:20 a.m. We had all day.

We waited an hour to let him bleed a bit. He'd stop to rest and would stiffen up and would be easier to catch up to. We went back and found our target rifles, tossed them into the stream, and covered them with rocks. What a waste. We then went into the hacienda with weapons more suited for the jungle. Wolkert had picked up a MAC-10, and I kept my government-issue Colt.45 automatic. His new weapon had been well cared for, and there was more than enough ammunition for it in the house. We ate what we could salvage of our victims' breakfast and freely drank Perrier.

With a belch, Wolkert announced that it was showtime.

We agreed that Number Two had probably fled directly into the jungle, and the nearest entry point was a few yards to the left of a certain dead tree. We didn't want to approach this across the open terrain, so we each picked a spot along the jungle's edge about a hundred yards to each side of our quarry's probable entry point. We ran to our spots in a crouch, keeping our eyes on the area by the dead tree. No shots fired. So far, so good. We listened intently for a few minutes, then we very cautiously made our way toward each other, looking for signs of our man's entry into the undergrowth. I inched along with the .45 cocked, scanning a thirty-degree area from the jungle edge into the bush and back again. Within ten feet of the dead tree, a half-drop of blood on the edge of a leaf seized my attention. I flattened out on the ground and listened. Wolkert, not fifty feet away, saw me go down and followed suit. I silently pointed to the ground in front of me, and he crawled slowly toward my position. I concentrated on the area to my right while Wolkert approached but heard nothing. When he arrived, I pointed to the blood, wiped it off the leaf, and rolled it between my finger and thumb. It was slightly inhomogeneous.

"This has been here for a while," I whispered.

We listened a while longer. All I could hear was the birds, and they gave no evidence of alarm. Maybe he was dead. I doubted it. He had covered a hundred yards, and the blood trail was pretty scant. He was in there, waiting.

As planned, I set out first at an agonizingly slow pace and Wolkert followed. I cautiously took a few steps, checked the area, then scanned the area by my feet. Every five or six feet, I spotted a quarter-sized blood spot on the jungle floor. He had been running, so this indicated a serious wound, maybe letting out three drops of blood a second. The blood was bright red; definitely arterial.

I passed a small tree with a tiny blood mark about three and a half feet above the ground on its bark. He had to have passed to its right; the other foliage would have blocked any other path. This indicated his wound was on his left side, probably on his upper arm or torso. Thirty yards beyond the tree I saw many scattered leaves and crushed ferns. He had fallen there. The blood was fairly fresh.

I hoped Wolkert was behind me. I couldn't see or hear him at all. Quietly, deftly, I continued my pursuit. The blood drops got closer together; he was slowing. I slowed. In several more yards and I found another spot where he had rested. There was a pool of red froth next to and partially on the trunk of a tree. He had coughed this up. This motherfucker had been hit in the left lung. He was ours. The droplets leading away from the resting site were now very fresh. We had disturbed him, and he was just ahead.

My heart was pounding now. Sweat ran into my eyes. Gnats swarmed in front of my face. Something crawled behind my left ear. I made no movement; I just studied the area ahead. Time was on my side; he was the bleeding prey. All I had to do was not make a mistake.

After five minutes, I inched forward on my knees and elbows. I paused again after I had covered about ten feet. I heard a muffled cough. He had to be less than thirty feet away. He was waiting for me. I stealthily proceeded ahead, arcing around about ninety degrees from where I had been but keeping the same distance from him. I would catch him on the next leg of his flight. There was another cough. I knelt to the right of a substantial tree, leaning against it to steady myself. I extended the .45 with a two-hand isosceles hold toward the target.

I knew Wolkert was behind me, and I was sure he must have heard the muffled cough. He must have known by the path I took that I had flanked our subject. He made some slight noise to pull Number Two's attention. From behind a tree, he leveled his MAC-10, and spray the noisy area with bullets.

The echoes of gunfire died away. No curious fool, Number Two decided to leave. As he stepped out from behind the tree on the opposite side from which he had fired, I shot him in the left side of the head. He disappeared, but I heard violent thrashing. The thrashing diminished to short spasms of noise, and then, finally, silence.

After a minute or two, I called out, "Wolkert! Are you okay?"

"Did you get him?" he asked.

A little more time passed, then I cautiously approached the victim. The area in which he lay was all matted down. There was blood all over. He had come to rest on his back with his left arm under him and his legs crossed at the ankles. I saw that the rifle bullet had passed through his left arm, about midway between he elbow and shoulder, and then penetrated his chest four inches from his left nipple. The projectile then exited his back just above the left kidney. The shot would have put most men down. The pistol bullet had entered his skull just behind his left earlobe and had not exited. It had rattled around inside his brainstem, no doubt causing all the thrashing. Wolkert took out the photo of Number Two, and we agreed it was he.

"A fitting end to a lousy motherfucker," he quipped as he pitched the photo onto the crotch of the corpse.

He pointed to the urine stains on my pants. My heart was still pounding. Looking at my face, his eyes widened.

"You son of a bitch, you're doing it again."

He was right. My hands were shaking. I had to sit down.

"We got that motherfucker, didn't we?" I exclaimed. "He thought he was a pretty macho mother, but we got him!"

"Just settle down!" Wolkert cautioned.

"Settle down, fuck. We just hunted the most dangerous game, and we got the fucker. Man, we hosed his ass."

Wolkert popped the top on a bottle of pilfered Perrier and offered me a drink.

"I don't want a drink, goddamn it. Jesus Christ, we had just hunted down a real badass with a machine gun in the fucking jungle and killed him with a pistol. And all you can say is 'settle down' and 'have a drink'? Shit, man. After thirty years, we're still good. That bastard didn't have a chance. He didn't know what he was up against."

Wolkert looked at me pensively. "I'm acting weird, right?" I said.

"No more than before," he replied.

"Goddamn! Don't you feel it?" I asked.

He didn't then and he didn't now. Well, it was good. His face said he thought I was a little out of control.

He gave me a few seconds to get my shit together. I brought up his screaming and cutting his way out of the tent that night on the mesa.

He stammered that that had been no nightmare; there had been a leech on his balls. Right.

After about twenty minutes, my heart rate had returned to normal, my hands had stopped shaking, and alas, the euphoria had passed. It was time to get the hell out of there.

CHAPTER TWENTY-FIVE

BEV JUMPED AT A clap of thunder. The storm had arrived. She paused long enough to go to the pantry and retrieve a flashlight in case the power went out. She didn't want to miss the rest of Connie's story.

We went back to the hacienda and gathered up everything we had brought. Quickly, we retraced our steps to the ridge, down the backside to the river, and north. From here we would take a path east about two hundred meters south of the compound to the barn. We found the path easily in the light of the noon sun. Neither of us had seen it the three times we had passed it before. We traveled about five minutes before the path led to a small clearing in which an abandoned, ramshackle barn sat. We observed the area for about ten minutes and concluded that no one was around. We circled the barn inside the tree line and entered through a stall door in the rear. It was dark; only a thin shaft of light entered through a crack. As our eyes adjusted to the dark, the form of a Bell 47G took shape. It sat in the middle of the floor like a giant dragonfly poised before the large doors.

Rhaspberry had come through again.

I suggested Wolkert go to the loft and keep a lookout while I readied the craft.

Without comment, Wolkert ascended the ladder, and I began. Starting at the left side of the helicopter, just behind the door, I unscrewed the cap on the hydraulic fluid reservoir. The red liquid was a little over the full line. Replacing the cap, I then checked the wires to the magneto and spark plugs. All were secure. Next, I opened the left fuel-tank and fuel-filter petcocks to drain any water. A few ounces of fuel trickled out of each onto the barn floor. I dipped a fingertip into the puddles and smelled the liquid, confirming the presence of aviation gasoline.

Moving back along the tail boom, I jiggled the tail-rotor driveshaft bearings and the cables to the tail-rotor pitch horns. All were tight and in order. The tail-rotor transmission box contained plenty of fluid, so I moved around the end of the helicopter to examine the tail-rotor blades.

I then inspected the small stabilizer just forward of the tail rotor. Its spring mechanism was fully functional. Taking another look at the drive shaft, I moved forward to the battery in the tail boom about three feet behind the engine. The contacts were clean, and the fluid tanks were full. Back at the engine, I checked the oil level and drained the sumps in the right fuel tank, again confirming the presence of gasoline. The spark-plug wires were properly attached and so was the oil cooler. Walking around to the front, I bent down to make sure the pitot tube was open.

The ground-level work complete, I stepped up on the left skid brace and reached up to unscrew the gas cap. I dipped my finger into the liquid and sniffed it to confirm the presence of gasoline. Since the tanks were crossconnected, I only had to check the one. After I refastened the cap, I climbed higher on the frame until I could see the top of the main rotor. After assuring myself that the Jesus nut was secure, I worked my way down, checking the various horns, plates, buffers, dampers, and shafts. After the check of the air-intake grid and the extra fuel tank inside the cabin under the seat, it was time to roll the baby out of the barn.

Propping each of the barn doors open with old pieces of lumber, I returned to the rear of the chopper, and with Wolkert's help, lifted the tail with a pry bar and wheeled the machine out into the clearing. I lowered the chopper to its skids and pulled off the wheels, discarding them and the pry bar in the brush. We didn't need the extra weight.

I untied the blade tether from the tail boom and pushed the rotor blade off-center to be sure it rotated easily. Wolkert and I then climbed aboard. Mentally, I began the start up procedure.

Head phones and intercom—check.

Starter breaker in—check.

Mag switch to right mag—check.

Battery on—check.

Engine primed with one twist and back to start detent—check.

Pedals and cyclic in neutral position—check.

Collective full down—check.

With my right hand on the mag switch, I pushed the starter button on the collective/throttle control. The engine coughed and died. I reprimed it and tried again. This time it caught. I quickly switched the mag switch to BOTH and increased the throttle to bring the rpm to 1,800. The centrifugal clutch was slowly accelerating the main rotor, and when the rotor rpm reached 200, I decreased the throttle to marry the needles and brought the rpm up to 2,200 for the warm-up. While the cylinder head temperature gauge was inching its way to 100 °C, I continued my mental check list.

Carb heat in green—check.

Starter breaker out—check.

Generator on—check.

Altimeter set to field elevation—check.

Flight clock set to zero—check.

Oil pressure in green—check.

When the head temperature reached 100 °C, I revved the engine to 2,800 rpm and then turned the mag switch first to the right mag, then to the left, then back to Both to ensure that both were functioning properly.

After a brief check of the gauges confirmed all needles in the green, I pressed the intercom button.

"Here we go," I announced.

Wolkert mumbled something.

I motioned to him that he had to press the intercom button to talk over the engine noise.

"Got it," he replied. "Do you really fly these things?"

He was about to find out.

I brought the engine up to 3,000 rpm. With a light touch on the right pedal, I slowly pulled up on the collective lever to my left, and the helicopter rose to hover about three feet off the ground. With the hover stabilized, I turned the machine into the wind. I barely moved the cyclic control forward, and the helicopter advanced slowly. At about twenty miles per hour, the translational lift set in, and we popped up. Keeping the forward velocity at 50 mph, we gradually attained altitude. I reduced power to 2,800 rpm and 20 inches manifold pressure when we were about 500 feet off the ground. I executed a slight right turn to get the 27-degree compass reading that would take us 475 miles to Pasto, Colombia. We were on our way.

Wolkert raised his eyebrows and turned down the corners of his mouth as if to say, "I'll be damned," but remained silent. With my smugness validated, I turned my attention to navigation. At eighty miles per hour, it was going to take approximately six hours to get to Pasto. That was a long time for two middle-aged men to go without a pit stop.

I knew not to keep eyeing the compass when trying to fly at a specific heading. Instead, I used the compass to get the right heading and then picked out an object on the horizon and flew to it. Once near it, I would adjust the heading, pick out another object, and fly toward it, and so on until we reached our destination.

The trip to Panama was long and, fortunately, boring. I even tried to teach Wolkert to fly to break the monotony. After several hours, he could hold a course pretty well. We flew on after dark, stopping for gas, oil, hydraulic fluid, food, and water. I put the chopper down for the last time, and as instructed, we left everything inside except our civilian clothes and personal papers. Rhaspberry had even marked the direction to the airport on the map.

With shirts untucked and sunglasses on, the two ugly—and, I might add, smelly—Americans made their way to the terminal. After a few hours we were in Mexico City and baking on a bus bound for Laredo, Texas. The trip north was every bit as delightful as the sojourn to Piura with Lupe. It had many commonalities.

We crossed the border at Laredo without incident, and we hailed a cab to take us to the Motel 8. The son of a bitch could have told us it was only two blocks away.

Wolkert went to the desk and asked for the key to room 213. The desk clerk promptly delivered it, and we casually drifted up the stairs. As Wolkert put the key into the lock, he turned and said, "You don't think they'll kill us, do you?"

I think my lack of surprise surprised him. If that was their plan, there was goddamned little we could to do about it.

Wolkert twisted the knob and the door opened. The room was empty, and so was the bathroom. A knock on the open door behind us gave us a start. A tall, lanky man with a floral-print shirt held out a letter. "This is for you," he said and left.

I opened the envelope to find a small slip of paper with only "Wait" written on it.

"Wait? How long?" Wolkert fumed. I smelled, he smelled, the clothes smelled. "Wittmond," he said, "you wait. I'm going out to get some clothes. I'll be back in no time."

"He says wait," I cautioned.

Wolkert reasoned that Rhaspberry probably had to fly down from DC. It'd take hours. Maybe he was right. I agreed and let him go.

Just after he left, I became apprehensive about being alone. The .45 was a mild comfort.

Wolkert had been right. He returned in plenty of time with clothes, underwear, socks, everything including two six-packs of Michelob Dry. We had Domino's deliver a garbage pizza and rapidly became re-Americanized.

The beer and pizza gone, we went to sleep. Several hours passed before I was awakened by shouts of, "Wittmond! *Wittmond!*"

"Another leech?" I asked

He responded with disdain that there was someone at the door.

He was right again. The very light rapping made its way through my mental fog. Before I could move, Wolkert was at the door.

"Who is it?" he said.

"It's Rhaspberry. Open up."

Wolkert left the chain on as he cracked the door to confirm Rhaspberry's presence, as though the chain would have done any good. Reassured, he closed the door, flipped the chain, and admitted Rhaspberry.

Rhaspberry flipping the room's only chair around and sat. We stood.

He asked if we had fulfilled his expectations, resting his chin on the back of the chair, staring at the floor.

"We have," replied Wolkert without qualification.

Rhaspberry's eyes rose to meet ours. He then offered to tell us what, exactly, we had done.

"I know *what* we did," I said. "I want to know *why*."

Rhaspberry paused for effect. "President Bush has been coming down hard on the drug people. This pressure has turned Colombia into a war zone, and most of the country's upper echelon have bought up vast isolated areas in Peru from which to continue their business. The brother of Number Two in your picture book was one of the lower-echelon people left behind to continue the struggle in Colombia. He was killed in a combined-forces raid this past December. Number Two didn't take this well, and in a fit of pique had the balls to plot to assassinate our president. This came to my attention in February, and I followed it along until I was convinced of its authenticity. Number Two was recruiting two professionals, and the high threat required that I inform the president. He and I discussed at length how this was to be handled. We didn't want to overtly violate Peruvian sovereignty, but we did want to stop the plot and we wanted to teach the drug lords a lesson: that we knew everything they were up to and that they could be taken out any time and in any place we chose. The bottom line was don't fuck with the pres. That's where you two came in. Your mission has been executed very deftly. The lesson is brutally plain and no one knows who the teacher is. I expect that we'll hear tangential reassurances from the cartel that Number Two was a rogue, et cetera, et cetera, and that the president should not expect that anyone will try it again.

"In any event, you did a good job, and both the president and I thank you."

"Now wait a minute," Wolkert said. "You mean that Wittmond and I were all that stood between the president and the assassins?"

"Not at all. There were contingency plans, but they would have had all kinds of political recoil. This way there will be no congressional bullshit, no media bullshit, no Secret Service bullshit; what needed to be done has been done. There's really nothing he could give you as a reward, but the Man wanted you to have a watch," he said, handing us each a stainless steel Omega Speedmaster. "There's a message on the back," he added.

We dutifully read the inscription: "I'd like to thank you personally, but it wouldn't be prudent. George."

Wolkert asked Rhaspberry if this were for real.

"It's for real. Don't you appreciate humor?" replied Rhaspberry.

Rhaspberry extended his hand. We each shook it, and before he turned to leave, Rhaspberry gave us our plane tickets home and wished us a safe journey.

"Wouldn't be fucking prudent?" Wolkert said, amazed.

When did prudence have anything to do with anything? We turned in to sleep out the rest of the night. My plane was to depart at 11:58 a.m., and Wolkert's would leave at 1:15 p.m., so we had several hours to shoot the shit after breakfast. About a half hour before my departure, we found our way to the airport.

It had been great seeing Wolkert again. I gave him my address and phone number and urged him to keep in touch. He agreed that we would. With a firm hug and a head butt, we parted and went back to our respective lives.

Bev heard the doorbell and put down Connie's journal. After greeting Vince at the door, she grabbed her raincoat and umbrella and hurried with him out to his car. She slid inside.

"Hi, Bev," Marilyn called from the front seat. "What have you been up to?"

"You wouldn't believe it," Bev said.

CHAPTER TWENTY-SIX

WITTMOND LEFT THE CABIN and made his way to the sentry stand, trying to be just as cautious as he had the first time he took watch. Arriving at his post, he took out his camo pack and was putting some finishing touches on his face makeup. He was commenting to himself that if his tongue were longer, all he needed was an electric guitar and he could join KISS. He was retracting his extended tongue when he heard a car pass the entrance to Wolkert's drive on the main road about one hundred yards away. It was the fifth car to pass in the last three days. The noise always brought Wittmond a twinge of concern. A few minutes later, he heard the noise again. Five in three days, and now two in five minutes.

His throat constricted and a new rivulet of sweat ran from his armpit down his left side. "Oh, boy," he said to himself. "Are the feces headed for the fan blades?"

He stood up and got comfortable against a tree that shielded him from the road and stomped slowly three times. After checking the chamber of the .22 to be absolutely, positively sure it was loaded and adjusting his hat and clothing for maximum concealment, he froze.

He hoped Wolkert and Rhaspberry were on their toes as he quietly clicked the safety off.

He rested his head against the tree, his eyes closed, straining to hear any unnatural sound. He detected, analyzed, and rejected the sounds of many birds, squirrels, rustling leaves, and bugs until he picked up on the objections of a disturbed blue jay off to his left. Someone was approaching the cabin on the road through the woods. From where he was, Wittmond wouldn't see him, or them. He remained motionless and continued to listen. He heard no more off to his left, strain as he might. A small fox squirrel flitted about several yards from where he stood. It hopped a few feet, looked about, and then dug in the leaves. Wittmond listened and watched it repeat the ritual. Suddenly, the squirrel stood upright and stared toward the road. It was motionless for perhaps thirty seconds before it scurried in the opposite direction. The new sweat felt like bugs crawling in Wittmond's armpits.

Perhaps ten minutes passed before the faint crunch of a footstep on gravel brought Wittmond to DEFCON 1. Someone was definitely approaching on the road, and he was very close. He was on the other side of Wittmond's tree. Wittmond's already rapid heart rate doubled, and his throat tightened.

He waited. The sweat was burning his eyes, but he made no move to wipe it away. The enemy was good; he made virtually no noise. Slowly his figure emerged into Wittmond's field of vision. Wittmond stood about thirty feet off the road, and the bad guy was paralleling the road about ten feet into the woods on the same side. He carried an M-16, and his deft moves indicated not only military training but experience. He was dressed in casual street clothes, and the large sweat stains in the armpits of his shirt that indicated more than heat was bothering him. For just a second, Wittmond thought he could smell him, but it was probably himself.

The enemy wore an earplug headset and paused his advance to press the piece deeper into his right ear. As his hand left his weapon and came up to his ear, Wittmond raised the pistol and set the sight a half-inch behind and a half-inch below the man's left ear and squeezed the trigger. There was a faint *click-clack* as the pistol cycled. The man disappeared from the sight picture.

Wittmond remained motionless. The man was down; he could see his gray pants leg in the brush not fifteen feet away. He watched the leg while listening for signs of any companions. An explosion ripped through the calm, and Wittmond flinched slightly. The leg didn't move. The blast must have been from one of the claymores. Leaning back slowly and looking from behind the tree down the road, he studied the path intently. Nothing.

After listening for a full five minutes, he was convinced that no one had been close to his victim. Wittmond slowly slid to the ground and wormed his way toward the body. His low approach soon brought his face to the bottom of the man's running shoes. Raising his head a little, he saw that the man had wet his pants—

another positive indication of his enemy's condition. Wittmond inched up on the man's left side, training the .22 on the nearest vital organ. The man was lying on his belly, his head turned to the right. Wittmond rolled over on his left side and turned the man's face toward him with his right hand, keeping his pistol ready in his left hand. The man's neck was flaccid; his head turned easily. Wittmond could see the tiniest trickle of blood behind the man's left ear. The man's eyes were open and rolled to the right. His face was expressionless; he had died instantly.

Wittmond removed the listening device from the man's head and put it on. He heard only static. Backing up to his tree, he stood up. After a few minutes of surveillance, he moved along the road toward where their car ought to be. During the fifteen minutes it took to get into visual range of the car, he heard nothing on the radio. He watched the car and surroundings for a while but saw no one.

A few quick steps out of the woods had him next to the driver's door. The car was empty. Wittmond opened the door, rolled the window down, popped the hood, and then quietly closed the door again. Raising the hood, he stuffed his handkerchief well into the intake opening on the air filter and gently closed the hood again. His handiwork done, he took up a position about ten feet into the woods from the driver's door. Wittmond put the .22 into his belt, drew his .45, cocked it, and positioned himself for an ambush. There was still no activity on the radio. He figured it must have been broken, so he discarded it. With no communications, all he could do was wonder what was going on. Another explosion ripped through the woods. The second claymore? He remained still.

If each claymore got one and he had gotten one, that should be all three guys, but who knew? Not ten seconds after the explosion came the rattle of automatic weapons fire. Two bursts of maybe six or seven shots each rang out from the same weapon, then silence. Wittmond waited. A few more minutes passed before he saw a lone figure picking his way through the bush toward the car. He was moving too fast for Wolkert or Rhaspberry. He was trying to get away. Wittmond waited.

When the man reached the car, he rushed to the driver's side and got in. He threw his MAC-10 onto the passenger seat and pulled the door closed behind him. Wittmond let him grind the starter for about five seconds, then stepped into view with the .45 pointed directly at the quarry's face. The man looked up and saw Wittmond. For a second his eyes shifted to the right as if to locate his weapon.

"Don't. Don't even blink," Wittmond ordered in a low, steady voice. "Put both hands on the wheel or it'll be a closed-casket funeral."

The man complied. Wittmond took up a position behind him, and opened the car door with his left hand, and backed away.

Wittmond kept his finger tight on the trigger of the .45. If his heart thumped hard, the man's brains would be all over the inside of the windshield.

"Go to the front of the car and keep your hands up."

Wittmond must have looked more ferocious than he felt. The guy was trembling. After the man was in position, Wittmond ordered him to unbutton his shirt and slowly remove it. He then ordered him to remove the rest of his clothing, revealing a backup .22 pistol in an ankle holder and a small knife in his belt buckle.

Wittmond ordered the man to turnaround and stay in the middle of the road. Wittmond then gave the signal: three shots followed by two more, one shot for every kill. With the first shot, the captive cringed, as he did with each successive shot. The signal was answered by three shots followed by one more.

"That's all three of you," Wittmond commented to the prisoner. "Come on, fuck face, back to the cabin."

"What about my clothes?" the man meekly protested.

"Fuck the clothes. Get going *now*, or I put one in your foot." He fired a round into the gravel between his captive's legs for emphasis.

"All right! All right!" the prisoner screamed, a little more frightened than before, if that were possible.

Wittmond had him walk about ten feet ahead of him up the road to the cabin. As they rounded the bend and came into view of the cabin, Wolkert and Rhaspberry, who were standing in the yard, started convulsing with laughter. A naked, bearded man covering his genitals with both hands and hopping about on the gravel road was amusing.

"What you got there, Wittmond?" Wolkert shouted.

"I have here the unluckiest son of a bitch in the world," Wittmond answered.

Wolkert smiled and retrieved a length of chain and a padlock and shackled the man to a tree.

With the captive secure, the threesome adjourned to the bunker. First they reconstructed what happened. The would-be assassins had come toward the cabin three abreast. Wittmond had killed the one on the road just before the other two approached the cabin. Being cautious, the remaining two opened the door without exposing themselves, and the first Claymore went off, ruining the door but not harming them. This, naturally, had put them on their guard. They completely searched the cabin and, finding nothing, went outside and headed to the basement door.

They approached the back of the cabin from both sides, and seeing nothing, one cautiously approached the bunker door. He was examining the lock when Wolkert remotely detonated the second claymore. The shrapnel balls shredded the man and put no small number of dents in the door. Immediately after the mine went off, Wolkert cracked the steel door and sprayed the foliage with two bursts of fire and just caught a glimpse of one man fleeing. Wolkert exited and took up a position across from the door, which Rhaspberry then secured, and they waited. That's when Wittmond caught the fleeing man at the car and brought him back.

Debriefed, Rhaspberry took over. "First, Wolkert, send your family home. They'll be safe now and you don't want them to see what comes next. Second, we have to stash the two bodies. We can put them in the car and torch it somewhere away from here. Wittmond and I'll do it while you get your family on the road. Third, we have to extract the necessary information from our friend, then we can wrap this thing up."

Wittmond packed the body of the guy with the head wound and most of the guy who had the encounter with the claymore into the bad guys' rental car. Rhaspberry followed in his rental car. They searched for and located an appropriate place to dump their trash. By the time they returned, Wolkert had moved the captive into the bunker and had his arms and legs shackled to the metal frame of a cot. He had generously allowed the man undershorts.

"Family all gone?" inquired Rhaspberry.

"Yep, they're on their way," Wolkert replied.

Rhaspberry approached the captive. "I don't suppose you'll be reasonable and answer a few questions?"

No answer.

Rhaspberry continued, "You know, you've presented a real threat to the families of these two. That wasn't a real bright thing to do, but you didn't know that. We have to know where you are going to meet the old man to prove that you have completed the job. That's all."

He paused. There was silence, so he proceeded.

"Did I mention that these two guys are doctors? The one you tried to kill is a surgeon. They are well-versed in the various aspects of pain."

Wittmond was sure the prisoner blanched a little. Rhaspberry went on.

"I personally would use a soldering gun on some of your more delicate parts, but I'm sure these guys' fertile imaginations will be much more inventive. So I think you have to recognize that you will ultimately answer; the only question is how much discomfort you are willing to tolerate beforehand."

Still silence, but Rhaspberry had his attention.

"Well, guys. I guess you'll have to convince him."

"I've been giving this a lot of thought," Wittmond said. "All that time I was sitting by that tree and in that heat. I think I've come up with an idea for a guy that kills children with plastic bags."

The captive's eyes rolled to the left to look at Wittmond. Wittmond returned his gaze without blinking. He could have killed him then and there.

"I'll need an ice pick, a swizzle stick, and a battery charger. Do you have any of those items handy, Wolkert?"

Wolkert looked puzzled. "Probably. I'll have to look." The captive was sweating. Rhaspberry was smiling.

CHAPTER TWENTY-SEVEN

WITTMOND FLATLY EXPLAINED WHAT he had in mind for the captive. "The problem with conventional torture for the purpose of extracting information has always been the inability of the inquisitor to turn pain on and off without the residual pain dulling each new application and the captive losing consciousness. Older methods of burning, twisting, gouging, and so on all had this drawback. I, however, think I have a system that will circumvent this problem."

Rhaspberry nodded and said, "Sounds interesting."

Wolkert said, "Go for it."

Another bead of sweat dribbled down the captive's face; his eyes darted back and forth.

Wittmond continued his lecture. "How does the brain perceive pain?"

"I don't know, but I am sure you will tell us!" Rhaspberry said.

"Through the nerves, obviously. Where can you get directly to the nerves easily without causing tissue damage and, in turn, residual pain? The spinal cord. In the spinal cord there are thousands of nerve tracks right to the brain. We'll do a spinal tap and then provide electrical stimulation to the nerves to the degree and for the duration necessary to achieve our objective. If the captive proves recalcitrant and we burn out the nerves at one level, we just do another tap a vertebra or two higher and start all over again. What do you think?"

Rhaspberry asked, "What's the swizzle stick for?"

"It'll work like this. We firmly secure him on his belly to the cot springs and attach the negative lead of the battery charger to the cot. Then we slide the swizzle stick over the ice pick and use the pick to do the tap. Once the ice pick enters the spinal canal, we push the swizzle stick forward so that it insulates all but the tip of the ice pick. Then we tap the positive electrode to the base of the pick, and voilà — instant, controllable, excruciating pain. Of course, if we get too vigorous he'll never walk again, but who gives a fuck. He'll talk."

"Sounds workable to me," Wolkert seconded. "Do it."

"You fuckers don't have the balls," the captive said, his voice quavering.

"Do you have any anesthetic in your medical locker?" Wittmond asked.

"I've got some ether," Wolkert answered.

"Fine, let's have it."

Wittmond soaked a rag in the ether and held it over the nose and mouth of the captive. The man tried to hold his breath, but after forty-five seconds or so he had to breathe. He was under in less than two minutes.

"Are you really going to do that?" Wolkert asked.

"I don't particularly want to, but then, I'm not that averse to it, knowing who he is and what's at stake," Wittmond said.

"Let's get on with it," persisted Rhaspberry.

Wolkert was sure that Rhaspberry just wanted to see if it would work. They attached the flaccid body to the cot, facedown, and snugly secured his limbs with the duct tape. While he was still out, Wittmond introduced the ice pick between the last thoracic and the first lumbar vertebrae. He felt the telltale pop as the point of the ice pick penetrated the outer sheath of the cord. Wittmond then advanced the plastic swizzle stick down the ice pick's shaft until only about two millimeters of point were exposed. He attached the negative electrode to the springs of the cot and plugged in the unit. "We're ready. Wake him up," Wittmond instructed.

Rhaspberry slapped the man's face a few times. "Time to wake up, asshole," he said.

It was perhaps five minutes before the man was fully awake.

"That mild pressure you feel in you back is the ice pick," Wittmond informed him.

The man strained to look back over his shoulder but couldn't see anything.

"I'm going to ask you one last time to cooperate. Where are you going to meet the old man?" asked Rhaspberry with inappropriate politeness.

"Fuck you," blurted the captive. He apparently didn't believe he had been wired.

Wittmond touched the ice pick where the metal entered the handle with the positive electrode. The results were dramatic.

The prisoner screamed and arched his back. Both legs jerked so violently the bed frame cut into his ankles. The damned cot jumped a few inches off the floor. A trickle of urine made a small puddle under the bunk, and he passed out.

"Jesus, Wittmond, is he dead?" asked Wolkert.

Wittmond checked his pulse. "No, just unconscious. What voltage setting is that thing on?

"It's on twelve. You think we had better back off to six?"

"It would seem so," Wittmond answered, almost certain he had detected mirth in Wolkert's voice.

A cold rag brought their boy around after a few minutes.

"Do you have anything to say?" queried Rhaspberry.

The captive didn't say anything, because of stubbornness or difficulty articulating, Wittmond didn't know, so he applied six volts to the man's central nervous system.

The results were almost as spectacular as before, except the man remained conscious.

"That's better," commented Wolkert. "Now we can get to work."

"No! No!" the captive screamed. He had had enough.

"Okay, asshole," said Rhaspberry. "I'm going to ask you a series of questions. Some of which I know the answers to, and some I do not. One false answer, and it's back to twelve volts and I'll have Wittmond zap you until you're a fucking paraplegic. Understand?"

The captive nodded his resignation. Rhaspberry proceeded with rapid-fire questions:

"What is your name?"

"Who are the other two you were with?"

"What is the old man's name?"

"When did you meet him?"

"How much is he paying you?"

"When and where are you to meet him to confirm the kill and give him the information?"

The man answered each question, and Rhaspberry gave no

indication that the man was lying, so Wittmond took his answer that he was to call the old man and set up a meeting in Saint Louis as true.

At the conclusion of the interview, Rhaspberry turned to Wittmond and said, "Put him out again."

Wittmond hit the ice pick again with the electrode and gave the captive a sustained jolt. After thirty seconds or so of exquisite anguish, the man was rendered unconscious.

"Goddamnit, Wittmond, I meant put him out with the ether," reprimanded Rhaspberry.

"I know," Wittmond answered. "That was for the kids in the plastic bags."

"Is he dead?" Wolkert asked, moving nearer to check his pulse.

"He's not dead, but if he's paralyzed. I'll carry him to the car," Wittmond volunteered.

"I think you've done enough, Wittmond. You two get him ready for travel. I've got something in the car that I want to attach to him," Rhaspberry said.

The medical duo proceeded to remove the tap and unbind the captive.

Upon his return, Rhaspberry fastened what looked like an ammunition bandolier around the man's waist, securing it with a small padlock. "He won't be able to get this off without a knife," he said, admiring his work.

"What is it?" asked Wolkert.

"It's a radio transmitter. It has a five-mile range and the batteries last about two days. You guys finish dressing him and I'll fill you in on where we go from here. As you heard, he's supposed to bring Wolkert's head in a bag for the old man to see. We'll substitute a bomb.

"We'll tell him we are going to let him meet with the old man so he fingers him for us to capture. When he gets in the car and says the old man's name, we'll blow them to hell."

"Do you think it'll work? I mean, do you think he'll believe we want to capture the old man?" Wolkert asked.

"He may, he may not. What choice does he have? He has to know that the only reason he's still alive is because he's of some use to us. He'll agree or die, and he knows it. Wittmond, you've already demonstrated what a ruthless bastard you are."

"Hey, I've never done this before, but in this particular case, I did enjoy it. Plus, there's a lot at stake."

"Fucking right, Rhaspberry," Wolkert joined in, somewhat defensive, somewhat inflamed. "It's very personal when they're trying to kill you and your family."

"Calm down, you two," Rhaspberry said. "I was just giving you a little shit to break the tension. Finish him up. I've got a call for him to make."

"He's kind of slow coming around. Hit him with a little cold water," offered Rhaspberry.

After a short while, the captive had fully regained full consciousness.

"He's okay now," Wolkert said.

"Fine. Bring the asshole over here. He's got a call to make," Rhaspberry said menacingly.

The look on the captive's face was a mixture of terror and confusion. With two guns tracking him, he took a seat next to the phone.

"Now you call and tell your boss you completed the job and have info on the other killer. Set up a meeting for him to get his proof and you your get money. Any nonsense, any at all, and by God I'll give you back to Wittmond, and when you get to hell, it'll be a welcome change. Understand?" Rhaspberry instructed.

The captive looked into Rhaspberry's eyes and nodded. The men watched closely as he dialed. His whole body was shaking; he was sweating like the pig he was. The phone rang twice and a female voice came over the speakerphone.

"Airport Hilton. This is Julie, may I help you?"

"Room 313, please," the prisoner replied with a hint of a quaver.

"Yes, sir, one moment," she answered.

The phone rang again with a different tone. On the third ring, a man answered. "Yes?"

"Mr. Cerro, please."

"Who may I say is calling?"

"Tell him it's the team manager."

"A moment."

There was silence for perhaps thirty seconds before the voice of a much older man came on the line. "Did you do it? Did you get my son's killer?"

"We did."

"Excellent, excellent."

"I have the information about the other one."

"Fine, do you have the proof?"

"When I get paid."

"Okay, okay. Where are you now?"

"About five hours out of Saint Louis."

"It's seven fifteen now. Do you know the parking area just off of Lindbergh Boulevard where people watch the planes take off?" questioned Cerro.

Our man looked at Rhaspberry; Rhaspberry looked at Wittmond. Wittmond nodded and then Rhaspberry did as well.

"Yes, I know it."

"We'll meet you there at 2:00 a.m. We'll be in a grey Buick. Don't forget, I want to see the head of that motherfucker."

"I'll see you at two," the captive replied.

"Adios, amigo." And the line went dead.

The prisoner about dropped the phone attempting to hang it up.

"Sounded okay to me," Wolkert ventured.

"I guess it's okay," confirmed Rhaspberry with a tone of minor skepticism, which clearly disturbed the prisoner.

"It's okay. Honest, it's okay," the prisoner pleaded, shaking more and sweating more. The big bad man was coming unglued.

Rhaspberry gave him a sidelong glance that did nothing to console him.

"Do we kill him now?" Wolkert asked blandly.

The prisoner's eyes bulged and his jaw dropped.

"No, I want the old bastard alive. He's the only one who can finger Cerro in the car before we close in," explained Rhaspberry.

"You mean this fucker is going to live through this?" Wolkert said, feigning disgust.

"He just might, if he does everything just right," replied

Rhaspberry. He went to the kitchen area and came with a white plastic grocery bag bulging with a round object about the size of a human head.

"Your head, Wolkert."

"What's in there?" Wolkert asked.

"Just a head of cabbage wrapped in a few towels; it should get him to the car."

"Then what?" Wittmond asked.

"The old man's guard will be driving; he'll be listening to our friend's story, and so will we. Wolkert will come up from the opposite side of the car and take out the driver and any bodyguards, and we'll have the son of a bitch."

"Why do you want him alive?" Wittmond said.

"I need him for a trade. I can't say more," answered Rhaspberry. "Have the prisoner take a leak and then put him in the backseat, behind the driver. Tape his mouth shut and secure him well. And goddamnit, be careful with your head there."

"My Allstate man is going to have a real hard time with this one," commented Wolkert as he gave his cabin a last wistful glance before sliding into the car.

"Yeah, I'll bet your premiums go up. They may even put in a claymore exclusion clause." Wittmond laughed.

"Shit," said Wolkert, shaking his head.

CHAPTER TWENTY-EIGHT

WOLKERT AND WITTMOND TOOK turns driving and the miles slipped quickly away. Rhaspberry stayed in the copilot's seat the entire trip and seemed to sleep most of the time. He would stir only at gas stops and to admonish the driver occasionally to slow down. The very last thing they needed was to be stopped by the Missouri Highway Patrol.

Wittmond noticed the Walther pistol in Rhaspberry's right hand as he shifted to sit more comfortably.

Fortunately, the trip was uneventful. As they entered the proximity of Saint Louis, Wolkert ever so carefully woke Rhaspberry.

"We're about thirty minutes out," he said. "We'll get off 44 at 270 and go north to catch 70 east. From there, it'll be about a mile north of 70 on the west side of Lindbergh."

Rhaspberry replied, "It's eleven thirty now. We have a few hours to kill. They'll probably be there a little early to do recon, so we'll need to be there a little earlier yet and set Wolkert out. Then, Wittmond, you and I will drink coffee until it's time."

The captive seemed to sleep. The density of the traffic and the haze of air pollution increased as they approached the city. Traffic then lightened on Lindbergh; it was after midnight on a Wednesday. A 747 roared across the road about a quarter mile ahead of the car on its approach. The clouds, which had thickened in the last few hours, finally started to release the rain.

"Pull over here. Okay, Wolkert, you walk up the road on the right side and check it out. If it's clear, cross over about a mile up and come back. Find yourself a good spot to hide on the north or west side of the lot. We'll park on the south or east side, depending on how Cerro parks. That way you can get the driver and bodyguard."

"Right. Got it," Wolkert said.

"Keep your head down," directed Rhaspberry.

With this, Wolkert was away, drifting along the shoulder like some bum.

"Let's get some coffee, Wittmond."

They drove into a Hardee's, and Wittmond got out and fetched two cups to go.

"What about him, doesn't he get any?" Rhaspberry joked.

"Fuck him. I'm not wasting fifty-five cents on that asshole," Wittmond replied. The prisoner's eyes still revealed terror.

Wittmond moved to a dark spot on the Hardee's lot, and they waited. Rhaspberry took what looked like a Walkman out of his pocket and raised an antenna. A small green light glowed as he flicked a switch.

"Say something. I want to test this thing," he said.

"Uh … the coffee's too hot, and even if it weren't, it tastes like shit," Wittmond offered.

"Excellent. It's working perfectly."

Rhaspberry pushed the little antenna down, switched it off, and put the whole unit back in his pocket. "We can't stay here too long, it'll raise suspicion. We don't need some nosy cop to fuck this up. Drive north for about four or five miles, then turn around and come back. That'll put us there about thirty minutes early."

Wittmond drove along Lindbergh north to its end at Highway 367, where a sign announced that if he turned left, it was seven miles to Alton, and if he turned right, it was seven miles to Saint Louis. He did neither. He turned around and went back. About halfway back, Rhaspberry told the prisoner to slide over, further behind Wittmond. With the Walther in his right hand, he leaned back and cut the man's nylon bindings with a knife he held in his left hand.

"Please don't do anything silly," Rhaspberry cautioned. "Now slowly raise your left hand and remove the tape from your mouth."

The prisoner obeyed, his eyes never leaving Rhaspberry's gun.

"Now put both hands on your knees, keep you mouth shut, and don't do anything to provoke me."

"The turn's just up ahead," Wittmond announced. "They're already here."

The Buick was parked so that it was pointed toward the exit. Wittmond pulled up parallel to it about thirty yards to the east but facing the opposite way, putting his side of the car nearest theirs.

"Reach down and get the bag with the cabbage," Rhaspberry instructed the prisoner as he turned on his radio.

"Walk slowly toward the door behind the driver. If you run or vary from the path, Wittmond will cut you in half. Get into the car, and if the old man is in there, say, 'Hello, Mr. Cerro,' then get down on the floor with him. If you do anything else, you'll die. Understood?" The prisoner said nothing but shook his head affirmatively.

"Now go!"

The door opened slowly and the prisoner stepped out. He was quite shaky. He stretched out some of the stiffness from the long ride then slowly and unsteadily walked toward the car, package in hand. The rear window came down, and over the radio Rhaspberry and Wittmond heard a voice.

"Get in, get in. Tell me all about it." It was the old man's voice.

As the prisoner's hand grabbed the door handle, he flung the bag over the car and dove inside. They heard him yell, "Drive, drive! Go, go! It's a trap!"

After a brief second, the Buick lurched forward and the rear door slammed closed.

"They've got a bomb! I threw it away! They're crazy! They tortured me!" the prisoner related in a high-pitched frenzy.

Wittmond screamed at Rhaspberry, "He threw the fucking bomb away!"

"Get down," cautioned Rhaspberry.

Wittmond scrunched down in the seat and watched Rhaspberry press a button on the Walkman. Wittmond then turned to look at the Buick as the back half became dust. He blinked as the shock wave rocked their car. The front end of the Buick rolled on for a few feet, made a forty-five degree turn, and stopped. The back end had the top ripped open and was lying flat on the ground like a smashed beer can. There was a brief burst of flames, and then it was still.

"Get Wolkert and let's get out of here," prompted Rhaspberry.

"The bomb was in the belt," Wittmond stated incredulously. Wittmond drove toward Wolkert, who dove into the backseat. They left the parking lot with restrained celerity.

"Don't speed, just drive," Rhaspberry said.

"Did you know the bomb was in the belt?" Wittmond asked Wolkert.

"Hell no. When that goddamned bag came over the top of the car at me I thought it was all over. Hell, I dug in as tight as I could. Good thing, too. The right rear door would have decapitated me if I hadn't. What was in the bag?"

"Just a head of cabbage," remarked Rhaspberry. "I had to let him think of a way to escape and still ID the old man. As he was coming out of his stupor, I saw his eyelids flutter a little and then I divulged the cabbage-bomb ploy. He saw a way out, so he went along with it, and boom. It'll be months before the police find out what happened to whom."

"Where do we go from here?" Wolkert asked.

"Well, I thought we'd drop you off at the airport so you can fly home, and then we'll drive back to Wittmond's place."

"Sounds good to me," Wolkert said eagerly. "I want to get back to my family. Do you think this is the end of it, Rhaspberry?"

"As far as I know it should stop here, but I can't say for sure," he replied.

There was a long silence. Wittmond finally broke it as they pulled up to the airport. "Hey, Wolkert, when you get Elise and the kids settled down, give me a call. We've got to get us all together before we die of old age. Or something else."

"I was about to suggest the same thing. I'll call you," he yelled as he left the car for the terminal.

"Now, I've got to get home," Wittmond told Rhaspberry. "Where will you be going?" he asked.

"I live with my daughter and her husband since my wife died. They have a place near Hilton Head on the east coast. I'm gone a lot, but that's where I call home."

"Is that the daughter I met in my office?"

"The one and only. She enjoys fussing over me, and to a degree, I enjoy it too. It's nice being so close to the grandkids. I missed a lot when I was younger, you know."

He seemed to drift but quickly caught himself before he said anything that might make him seem human. He looked up at Wittmond. "What the hell are your grinning about?" he snapped.

"Well, it's taking some adjustment to get used to thinking of the meanest, most calculating son of a bitch I have ever known as a kindly grandpa type," answered Wittmond.

"Well, I am, goddamnit. I'm a regular Wilford Brimley."

"Sure you are. Would you want to get together with Wolkert and me? You know, have a few beers and burgers?"

"It depends on what's going on at the time. You're not the only people with trouble, you know."

"You mean other people who have worked for you have had this kind of difficulty?"

"Occasionally," he answered, rather nonplussed.

Wittmond took this as a polite refusal and let the matter drop. The rest of the trip was quiet; they both were pretty well spent.

CHAPTER TWENTY-NINE

THE ONLY PROBLEM VICTORIA had on her trip to Saint Louis was fighting the boredom. The road was straight and flat, and unless you were into corn or soybeans, the landscape held little interest. During the four-hour-plus drive, she had played all of her tapes at least twice. So she was quite relieved to see the sign for the exit to Highway 3 north. Now she was but a few minutes from the Holiday Inn from which she would conduct her surveillance.

When she arrived, she parked and walked into the lobby and up to the front desk.

"You have a reservation for Barbara Niesen?" she asked the clerk.

"Why yes, room 122," replied the clerk. "May I charge this to your credit card?"

"No," Victoria replied. "I'll pay cash."

"That will be $187.35 for the three nights."

Victoria gave the clerk four fifty-dollar bills and instructed the clerk to keep the change for incidentals and waited for the key. The room was the quintessence of typical. Victoria didn't unpack; she just put her suitcase in the closet and made for the restaurant.

After a light lunch, she drove to Saint Louis International Airport and placed her car in the long-term parking lot. She then caught the airport shuttle back to the main terminal, where she had a car rental reservation. It was about four in the afternoon by the time she got back to the hotel.

The Alton-area phonebook gave her not only the address of her intended victim's office and home but also a street map showing how to get there.

She made a rough sketch of the route to each address from the inn. She also made a note of his office hours. There remained several hours of daylight, so she drove to his office. It was located in a professional building next to a hospital. With some difficulty, she found a parking space and, on foot, checked out his parking spot, his office door, and the layout of the facility. She didn't see his car in his space, so she called the office from a disposable cell phone. The information she received confirmed that he would not be in for a few days.

"Just great," she thought. "He's out of town. Or maybe he's just at home sick."

There was only one way to find out. Following her map, Victoria drove to the area of Wittmond's house. The house was located in a remote rural setting on a two-lane oil-and-chip road. As she drove by the property, she could just glimpse parts of the house through the trees. It had to be about two hundred yards off the road. She also noted that there was a subdivision about a third of a mile in each direction from the driveway.

"Very secluded. That's good," she said to herself.

The gate at the entrance to the driveway bore a sign that was explicit about trespassers, so she decided not to risk going down the drive in daylight. She would check it out on foot tonight. Victoria glanced at her watch.

"Hmm, time for supper."

This time of year it wouldn't get dark until about 9:00 p.m., so Victoria had several hours to waste after she ate. She watched the local and national news on TV and then took a nap. Her alarm went off at 8:30, and she prepared to reconnoiter Dr. Wittmond's estate. She drove her car to the subdivision just north of the doctor's house and parked it in front of a house with a For Sale sign in the yard. Decked out in dark jogging attire, she padded her way down the road, looking like any other health nut. Fifty feet before the doctor's driveway, she scanned about but saw no one. Without missing a stride, she turned into the driveway and then quickly darted into the trees. Stealthily, she made her way to within seventy-five yards of the house and froze when a dog barked. It sounded like a very big dog. After a few minutes, the dog stopped. The animal would have to be dealt with. From her fanny pack, she extracted a notepad and pencil made a sketch of the layout of the yard and house. A small pair of binoculars allowed her to scan the house and get a feel for the floor plan without getting closer. She had the house under observation for about an hour when a car turned off the road and into the drive. Victoria had to crouch down to avoid the headlights. She used the binoculars to watch a woman exit the car and wave at the remaining occupants. As they drove off, Victoria hid again as the car drove by her on the way out.

With the auto out of sight, she turned her attention back to the house. She caught a fleeting glimpse of the woman as she made her way through the house and upstairs.

Victoria saw a light come on behind a single window at the northwest corner of the house.

"Probably the bedroom," thought Victoria. A little later, a smaller window next to the bedroom illuminated.

"No doubt the bathroom," she muttered as she labeled the sketch on her notepad.

Fifteen minutes later, all the lights were out.

"No sign of the doctor. Damn."

If the house had been in town or a subdivision, she could have just parked her car and waited, but any parked car on the road here would certainly draw attention.

So Victoria had to figure a way to determine when Wittmond got home without sitting in the woods all night. She could call the exchange, but they wouldn't give out that kind of information. She could also call the house and wait for him to answer, but after a few calls, that ploy would raise suspicion. Try as she might, she couldn't think of any way other than constant nocturnal observation that would tell her of Wittmond's earliest arrival. She was hot sitting on that log. The mosquitoes were biting, and that goddamned dog was still about. She tried to sleep but couldn't get comfortable. She was miserable.

"From now on, no Cubans and no farmers," she swore.

In spite of the discomfort, she did doze off. A car speeding down the driveway woke her. She looked at her watch: 3:24 a.m.

"It's got to be him," she murmured.

By the moonlight, she watched a figure emerge from the driver's side of the car. The passenger slid over to the driver's position. After extracting a duffle bag from the trunk, one man trudged toward the porch. A few seconds later, the bedroom light came on, and a few seconds after that, the porch light. A pair of arms shot out of the darkness of the house and gathered the figure inside as the car made the circle in front of the house and left.

"Finally, some good luck," she thought. She was in a better mood now as she jogged back to the car. Driving back to the motel, she decided she would sleep late and go after the doctor late the next evening.

● ● ●

When Bev had been out with Vince and Marilyn earlier, they sensed her concern. After they made several attempts to get her into a better frame of mind, she decided to go home early. Marilyn assured her that everything was going to be all right and Vince echoed. She apologized for being a wet blanket as they dropped her off at the house. Sure she was safely in the house, they drove off into the dark. By the time Bev was ready for bed, Leno was coming on. The show was a repeat, and after a quick scan of the other channels did not yield anything worth watching, she turned off the TV. Sleep didn't come easily, and she saw the digital clock blink 12:21, 12:54, 2:13. Just when 3:24 came, she heard the dog barking. She went to the window, and after about thirty seconds, saw headlights coming down the drive. "That dog is amazing," she thought as she put on her robe and hurried downstairs.

"This had better be Connie. He had better be okay, and the story had better be good," she muttered, closing the distance to the door. She flipped on the porch light and peered though the curtain. Sure enough, it was Connie, apparently saying good-bye to the driver of the car. After a few seconds, the car completed the circle in front of the house and departed. She flipped on the porch light when she saw Connie, opened the door widely, and held out her arms.

"How you doing, kid?" he said wearily as they embraced.

"You look terrible," she commented.

"It's been a rough few days and it's good to be back home."

"Let's get to bed and talk about it in the morning," she offered, though she really wanted the answers now.

She put her arm around him as they went up the stairs. The butt of the .45 poked her in the ribs.

"Give me that. I'll put it in your office." Taking the weapon, she noticed the business end was sooty.

"You have been busy, haven't you?"

"Come on, let's hit the sheets," he sighed.

After a quick shower, he collapsed into bed. Together again, sleep came swiftly.

CHAPTER THIRTY

IT WAS ABOUT 9:30 the next morning before Wittmond began to stir from his deep slumber. Bev was already awake and was lying next to him, watching him sleep. She was so glad he was back and in one piece. They took an hour to get reacquainted. She had mercilessly reduced him to helplessness. Now, he became pensive in his recuperation. Something was on his mind; Bev knew what it was, but she didn't press him.

"I've been keeping something from you with the idea that it was for your own good, maybe our own good," Wittmond said. "At any rate, recent events have changed my mind, so I want to fill you in on some things."

Bev raised one eyebrow and said, "Oh, and what might those things be?"

"I've kept a diary of some exploits that I have been involved in. It dates back over thirty years, even before you and I knew each other," he explained.

It was a good opening, so Bev let him continue.

"I kept the diary to explain these events to you and the kids, in case something happened to me. These jobs were always far removed from our daily lives. Recently, though, consequences of one of them has brought things much closer." He paused.

"I read the diary," she interrupted, "while you were away."

"And you're not smoked?" he stammered.

"Of course I am. But it wasn't all that bad. At first I was put out about being kept in the dark all those years, but after mulling it over, I can understand why you did what you did. Almost."

Wittmond's surprise slowly melted into a smile of relief. "Then you don't think of me as some kind of ogre?"

"No more than I did before I read it. Actually, I was intrigued, and I'd like you to tell me more about those days. But that can wait. What in God's name has been going on this last week?" she demanded.

"Let's get some lunch and go out on the patio," he answered. "Have I got a strange tale to tell you. Remember Wolkert? From the diary?"

Bev dutifully followed his suggestions, and they got comfortable at the patio table.

"And of course you remember Rhaspberry driving up late the other night?" he opened.

She nodded.

● ● ●

Victoria had slept well into the late morning hours and awoke rested. She decided to perform a modified workout before she showered. As usual, she stood in front of the mirror clad only in her panties and went through her ritual.

After expertly indulging in some self-gratification, she remarked to herself, "That was a good one." It was a very mellow Victoria that stepped into the shower.

She spent the rest of the day lounging about and getting her equipment ready.

At 9:00 p.m., a well-rested Victoria donned her jogging suit and drove again to the subdivision north of the house. Selecting a different house for sale, she parked her car, checked that her Ruger was ready, returned it to her fanny pack, and proceeded to jog down the road. As before, when she was sure no one was around, she cut into the doctor's driveway and made for cover. She was downwind of the house, so the dog didn't detect her until she was within about twenty-five feet of him. He barked but didn't advance. When he paused, she fired three shots from the silenced .22, and he died without another sound.

Victoria changed magazines and proceeded toward the house. The only lights were in an upstairs room on the northwest corner of the house, the bedroom. Victoria Charles waited for five minutes to see if anyone would investigate the dog's barking.

CHAPTER THIRTY-ONE

"WHAT'S THE DOG BARKING at, Bev?" grumbled Wittmond.

Beverly moved to the bedroom window. Her scan revealed only darkness.

"I don't see anything out there," she replied.

"Oh well." Wittmond yawned. "Probably a raccoon or a deer." They settled back to watch the news.

● ● ●

Victoria easily entered through the french doors on the side of the house. She covered a pane next to the knob with duct tape, then placed a Phillips-head screwdriver at its center, and slowly pushed on the screwdriver until the pane fractured. After the quiet *pop*, she pulled out the glass and reached in to turn the doorknob. She had taken but four steps into the room when she detected a small red light ahead of her, high on the wall.

"Goddamnit," she mumbled to herself as she froze in fear.

After a few seconds, the LED of the motion detector went out. No alarm sounded. It was not activated.

As she approached with the aid of a penlight to the center of the room, the LED flicked on and then off as she moved under it. She gained the stairs without detection.

● ● ●

The small LED on the alarm console in the bedroom came on silently and went out for a few seconds.

"Connie! Look!" Bev whispered loudly. The light went out for a few seconds then came back on.

"Someone's downstairs," Wittmond said. He moved to the closet, then turned back to Bev. "Where's the shotgun?"

"You left it downstairs in the music room when Rhaspberry was here, remember?" Bev replied.

"Oh, shit! Twenty guns in this place and they're all on the other side of the house. Goddamn! Weapons! Weapons! What can I use for a weapon?" he thought. He frantically rechecked the closet—nothing. Next to his wallet , on top of the bureau, he caught sight of the aluminum butt of his Boy Scout sheath knife.

"Ah!" he grunted, seizing the weapon. He stripped off the sheath revealing seven and a half inches of dark steel. He felt less naked now.

"Bev! Go in the bathroom, lock the door, and get in the tub; it's the safest place," he instructed in a whisper.

"But ... what are you going to do?"

"I have to take the fight to them. If we wait, they'll kill us both. Now go and be quiet. Please," he pleaded.

Reluctantly, she complied. With a forced smile, she closed the door, and he heard the lock click.

He assessed the situation. The intruders would come up to the lighted room not knowing they had been detected. He would intercept them from the room across the hall. Quickly, he moved across the hall to his son's darkened room and set up a position next to the door frame. From there, he could see the intruders outlined against the glare of the television. The first one would be easy, the second or third were going to be rough. His heart was pounding now that he fully realized his situation. He fought to control his breathing. He strained to hear any slight sound.

● ● ●

With the pistol extended in front of her in one hand and the penlight directed at the steps in the other, she slowly, quietly ascended the stairs. She felt her heart rate increase and she had to make an effort to control her breathing. At the top of the stairs, she saw a long dark hall leading to a doorway on the right and the flickering light of a television inside.

Still there was no sign of the alarm. "Maybe they're both asleep," she thought. That would make it easier. There were three open but dark doorways down the hall on her left; probably other bedrooms. Her target, however, was at the end of the hall on the right. She pocketed the penlight, and with the pistol at arms' length in a two-hand hold, she started down the hall. She passed the first doorway on the left and glanced inside—completely dark. She proceeded. Now she could hear the TV weatherman discussing tomorrow's weather. She silently passed the second door on the left and paused.

The room was completely dark, and so was the third. Pressing on, she was within five feet of the lighted doorway. Adjusting her grip on the Ruger, she prepared to enter the room.

● ● ●

For the next few minutes, it seemed as though time was suspended. Nothing moved except the flashing light from the TV. Wittmond's heart about stopped when he saw the silhouette of a pistol and then a woman. She turned and looked directly into the room where he stood. He could smell the soap she had used, yet she didn't see him. As she turned away, he got a better look at the pistol extended in front of her.

Intent now on the lighted room, she moved slowly away from him.

In his stocking feet, he moved toward her. He took a quick glance down the hall but could see nothing. His attention was back to her in a split second. She had taken another step toward the light. He took a deep breath, and in one large stride, he was behind her.

His left arm shot over her left shoulder, crossed her chest, and grabbed her top below her right armpit. Jerking her back and up off her feet, he inserted the knife blade to the hilt parallel to her ribs on the right side of her body, where the aorta lay in front of the spine. She fired a muted shot then dropped the pistol to the carpet silently. He pulled the end of the knife's handle toward himself, directing the tip of the blade forward to sever the large vessel. He felt her stiffen with pain. She let out a light gasp, then she went limp, unconsciousness. He did a 90° turn to the right without releasing her, putting her body between him and the next assassin.

There was no next assassin. He felt her heart pounding against his forearm. It became more rapid but fainter until it stopped. He gently lowered her body to the floor. Leaving the knife in place, he felt blindly across the carpet and located the pistol. Wittmond stepped back into his bedroom. Looking down the hall, gun ready, he switched the hall light on. It was empty, except for the body.

"Bev! Bev! Come on out, it's okay." His wife emerged from the bathroom wet-eyed but in control.

"Watch the alarm control panel for activity," he instructed as he continued to watch the hall. They were silent for more than five minutes. There was no sign of anyone else in the house, but he had to be sure. With the assassin's pistol in hand, he made his way to his office and retrieved his .45. Now he felt quite secure. After an anxious ten minutes, he had made sure the house was empty and returned upstairs.

"Who is she?" Bev asked.

"I don't know," he answered. "But she has to be connected to that Cerro thing. Rhaspberry didn't know I had been made. Come to think of it, Cerro didn't make a big deal about my identity; it didn't matter. He already had the plan for me in motion."

"What do we do now?" asked Bev "Call the cops?"

"Hell no! How would we explain this? I'll clean up this mess and call Rhaspberry in the morning."

"I think we both need a drink; I'll get some brandy," offered Bev.

She carefully stepped over the body and went down the hall without looking back. Wittmond knelt beside the body and withdrew the knife. There was little bleeding. He took the knife to the bathroom and washed it, then returned it to its sheath. This small task completed, he returned to the body. Placing a towel under the wound, he rolled the assassin over on her back. Her eyes were half open, her gaze fixed. A look of slight disbelief remained on her face.

"Must be about thirty," he thought as he examined her clothing and fanny pack. In the pack, she had two car keys, a hotel key, two full magazines for the .22, and a camera. Nothing that would identify her.

"What a waste," he mused, looking at her tight, athletic body. He adjusted her clothing and went down to the kitchen with the keys. There, he sat down at the table and Bev poured a snifter of brandy for each of them.

"I found three keys, two for cars and one other to a room at the Holiday Inn," he said. "First I want you to drive me to the motel. I'll search the room, and then we'll look for the car."

"Do you think this is the right way to handle this thing?" Bev asked.

"It's the only thing we can do. We don't want Pandora's Box opened, now do we?" he countered.

After they finished their drink, both felt a little less shaky. They pulled out of the driveway in the 460 SL and headed for the hotel.

The hotel room contained only a suitcase, which Wittmond took out but didn't open. He left the room and then the hotel through a side door to avoid the front desk. Back home, he and Bev investigated the contents of the bag at the kitchen table. It contained a wallet with no ID, $130.00 in cash, two changes of clothes, and a rental car receipt for a Lincoln Town Car. Connie found the car in the subdivision after a twenty-minute search and drove it back to the house.

Back upstairs, Wittmond took an ink pad and took the dead woman's fingerprints. He then carried the body down the stairs over his shoulder and placed her in the backseat of her car with her luggage.

"What's the name of that topless place in Sauget that's always in the news?" he asked Bev.

"TJ's or TP's or something like that," she replied. "I'll look it up."

The phone book revealed the name was PJ's.

"You drive there and wait for me," Wittmond said. "We'll dump the car there."

"You want me to wait in the parking lot?" She smiled.

"Yes, in the parking lot." He smiled back and shook his head.

They set out on their separate missions, Bev to PJ's in the 460 SL, Wittmond to dispose of the body. First, he drove the rental car down highway 3 to East Saint Louis, where dead bodies appeared regularly. Seeking out a deserted street in an area that looked like London during the Blitz, he parked in a likely place and turned out the headlights. His watch flashed 2:32 a.m. He waited for about ten minutes; no activity anywhere. He exited the car on the passenger side after removing the bulb from the dome light. Dragging the body from the backseat, he quietly pushed it into the weeds on the other side of the crumbling sidewalk. He returned to the car and again watched until he was sure no one had observed him. Confident his deed had gone unnoticed, he drove to PJ's parking lot. He noticed that the lot was still full. No doubt the patrons were still enjoying themselves inside.

"Good!" he said to himself. "Good cover." He spotted the 460 SL sitting empty. Driving to the opposite end of the lot, he parked the Lincoln, wiped the wheel and door handle, and then locked the car. He pocketed the key and made his way to the Mercedes by an indirect route. The car was locked. He tapped on the window and Bev appeared from out of the darkness. She had been lying on the seat, face up, with a Walther PPK/S in her hand, resting on her chest. She unlocked the door. He got in, and they drove off together.

"Do you come here often?" she joked. Somewhere around Collinsville, he threw the car keys out the window into the blackness. They drove the rest of the way home in silence.

The next morning, Wittmond contacted Rhaspberry and recounted the events of the past evening.

"She must have been given the contract during that episode with Wolkert's family," Rhaspberry suggested. "Any ID?"

"Nothing on her," replied Wittmond, "but I printed her. I can fax the prints to you if you'll give me a number."

After giving the fax number, Rhaspberry assured Wittmond he would look into it and get back to him.

He did call back some days later. He told Wittmond that Victoria Charles had been the wife of a suspected professional killer who had been killed in an auto accident. She had obviously kept the business going. "She worked alone. With Cerro dead, no further threat exists," Rhaspberry said.

"Where have I heard that before?" Wittmond mused aloud.

EPILOGUE

THE HOUSE WAS DIFFERENT after that dark night; the Wittmonds' lives were different as well. They moved away some six months later. He retired, and they set up a small farm. Occasionally, Bev filled in as a substitute teacher at the high school, and Conrad would cover for the local doc when he went on vacation. They saw the Wolkerts once since their move, around Easter last year. The Wittmond kids were all out of college now and dropped in now and then. To the outside world, the pair was the essence of calm and gentility. Time attenuated the memory of that dark night. Conrad's journal was clasped once again.

THE END